WHAT I WOULD TELL YOU

A NOVEL

A NOVEL

WHAT I WOULD TELL YOU

LIZ TOLSMA

What I Would Tell You ©2023 by Liz Tolsma

Print ISBN 978-1-63609-459-5
Adobe Digital Edition (.epub) 978-1-63609-460-1

Published by Barbour Publishing, Inc., 1810 Barbour Drive, Uhrichsville, Ohio 44683, www.barbourbooks.com

Our mission is to inspire the world with the life-changing message of the Bible.

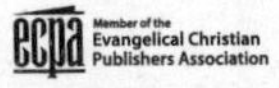

Printed in the United States of America.

DEDICATION

In memory of the 48,000 Salonikan Jews who perished in the Holocaust. Seeing where you lived, where you worked, where you loved touched me deeply. History remembers you. Now I hope the rest of the world will too.

Far be it from You to erase our memory. Look towards us with mercy, for Yours, O Lord, are mercy and forgiveness. A man, whether he be a year old, or whether he lives a thousand years, what does it profit him? For is it not as if he has never been? Blessed be the True Judge, Who brings death and restores life.

From the Tziduk Hadin, a Jewish funeral prayer

But God will redeem my soul from the power of the grave: for he shall receive me. Selah.

Psalm 49:15 KJV

AUTHOR'S NOTE

Because Sephardic Jews were forced to leave Spain in 1492, they brought with them a form of the Spanish language mixed with Hebrew and even some Portuguese. This language is called Ladino. By the 1940s, after over twenty years of Greek rule, Greek was the official language of Thessaloniki and the language of the schools. Many of the younger generation began to lose Ladino. Mathilda and Asher would have been right on the edge and likely would have spoken both, though their parents would have used Ladino exclusively. To avoid having to use too much Greek, one of the hardest languages for native English speakers, I have chosen to have them speaking Ladino to each other and to their Jewish friends. After WWII, when so many of the Jews perished, Ladino almost died out. There is a movement underway to preserve the Ladino language. That is why you'll see words that appear to be Spanish. Some of the spellings are different from what we're used to. Ladino is mainly written with the Latin alphabet, but it can also be written in the Cyrillic and Hebrew alphabets. Again, I have spared the reader and chosen to write it in the Latin alphabet.

GLOSSARY

Ladino Words

Adyo *– goodbye*
Avuela *– grandmother*
Ayuda *– help*
Buenos diyas *– hello*
Denada *– you're welcome*
Dio *– God*
Gracyas *– thank you*
Mi alma *– my soul*
Mi amiga *– my friend*
Mi corasón *– my heart*
Por favor *– please*
Te amo *– I love you*
Tia *– aunt*
Vinido bueno *– Welcome*

Greek Words

Bakaliaros *– salted cod*
Kalamari *– squid, not necessarily fried*
Kaliméra *– good morning*
Opa *– similar to "whoops." Usually used when you drop something on the floor.*
Pappoús *– grandfather*
Trigona *– a triangular dessert made of fried phyllo coated in honey and filled with vanilla cream*
Yiayia *– grandmother*
Yassou *– hello*

German words

Raus *– out*
Schnell *– hurry*

CHAPTER ONE

Sunday, April 6, 1941
Salonika, Greece

This is the day I dreaded, the day I feared might come, the day I prayed never would. Greece will never be the same. Will the Nazis treat the Jews here the same way they are treating them in Poland and in Czechoslovakia? We've heard the whispers about the camps.

We must do whatever we can to stay out of them.

—From the diary of Mathilda Nissim

The words from the polished brown radio set in front of Mathilda echoed in her ears, but she couldn't believe them. The man droned on in Greek, but she shut out what he said. His words made what was happening to her country all too real. If she didn't listen, maybe they wouldn't be true.

But her heart said differently. Told her that this was no nightmare from which they would awaken. This awful dream was their life.

German boots now soiled the land of her beloved Greece.

Her blood chilled.

Not much time had passed since they had defeated the Italians and sent them back across the Ionian Sea. Now the Germans took their place. At the synagogue yesterday, this had been all the talk. Would Hitler come and usurp the Italians? Would he fill the void?

Many had argued he wouldn't do such a thing. Though the thought bordered on the preposterous, deep down, Mathilda had no doubt he would. He was insane enough to make the move.

Now it had come to pass.

The man on the radio continued to read the bulletin, but very little of what he said registered with Mathilda, and not because her Greek was imperfect. She leaned forward in her red-and-gold embroidered armchair, closer to the radio, as if that would help her make sense of what she heard.

Life around her shattered, like a looking glass smashed on the cool tile floor. Because they all knew what awaited them. They had spoken of it in whispers behind closed doors, as if speaking aloud would bring it about.

Those who had tried to make themselves believe Hitler wouldn't do this had fooled themselves. Well, no longer. The tone of the words changed. The Greek language, flowing like water over rocks, turned to guttural German. The harsh voice on the radio demanded the people pay attention.

If only they had paid attention years ago. England and France had failed the world. They had failed every citizen in Europe and every Jew on the continent.

Including Mathilda and Asher.

At that moment, the door to their flat crashed open, and her husband raced into the apartment, panting as he stopped in front of her, his Hamburg hat askew, his blue necktie loose, his round face flushed. "Did you hear? Did you?"

She motioned to the radio in front of her. "I heard." Tears thickened her throat. "We have to do something about it. There must be a way to stop them from doing this."

"What would that be?" Asher dropped his hat on the table near the door. "Soon Greece will fall to them. There's no doubt about that. They're coming with their tanks and their guns. We have nothing."

"No, that's not true." She swallowed hard and rose from the chair, not clicking off the radio. "We have the power of our words.

I have to get a special edition of the paper out to keep the people informed of what is happening and prepare them for when the Nazis arrive in Salonika."

Asher, his dark hair mussed, crossed the small distance between them and grabbed her by the shoulders. Gave her a small shake. "No, you will not do such thing. When they get here, they'll find your writings. You'll be under arrest for sure. Instead of producing more, we have to destroy everything you have. All of your work. Every paper you ever published. All the printing machines, the ink, all of it. Without delay."

"*Por favor*, don't ask me to get rid of it. It's more important than ever now. How can we call our people to action if there isn't a Jewish newspaper?"

"They're going to shut down all the newspapers, both the big ones and the small ones like yours. Do you believe the Nazis will allow you to continue producing such inflammatory rhetoric?"

She stepped back, out of his grasp, as if he had struck her. "Inflammatory? How can you say such a thing? I thought you supported me and my work."

"I didn't mean that." He softened his voice. "The Germans will see it as such. They will only allow their own propaganda to be printed. Especially nothing Jewish. Jews in other countries have lost their businesses, their homes, their very lives."

"Now you understand why I have to keep writing and publishing. So that we don't lose our voices. There is so much I have to tell."

"At what cost?" Asher stared at her, his eyes dark and stormy.

"At whatever cost it might be." Too many Jews had already died. If she could prevent one more death or ten or a hundred, it would be worth whatever *Dio* demanded of her.

He shook his head. "No. *Mi corasón*, I couldn't stand to lose you. I can't allow you to put yourself in so much danger."

"No matter whether I stop writing or not, I fear we are all in danger. You have heard the stories from Germany and Poland and the other occupied countries. No Jew is safe in a Nazi-controlled land. Any moment, any one of us could be taken—"

With a touch to her lips, he shushed her. "Put those thoughts out of your mind."

She kept her words soft, almost whispering in his ear. "We have to think about such things."

He hugged her hard, trembling from head to toe.

"I'm scared too. So afraid. What will become of us? But the entirety of Europe's Jews may well be wiped out if we stand aside and remain spectators to own destruction. I am more afraid of what will happen if we do nothing than of what will happen if we do something."

Asher stroked her cheek. "How did I manage to marry someone so wise and brave?"

"You will let me keep writing then?"

He gave a single nod. That was enough for her. "I will concede that I can't continue to publish in the open as I have, but we don't have to destroy everything. We can hide it. Take it out only at night. We have to become clandestine."

Asher gave a deep, long sigh. "Then I'll help you, come what may. But I'll fret about this and lose sleep. I'm so afraid for your safety. What would become of me if I lost you?"

"Let's not worry about what may or may not happen, things that are out of our control. Right now, we have to find a hiding place for everything."

Asher nodded, a dark lock of hair falling over his high forehead. She itched to reach out and stroke it into place, but there was no time for that. As Salonika was an important port city, the Germans would arrive here sooner rather than later.

Together, which was how they worked best, they searched for a spot to hide her equipment. She entered the bedroom, Asher following. A big bed covered with a red chenille spread in the middle of the room and a large wardrobe in the corner engulfed the small space.

Asher motioned for her. “In here. This is the perfect spot.” He went to the wardrobe and pushed aside a few dresses and some of his slacks. “I can build a false back, and we can store everything in that space. Good that you only have a small press and not many supplies.”

“Behind a false back which is behind all of our clothes? That won’t be convenient. No easy access to what I need.”

“That’s what makes it so perfect. If the Germans come to search here, it will be a great deal of work for them to find this, so it will be well hidden from their eyes.”

“Of course. That makes sense.”

“Take these clothes out of here so I can measure. Tomorrow I’ll bring home the wood we need to build it. Maybe we can even have a hidden hinge to make it easier for you to open.”

“For tonight, we’ll hide it under the bed.” Asher dropped to his knees on the wood floor and lifted the spread. “I doubt the Germans will make it here in such a short amount of time, but I want to be safe. This is not a good hiding place, but it will have to do until tomorrow.”

With great care, she moved her small printing press, all the ink she had, and her stack of blank newsprint under the bed. Even a pair of stained gloves. It wouldn’t do for her to wander the city with black fingers.

Asher reached for the stack of articles and newspapers she had produced. And her diary.

“No.” She grabbed him by the arm to stop him. “They have to be separate. If the Nazis discover the press, then so be it. But my journal, I want that somewhere else. Perhaps if the Germans discover what I have been up to, they will be satisfied with the tools of my trade.”

Asher kissed her cheek and squeezed her shoulder. “I understand.”

And that is what she loved so much about him. He always understood. Maybe he didn’t agree with her writing so much.

And he was correct. The Nazis would find it inflammatory. Some of the Greeks already did. But he never disparaged her work. He always fully supported her.

He pried up a few of the wood floorboards, creating an opening between a couple of the joists. The space was just enough for her to place her precious book of thoughts, her private ramblings. And now her witness to the events that were about to take place in her homeland.

When she and Asher had moved to this flat, they had dreamed of this room being a nursery. Dio had different plans for them. Though married three years now, no children had come along. In these times, that was a good thing, a blessing from above.

With the Germans here, a child would not have a good life. He would grow up in fear, being hated, scorned, and always under the threat of being taken away. No, it was better that it remained just her and Asher. Together the two of them could stand strong against the Germans, the *Schuss*.

As Israel of old had stood firm against the Philistines, David defeating the giant, so they would stand against this giant who once more taunted the people of God.

CHAPTER TWO

April 9, 1941

The thumping of jackboots against the ancient streets of Salonika reverberated deep in Mathilda's bones. Where the Christians said the apostle Paul had once trod, now the feet of filthy Germans marched on the roads. Hundreds of them. Maybe thousands. All with a steady thump, thump, thump.

This ancient city, devastated by fire not yet twenty-five years ago, then devastated by Italian bombs dropped from Italian planes, now devastated by Nazi bloodlust. How much longer would they suffer? Would anything of Salonika remain by the time their conquerors left?

Would they ever leave?

No longer did gulls cry overhead. Now the crying came from women, children, even some of the men. The noises were too much to take and sent Mathilda pacing the small flat, her hands fisted, her jaw clamped.

She didn't dare raise the dark blue curtain to peer out the window. She couldn't meet their stares, their cold blue eyes filled with hate and vengeance, intent on bringing the world to its knees, bowing before them in submission.

Though the movement warmed her, she couldn't stop. She'd heard the stories. They talked about them at synagogue almost every week, of what was happening to Jews in Germany, Poland, and Czechoslovakia. Horrible, unspeakable things, yet the tales passed their lips in whispers, as if that might shield them from the terrors.

With the grinding of tanks over the cobblestone streets, their world shattered.

Mathilda shuddered, unable to draw a normal breath, heat rising in her chest.

Asher was out there somewhere. This morning, as every morning but the Sabbath, he left their little flat above the spice shop in the old Jewish market and walked the six blocks to the pharmacy.

In vain, she wiped the tears from her cheeks with the corner of her shawl. What was happening to her husband? Everyone knew what the Germans did to their Jews on Kristallnacht, how they were dragged from their homes and businesses, beaten, some of them taken away, never to be seen again.

Was that what was happening to Asher? Her throat tightened.

She clenched the black shawl in her fists. Her chest heaved. On her next circuit of the flat, she moved through the bedroom and into the little living area, then leaned over the table beside the sunny window and parted the curtain the slightest of bits. Though she had vowed not to watch them, she had to know what was going on right outside her window.

A stream of soldiers flowed down the street, unending, unceasing. The tromping of their feet turned to background noise. Screams rose above the din. The kosher butcher was dragged from his shop across the street, his bloody apron tied around his waist.

Mathilda's stomach dropped, and she trembled. No, no, not Samuel. The kind man who always put a little extra meat in Mathilda's package and never charged her for it. Told her it would build her strength. The sweet man who always had a word of advice for her. The gentle man who had a hug for her when, as a little girl, she lost her father.

With the butts of their guns, the olive-clad Germans beat the gray-haired man. Mathilda bit her fist to keep from screaming. They continued their torture until Samuel's legs gave out. With a thud, he fell to the ground.

How could these monsters do such a despicable thing to such a wonderful man?

Before she knew what she was doing, she ran down the stairs and out the door onto the street. The ceaseless parade of victorious Nazis maneuvered around their colleagues beating a helpless, innocent old man, uncaring of the senseless violence. Such were these people.

No one else from her neighborhood ventured from their homes. The market where their flat was located was bereft of everyone but Germans. Stalls of meat and fish and olives stood forsaken and forlorn. Where were the citizens? The soldiers? This was how the Germans defeated the people of Europe. No one was willing to stand up to them.

Moments ago, she had been unsure of her actions, hopeless to do anything. No longer would she hide and allow the Germans to decimate her city.

She dashed down the street, but the tide of gun-toting soldiers separated her from Samuel. Somehow she had to make it to him. Had to help him.

If only she could reach him.

She stepped into the flow of Germans. "Excuse me, por favor."

They pushed her. She fell onto the narrow walk, scraping her hands on the rough surface. Between their perfectly straight lines, she glimpsed Samuel, now lying still on the street. The soldiers marched right over him. One stepped on him.

She had to get to him. "*Ayuda*! Ayuda! Help me!" But none of her neighbors dared to peek through their curtains.

Well then, she would have to do what had to be done. She rose from the sidewalk and steeled herself. Her shawl slid from her shoulders, but she didn't stop to pick it up. Though these men rose a head taller than her, she plowed her way through their ranks.

One reached out to grab her. She yanked from his beefy grasp and moved forward. Another one kicked her, dropping her to her hands and knees. Pain raced through her legs and already-bruised palms. She couldn't allow him to strike her again. Drawing on every bit of strength she could, she rose and ran.

He didn't follow.

There was Samuel, just ahead. She stumbled on the old, uneven cobblestones but managed somehow to keep upright.

"Mathilda Nissim, what are you doing?"

Mathilda glanced at the window just above her where the elderly Mrs. Benjamin lived. As always, a scowl marked her lined face.

Mathilda reached the other side of the street. Reached Samuel.

"Mathilda, get in here right now. You're a fool girl who has no understanding of the world."

If anyone was the fool, it was Mrs. Benjamin, who would yell from her window onto the street but not climb down a flight of stairs to help the man who had been like a father to Mathilda.

The wave of Germans came to an end. As if a storm had passed, the birds once again chirped as they hopped along the rooflines. The sun fell across Mathilda's shoulders, caressing the back of her neck like Asher did. A peaceful stillness covered the neighborhood.

Mathilda bent over Samuel.

But it was too late.

Only the dim light of the bulb above the table in the alcove lit the apartment. The stove had gone cold. How Mathilda had gotten home, she had no idea. One minute, she was leaning over the body of the man who loved her as much as a father, and the next, she was sitting in her flat, a cold cup of coffee in her hands scarred by a long-ago fire, cheery yellow flowers in a vase in the middle of the lace tablecloth.

She rubbed the back of her aching neck in an attempt to rid

herself of this awful headache. It didn't work. Nothing would work, because every time she closed her eyes, the image of Samuel, bloodied, beaten, beyond hope, flashed in front of her.

An image that would be seared into her brain for all eternity.

She closed her eyes. If only she could weep. If only the tears would come and wash the blood from her hands, the screams from her ears, the memories from her mind. Though the clock on the table in the living room ticked away the minutes, no tears came. On the street, she had been unable to stop them.

Now, when their coming would be a blessed relief, nothing.

Nothing at all.

No pain.

No sorrow.

No wailing.

The door clicked open, but she didn't turn toward the sound. An instant later, Asher was at her side, the sweet smell of his cologne wafting to her as he knelt beside her. Then he grasped her by the hand, his own fingers long, the nails neat, the creases in the knuckles deep. She would know those hands anywhere.

"Mi corasón, I came to you the moment I heard."

Still, she didn't face him.

"I am so sorry. Sorry that this happened. Sorry that you saw it."

She shifted in her seat but kept her gaze forward. "I was too late."

"What could you have done against a mass of armed soldiers?"

"No one else came to his aid. No one other than Mrs. Benjamin even peered out of their windows when they heard him crying for help." She covered her face. "Why? Why was I the only one? They are content to sit in their houses and let the Nazis come and take away everything we have. Including our lives."

She turned to her husband. Tears filled his hazel eyes. He shook his head, his brown hair mussed and unruly, so unusual for him. "What good are we going to be? Look at the Polish. They had armies and couldn't stand against the blitzkrieg. A few Jews in yarmulkes aren't going to mount a defense against them."

"No, maybe we were unable to defeat them in war, but we could have stopped them from harming Samuel. And however many other men they killed today."

Asher winced. *Si,* he knew. Out on the streets, he must have witnessed others meeting their demise at the hands of their captors. "We would all end up dead ourselves."

"But Samuel. Why him? Of all the people in this city, why him?"

"Only Dio knows those answers. We can't understand His ways."

"After my own father died. . ." Finally a lump formed in her throat. Her father was nothing more than a shadowy figure in her memory. "After he was gone, Samuel looked out for us, watched me and my sisters when Mama had to go to work. He—he has been everything to me for almost twenty years. And now Dio has ripped him away from me. Today I lost another father."

With those words, the dam inside her split wide open. All the tears that had refused to come released themselves in a torrent. She launched herself into Asher's arms and, for many long minutes, wet his pale blue dress shirt with those tears.

At last, when nothing more than hiccups remained, Asher held her away from him and peered into her eyes, searching her. He withdrew a handkerchief from his pants pocket and wiped her eyes, her cheeks, her nose. "I don't know what to say."

"There are no words."

As the darkness deepened, they sat together on the kitchen floor and held each other. As if by some unseen pathway, Mathilda drew strength from Asher. His heart beat against hers, its rhythm steady. Like he always was. Never flinching, never faltering, never failing.

With a final gasp, she released her hold on her husband. She traced the edge of his face, his jawline rounded. That face that had first attracted her attention. That face she had fallen in love with. "What have I done to deserve you? When all the good in my life is gone, you are still here."

"Then I hope not all of the good is gone." He smiled, tentative at first, then growing until the dimple appeared in his right cheek.

"No, you're correct. Not all the good is gone. Dio hasn't taken everything from me. But how will I go on without Samuel?" She couldn't voice her other question. How many more men had to die? She choked back a fresh round of tears. They would do no good. They would not return Samuel to her.

But this ache in her heart. She hadn't known pain quite like this even for her own father, the man who was nothing more than a smoky figure and a pair of strong arms to her. Samuel had been in her life for as long as she could remember. How would she break the news to her sisters? Would she even be able to get word to them in America?

Because of his pharmacy, she and Asher had stayed behind, just the two of them in this land.

Praise Dio, Mama and her sisters were now safe across the ocean. Only she was left here in Greece to face what must be faced. In that was a measure of solace.

Her husband came to his feet and helped her stand. The world spun, and she wobbled. He steadied her. Her rock.

"Have you had anything to eat today?"

"Not since this morning."

"Sit down and let me make you something."

Through the pain that sliced across her soul, she managed a small laugh. "You haven't cooked a meal in your life."

"I watched my mother, and I watch you. I think I can fry a lamb chop and a potato."

As the aromas of the meal filled the flat and set her stomach to rumbling, a pounding came at the door. "Mathilda, Mathilda."

Panic infused the voice of her friend Perla Yacoel. Now what? Mathilda opened the door to find the tall, thin woman as pale as a winter's moon. She drew Perla inside. "What is it?"

"The rabbi. You must come as fast as you can. Please hurry."

CHAPTER THREE

Pittsburgh, Pennsylvania, May 2019

I just don't know how much more I can take. Between finals coming up and things going on at home, I'm super stressed out. Jay is, well, Jay, just like he has been since the day he and Mom got married. I'll never know what she sees in him or why she had to ruin the relationship the two of us had after Dad died. We were doing great. We didn't need him.

—From the journal of Tessa Payton

The words in the child psychology textbook blurred in front of Tessa Payton's eyes. The final was tomorrow, and she needed a good grade, but for whatever reason, she couldn't concentrate.

She rubbed her temple where a headache throbbed. *Okay, Tessa, get with the program. Focus.* But no matter how much she coached and cajoled herself, she couldn't keep her mind on Jean Piaget's theory of child development.

She was going to fail. For sure.

The room was quiet, as was the floor. Everyone was studying. Even her roommate and cousin, Riley, had gone to the library. Maybe that's what she should have done.

But it wasn't noise that kept her from studying. No. Instead, over and over she replayed the conversation she'd had with her mom earlier in the day.

"Jay is really upset, you know."

Jay, Tessa's stepfather, was always upset with her. Had been for the entire ten years he'd been married to Mom. "What is it now?" She worked to keep the exasperation from her voice.

"Don't be like that."

Tessa suppressed a sigh.

"When you were home last weekend, did you throw some chocolate wrappers in the trash in your room?"

Oh no. This was not going to a good place. "Yeah, I guess I did."

"Well, Gigi got into your garbage can, ate the wrappers, and then was sick. Jay wasn't happy."

No, he probably wasn't. His little Chihuahua was forever getting into trouble. But Jay's reaction to the situation was nothing new.

"You can't do that, Tessa. Jay was left to clean up the mess. He gets mad at me when you do things like that."

"I'm sorry, Mom. I'll try to remember from now on."

That's what Jay did best. He pitted Mom against her and made himself the victim. Lily, his daughter, still lived at home and shared a room with Tessa. She should have closed the door or emptied the trash before she went out and left Gigi alone.

"Thank you. Well, I'd better run and get dinner on the table. Hope your exams go well. Love you." Mom hung up.

Now Tessa couldn't get the conversation out of her head. And she couldn't cool her boiling blood. She had to do well on this exam so she could get an internship this summer and get out of that house. Away from Jay. He couldn't find fault with her if she wasn't there.

But that wouldn't stop him from trying.

She stood, arched her back, and rolled her shoulders in an attempt to release some of the tension. The little twinkle lights sparkled in the room's darkness, transforming it from a concrete-block cell into a soothing haven. The only other light came from her desk lamp.

To try to focus, she paced the tiny room, reciting to herself

Piaget's stages of cognitive development. This should be so easy. She'd studied him last year in Psych 101.

But she couldn't remember a thing. Not a blessed thing.

She caught a scream in her throat. No need to disturb the girls in her dorm who actually could study.

Just as she remembered the sensorimotor and preoperational stages, the room's door flew open. Riley burst in and flipped on the fluorescent overhead light. She plopped a large box in the middle of the floor. "Look what we got."

Tessa stared at the monstrosity. How had tiny Riley ever been able to carry such a large package? "I think you mean what you got."

"Nope. Mom addressed it to both of us."

Aunt Fran did that because she knew Jay would never allow Mom to spend the money on such frivolities as a care package from home. He was paying enough for Tessa to go to this small Christian college.

Riley dug in her desk drawer, drew out a pair of scissors, and sliced open the tape. "Look at all of this stuff." She bounced up and down, her blond ponytail keeping time.

With Riley's enthusiasm so contagious, Tessa peered at the box's contents. Aunt Fran did send the best care packages. This one was stuffed with homemade cookies, bags of chips, jars of nuts, and lots and lots of chocolate. At least Gigi, that stupid dog, wouldn't be around to eat the wrappers. "Your mom is the best."

Riley gave Tessa a side hug. "You know what else? I got my genetic test results today. Did you?"

"I've been trying to study. Haven't really checked my email."

"Well, you'd better do it because I'm dying to see your results. Though they should be similar to mine since our mothers are second cousins. Or whatever it is when you have a common great-grandmother."

Piaget would just have to hang on. Tessa had been waiting for these results for weeks. She couldn't define what drove her to be so excited about this, but she was. Maybe she would discover more about Dad's family. After his death, she didn't see Granny or Gramps very much, and when she did, they had so much more to talk about. "Any surprises?"

"Not really. Mostly Greek on Mom's side and Russian on Dad's. Kind of boring. But I'm excited to see what you have."

"Well, we know most of what it will be from Mom's side since we're related." She unlocked her phone and pulled up her email. She tapped to see the results.

Riley peered over her shoulder. "What does it say?"

Tessa wrinkled her brow. "I don't understand this. Let me see yours."

Riley had hers up on her phone in record time. Tessa leaned over for a better look. She scrolled down. This didn't make sense. They should have at least some overlapping genetic types.

She handed her phone to Riley. "Look at this. It says that on my mother's side I'm Spanish and Sephardic Jew. Whatever that is. And a little French. Yours says you're Greek and Slavic. That can't be right."

"You're Jewish? I've never heard of Sephardic Jew."

"The point is that these results can't be right. Our moms are cousins. They have the same haplogroup. We share a common ancestor on our mothers' sides. There should be some overlap at least. I took biology for my science requirement. I know."

Riley stared at Tessa and shook her head, her hair slapping her cheek with the motion. "What are you saying?"

Tess gulped. A shiver coursed through her. "Either the lab got my sample mixed up with someone else's or we aren't biologically related. Maybe I'm even adopted."

Mom would probably be mad that Tessa was calling this late. Jay would be for sure. They went to bed super early. But this couldn't wait. Not for her to get home for summer break in a few days. Not even for the morning. Tessa had to know now.

The phone rang and rang until Mom picked up, her voice heavy with grogginess. "What's wrong?"

"Hello, Mom."

"You don't call at this hour if there's nothing wrong."

"It's only 10:30."

"You know Jay gets up early for work. Hang on." A rustle came. Mom was getting out of bed to talk without disturbing Jay. "What is it?"

"You know that DNA test I did when I was home over spring break?"

"That's what you woke me up for?"

"Listen, Mom. It's weird. Riley got her results too. We should have similar backgrounds on our mothers' sides. Some overlap at least. But we don't. Not a single thing."

"Huh?" Mom took medication to help her sleep. She wasn't real with it after she did.

"Hers came back Greek and Russian. Mine came back with Sephardic Jew and Spanish mixed with a little French."

"I don't understand."

"Either the lab made a mistake, I'm adopted, or you and Aunt Fran aren't biological cousins."

"You're not adopted." Her voice was flat.

"You're telling me the truth?"

"Of course. Don't be ridiculous. I'd never keep something like that from you. Besides, how many people have told us we look like sisters?"

A lot. "Are you adopted? Or is Aunt Fran? Or anyone else in the family?"

"No."

"No whispers or anything that someone adopted a Jewish child?"

"Oh honey, it's the middle of the night."

"Not really."

"To me it is."

"Do you remember any talk when you were growing up about there being any Jewish in our family?"

"No..." A creak. Mom must be moving about.

Tessa swung her legs over the side of her unmade bed. "That didn't sound convincing."

"Why are you bringing this up? Why do you want to know about this so much?"

"I don't know."

Riley waved as she left the room. She'd said she was going to La Café for a La Latte to keep her awake a few more hours so she could study.

Why did Tessa want to know about her ancestry so much? Maybe because no one in her family ever spoke much about the past. If only Grandma were still alive. "Did *Yiayia* ever say anything to you about anything like this?"

"No..."

"You're hesitating again."

"I don't know. To me, Aunt Katherine and my mother didn't look very much alike. But that was a long time ago. Both of them are gone now. I was only a little girl when my aunt died, so my memory may be foggy."

"What are we going to do?"

"What difference does it make? That was so long ago, and like I said, neither of them are here anymore."

"Don't you want to find out if you're adopted?"

"Not really. And you should just drop this. None of this changes who you are. Who I am."

"What about Aunt Fran?"

"I've seen pictures of Aunt Katherine pregnant with Fran."

"Then either Yiayia or Aunt Katherine was adopted."

"You have studying to do. Put this to the side and concentrate on that. The past doesn't make a difference now. You have a future to think about."

"I know that." But deep in her belly, Tessa had to know. Something undefinable drove her. "Thanks, Mom. Sorry I woke you."

After they hung up, Tessa was back on her computer, not for the educational psychology final, but to research Sephardic Jews.

Because she doubted the lab had made a mistake. She would call them first thing in the morning and talk to them.

She was still knee deep in research when Riley came back. "How's your studying going?"

"It isn't. Listen to this. Sephardic Jews are Jews from Spain who were kicked out of the country by King Ferdinand and Queen Isabella. Those are the ones who financed Christopher Columbus. Anyway, many of those Jews ended up in Greece."

"You should have been a history major." Riley set her coffee on her desk and pulled her laptop from her backpack.

"That's why there is Spanish in me."

"You don't know that. I think there was some kind of mix-up."

"Maybe. But isn't that interesting?"

"If you say so." Riley yawned, then sipped her latte. Probably not her first one. "You aren't going to let this go, are you?"

"If it's true, it means that someone along the line—either one of our grandmothers or one of our mothers—was adopted. And it means I'm Jewish."

"That's kind of cool." With that, Riley was lost in her paper for some nursing class she was taking, tapping away at her keyboard.

Tessa couldn't sit still. Yiayia had had a picture of herself and her twin sister on her end table when Tessa was growing up. Two sweet little girls, big bows in their hair. Yiayia had said the photo was taken when she was two or three years old, soon after her family came to America.

Everything about Yiayia was darker. Her hair, her eyes, her skin. Not that Aunt Katherine was fair, but she was so opposite Yiayia.

She had a round face. Aunt Katherine's was long. Yiayia had curly hair. Aunt Katherine's was straight. They looked nothing like twins.

Like a bubble, a bigger question rose from deep inside Tessa.

If she was indeed Jewish, what did that mean for her? Did that change her in some way?

CHAPTER FOUR

Somehow Tessa managed to survive finals, and Mom had arrived with Jay's truck to move her home for the summer. Not a place she wanted to be, but the internship she had gotten was virtual, so home it was.

She carried a box full of teacups and loose-leaf teas down the stairs to where Mom had parked in the circle drive in front of the dorm. Just as she reached the bottom step, her phone rang. Even though she didn't recognize the number, she set the box down and answered it.

By the time she hung up, her hands were shaking. She shouldn't carry a box filled with such delicate items when she might drop it any minute. Finally, she arrived at the truck and was able to set the box inside without damaging the contents.

She had to sit on the tailgate to regain her composure.

Mom returned with a plastic bin that she set in the truck beside Tessa. "What's going on? You look upset."

"That was the DNA lab. I had left a message with them the other day asking about the test I took to see if there could be any mistake." Tessa drew in a deep breath. "She finally got back to me and said there wasn't."

Mom pinched together her perfectly plucked eyebrows. "Oh." Another flat tone to Mom's voice. Other than the eyebrow thing, not much of a reaction from her.

Tessa nodded. "We're Jewish. Sephardic Jews, to be exact. From Spain to Greece."

Mom pushed the box aside and sat next to Tessa.

"The Jewish DNA came from your yiayia. The amount in me is equivalent to great-grandparents." Tessa couldn't stop her foot from jiggling. "I was thinking about the pictures we have at home of Yiayia and her sister when they were little, soon after they came to this country. Yiayia is so much darker skinned than her sister. Before this, I never thought twice about it, but now it makes me wonder."

"Has this been bothering you since you got those results?"

"Yeah, kind of." Tessa and Mom could have these kinds of talks when Jay wasn't around, and Tessa cherished them. "For one reason or another, either Yiayia chose not to share her story with anyone, or her mother forbade the telling of it. But why keep this secret?"

Mom shrugged.

"They must have had some reason. Thessaloniki was occupied by the Germans during the war when Yiayia and her mother were there. Perhaps that's why they kept their heritage secret." She turned toward Mom, her foot jiggling more than ever. "I want to go to Greece and find out."

"Who's going to go with you? I can't take time off work. And where would you get the money? That's an expensive trip."

Though she hadn't put much thought into the idea until just now, it came into focus with a great deal of speed. "I don't need anyone to come with me. In fact, I want to do this on my own." She'd never had an adventure before. It would be fun and different. "I have the money in the bank that's been there forever."

"That's to be used for education." Mom swiped a graying strand of hair from her damp forehead. "What about your internship?"

"That's the best part. It's remote, so I can work from anywhere in the world I can get internet access. This is the perfect time for me to go and do this, before I graduate next year and have to start working for real."

"I don't like the idea, and I don't think Jay will be fond of it either."

"I'm an adult now, and if I want to do this, neither of you can stop me."

Mom sucked in a breath. "I've never heard you so defiant. This isn't like you."

No, all her life, she'd been the good girl, first to please Mom when she was grieving Dad's loss, then to please Jay and keep peace in the tense house. This was her chance to get away from the drama, from Jay's demands and Mom's pleading looks, to live her life the way she wanted.

An entire summer of freedom left her head spinning. "I'm going to do it. My passport is up to date from my mission trip over Christmas break."

"You know nothing about Greece. Where would you stay? How would you get around? What do you hope to accomplish by going?"

"I'll learn. I think the same group that ran the mission in the Dominican Republic has an organization in Greece. If I contact them, I'm sure they can help me. I can even volunteer with them a little bit."

Mom crossed her arms, her lips drawn tight. "You seem set on this."

"I am. We aren't who we thought we were. We're Jewish, part of God's chosen people. I need to find out more about that. In your day, you would say you had to find yourself. I guess that's what I'm doing."

"I never had to find myself." Mom stood. "You're Tessa Payton, my daughter, psychology student, Pennsylvania resident, descended from Greeks. What more do you need to know?" She marched off.

Tessa sighed and slipped from the tailgate, thumping to the asphalt driveway. She trudged up the stairs to her room. By the time she got there, Mom was already on her way back down with a suitcase Tessa had crammed full. Riley was pulling the sheets off her bed and folding them.

"I'm going to Greece."

Tessa's announcement stopped Riley cold. "You're what?"

"Going to spend the summer in Greece to try to discover what secret Yiayia held." She lowered her voice. "Not having to go home is a huge bonus."

Riley shrugged and continued folding. "Sounds fun. I only wish I could go, but some of us have real jobs." She laughed.

Tessa joined her. "Sure. You have to get up at five to be at the nursing home by six. Sounds like a blast to me. I get to experience another culture, our culture, and I can work anytime I want. In fact, six in the morning will be... I don't know, but probably sometime in the afternoon in Thessaloniki."

"You're sure about this?"

"More sure than I've been about anything in my life."

"You aren't going." Jay thumped his rather large fist on the kitchen table, jiggling the silverware and glasses on it. "You certainly aren't going to take that money and leave me with the bill for your final year of college."

Tessa bit the inside of her cheek. Asking Jay for permission to go to Greece had been pointless. Bringing this up to anyone was. She should have just left a note and snuck off in the middle of the night. She fisted her own hands. "I'm not who I thought I was. I'm a Jew. That changes everything about me. Somewhere back in the family was a huge secret, one that I'm going to uncover." Breathing hard, she slid from her chair. "Don't worry. I'll drop out of college if I have to."

Too hot to say another word, she stomped from the kitchen

and up the stairs to her bedroom, slamming the door behind her. When she was at last alone, she released her breath, tears stinging the back of her throat.

Truth be told, the entire idea of going to a foreign country by herself and trying to find her way around terrified her. Other than that trip with the school group over winter break, she had never been out of the country.

Anything, though, was better than staying in this house for three months. She couldn't take it anymore. Ever since she'd been young, Jay had had it out for her, had made her life miserable. The worst was when he'd left her behind at a gas station when the entire family, including Jay's parents and some of his daughter Lily's cousins, was on a vacation to Yellowstone. There were so many of them that they'd had to take two cars.

She'd sat there for hours on the concrete sidewalk, the summer sun beating on her head, sweat dripping down her face, until the family's red car had returned. She got inside, buckled her belt, and Jay headed back to the highway without a word.

Mom had turned and smiled at Tessa, her eyes glistening but her lips tight. Her stepsister had this Cheshire-cat style grin plastered on her face. It was all Tessa could do not to knock it off. Only Jay's potential ire kept her hands folded in her lap.

Later Mom explained they believed Tessa was in the car with Jay's parents. That's what Lily told them, anyway. But Mom and Jay should have checked and made sure that's where she was.

That's why she had to leave Pittsburgh and do this. She didn't belong in this family. Jay had made that crystal clear. So where did she belong? Whose flesh and blood was she?

She swiped her laptop from her desk and plopped on the bed with it, then opened tab after tab on her browser: searching flights to Thessaloniki, where Yiayia had come from; what the city was like; how to get around; where to stay; what to do. She watched YouTube videos and read articles and blogs until her eyes were bleary.

By midnight she had a plan. Inhaling long and slow, she pressed PURCHASE for the airline ticket. One way. Then she booked an inexpensive rental for a month in the center of the city. That should help her get around by walking and conserve her funds.

Jay would be furious, and Mom would probably cry, but she was going to Greece in two weeks.

She'd wait to tell them until a couple of days before her flight.

Once she closed her laptop, she picked up her phone and called Riley.

"What's up? Miss me already?"

Tessa chuckled. "Hardly. I'm sleeping so much better now that I don't have to listen to your snoring."

"So funny."

"Hey, I'm calling to ask you a favor."

"Um-hm." Riley chomped on what sounded like a chip. Lucky girl that she could eat whatever she wanted and never gain an ounce.

"I need you to drop me off at the airport two weeks from yesterday."

The chomping stopped. "You're going, aren't you?"

"Against Mom and Jay's wishes, yes. I just made my plane reservations."

Riley squealed, and Tessa had to hold the phone away from her ear to keep from going deaf. "I'm so excited for you. What a great adventure you're going to have. And all those Greek guys."

"No guys for me. This is strictly a business trip, just to find out why—how—I got to be Jewish."

"I can explain that to you."

Both girls ended up in peals of laughter so loud that Mom shot Tessa a text from across the hall to knock it off. Jay was sleeping.

Soon she wouldn't have to worry about that. From what she'd read online, life didn't really start in Greece until nine in the evening. Then again, she'd be alone. "I sure wish you could come with me, Ri."

"I know. Me too, but you'll do great. You were always the first one to try anything new, so this is very keeping in your character. Wait till I tell my parents."

"You can't." Tessa struggled to keep her voice at a low whisper. "I'm not going to be able to endure Jay's wrath—and Mom's too—if I tell them now. No one, and I mean no one, is to know until just a few days before. Nothing comes out of your mouth or your fingers about this until I give you the go-ahead, got it?"

"Will you be back for the start of school?"

"I have no idea." Tessa had no idea about anything anymore.

CHAPTER FIVE

Everything's different. Nothing is what it was just weeks, even days, ago. The world has turned on its head, the North Pole now the South Pole. When you feel like you are falling from the face of the earth, how do you endure?

—From the journal of Mathilda Nissim

Mathilda's shoes tapped a hurried rhythm as she made her way over the ancient cobblestone streets toward the rabbi's house. What in the world did he want with her, especially with the new curfew in effect?

She held fast to Asher's hand as they wound their way through the Kapani market toward Rabbi Koretz's house. They knew him from the high holy days and when they attended synagogue each Saturday, and to Mathilda, the rituals were comforting but not very spiritual. They lacked something, but she couldn't put her finger on what that might be. "Why do you think the rabbi wants to see me?"

They turned the corner where the fishmonger had his stall, the salty stench of hake, anchovies, and *kalamari* coloring the air, and continued down the narrow, shop-lined street. Asher squeezed her hand. "My hope is that he intends to talk sense into you. You must know that you can't continue writing your paper."

She kept pace with her husband and bit her tongue. They had agreed on this earlier, but starting an argument now would do no one any good. For all they knew, the rabbi might have a special task for them. Perhaps he was going to encourage her to continue the paper to keep the community engaged and ready to push back against their aggressors.

Broken glass scattered across the road shimmered in the dying daylight. All around them was still and dark and quiet, the stalls already shuttered for the night. Far too early considering that dinner wasn't usually served until after sunset.

Not too long after they set out, they arrived at the building with large archways on the first level and a scattering of scrolled iron balconies on the levels above. With each stair they climbed, their steps in sync with each other, Mathilda's stomach trembled more. Her thoughts whirled in her brain until they were a tangled mess.

They knocked on the heavy oak door that separated them from the rabbi. He answered it so fast, he must have been standing on the other side, and ushered them in with urgency, shutting and latching the door behind him. "*Vinido bueno.* Thank you for coming so fast. There is much to do."

He led them into the light and bright living room to a large sofa across from a polished radio. "Por favor, have a seat." Rabbi Koretz situated himself in an armchair across from them.

In all this time, Asher hadn't released his grasp on Mathilda.

"I have read your newspaper, Mrs. Nissim. You are well informed, articulate, and…" He rubbed his beard. "Well, you are opinionated."

She bit her bottom lip. "As a writer, that is my job, to state my beliefs and to urge the population to action, no matter what the situation may be."

The rabbi nodded. "Be that as it may, I have already been visited by our new occupiers, who had much to say about the Jews of this city. I fear difficult days are ahead. We must watch our steps and be careful and thoughtful with what we say. They want all Jewish newspapers to stop. Immediately."

"I'm afraid I can't do that."

"Mrs. Nissim, I'm not asking you. If you do not, you risk many lives, including your own."

Rabbi Koretz was Ashkenazi. He didn't understand the Sephardic ways, and that had been a sticking point between him and the Jews of Salonika for years. "It is imperative that I continue. How else will we fight against this enemy? Will we allow them to destroy us as they have so many others?"

The rabbi turned his attention to Asher. "Be a good husband and make your wife submit to you. Help her to understand the gravity of the situation. We will be wiped out if we do not cooperate with the Germans. If we do as they say, they may spare us."

Mathilda squeezed her husband's hand so hard she might have broken his fingers. To his credit, he didn't wince, just withdrew it and pulled her close. "Rabbi, we honor and respect you as the head of our community. My wife is an intelligent and capable woman, gifts given to her by Dio. In good conscience, I cannot take those away from her. We discussed this at home and have taken measures to hide the equipment and to make sure her work will not be discovered. I may not like it, but I will support her."

"You can't know that you'll be able to keep this secret." Rabbi Koretz slid to the edge of his chair and leaned over his knees. "As I said, I am not requesting this. It is an order from the German government, the one now in charge of Salonika. Dio commands that we obey them."

Mathilda could no longer rein in her tongue. "If we obey them, we die. If we resist, we have a chance at life."

"You don't know if the Jews from other countries have died. They have gone to Poland to work and to start new lives. For many centuries, our ancestors have been forced from their homes to live in foreign lands. This is no different but a continuation of the way we have always known life."

Mathilda stood, as did Asher and the rabbi. "My words are important and vital. They cannot be bottled up and put away until the time is safe again. I believe we must do what we can to stand against the Nazis so that we'll live. Poland is not the Promised Land." A place where she desperately wanted to go.

Heat rising in her chest, she turned on her heel and headed for the door. *"Adyo."* She marched from the flat and down the stairs.

Asher's quick steps soon caught up with her on the landing. "Why did you say such things to the rabbi? Don't you respect him and his knowledge?"

She stopped and turned to face him a step above her. "You defended me to him, and now you question me?"

"I believe he perceives much, and his words should be given the consideration they're due. Whatever you decide, I'll support you. You must at least think about what he had to say. Perhaps Poland is not the worst place to go. It doesn't have the warm sunshine and clear blue water of Greece, but we could make a home there and be happy, if that's where they send us."

"You know better, Asher; you know better. They don't merely drive us out. They destroy us along the way. The Germans have made no secret of their hatred for our race. What if we all rose up and resisted them to protect our homes and our families?"

Asher stepped down so he was level with her, his rather rumpled suit smelling of rubbing alcohol and other things he handled at the pharmacy. Odors which she had become familiar with over the years she had known him. "If the entire Polish army, if the entire Greek army, the French and Dutch armies were not able to stop them, can a handful of untrained Jews do any better?"

"I don't know." She spoke as she stared into his eyes. "But if we do nothing, our doom is sure. That much I do know."

"We must trust Dio in this and every circumstance."

Trust Dio. For so many of her people, that was an easy task. They just did it. For Mathilda, that was too much to ask. Visions of flames leaping from buildings all around her rose in her mind. And her father, rushing into those flames in a vain attempt to rescue some.

She rubbed the scars on her arm.

How could she trust a deity who didn't love her enough to spare her father? He was every bit as vengeful as the Torah said He was. And now this threat had arrived at their gates. Action was what was called for. "I beg of you, Asher. I know you are concerned for me and for many others, and that's why I love you so much. You love people with a genuineness that I will never understand. You speak of trust. Now is the time for you to trust me. Allow me to continue my work."

"You will do it whether or not I permit it." He rubbed his hairy cheek against her smooth one. There was no harshness in his voice, as there would be with many men, just acceptance. It wasn't that he was weak. Instead, he believed in her and her gifts and calling.

"This is essential to our survival."

"Then I won't stand in your way but will stand beside you. Promise me one thing?"

How could she deny him anything? "What is it?"

"That if the situation becomes too dangerous and your life or the lives of others are in jeopardy, you will stop when I ask. No arguing or going behind my back—you will simply stop."

She reached up and stroked his cheek. He had been so good to her. When other men would have demanded full obedience of their wives and would not have tolerated them to have jobs, Asher stood by her and loved her. He was giving her this gift of her words. Now it was time for her to give back. "I will. The moment you tell me to stop, my little press will cease until it is safe again."

He pulled her close until it was impossible to tell where one left off and the other began. He kissed her behind her ear and whispered, "*Te amo*, Mathilda. I couldn't bear it if any harm befell you. Promise me that you'll be more careful than you have ever been in your life."

"I won't be reckless, Asher. I would never do anything that would bring harm to you. You are my life."

"When we married, I vowed to protect you. I will do that to the best of my ability. My fear is that it won't be enough. Still, I trust that Dio will do what is best for us. I trust Him to direct us."

For the longest time, they stood in the deserted stairwell, body against body, breathing in unison. She was so blessed to have him in her life. He was the best man she had ever known, although Samuel had been a very close second.

Samuel. With the summons from the rabbi, she had put away her grief for a short time. Now, here, it hit her with full force, a wave slamming against the shore. She sobbed and sobbed until her nose ran and Asher's shirt was soaked.

"I know, mi corasón, I know."

"What they did to Samuel was inhumane. Who will give me a little extra meat? Who will greet me with a smile and ask how my family is and what I've heard from America? I am scared, Asher. Terrified. I watched the life leave Samuel's body. None of the Germans stopped. Do you know that one stepped on him? They were cruel to an old man who had done them no wrong. That's why I must put away my fear and continue writing. Oh, but my heart aches."

"Grieve as you must. His loss is great, and many will miss him a good deal. Who knows why the Nazis picked him, of all people, to show their might and frighten the rest of the citizens. Let it serve as a warning to us, that we have to follow their orders if we want to live. If we do that, we will be safe, no matter where they resettle us. As long as I have you by my side, my life will be complete."

A light mist fell as they exited the building into the night. The mouth-watering aroma of roasting meat and oregano filled the air, but it only turned Mathilda's stomach sour.

Asher tugged on her. "We must hurry home before we are caught breaking curfew. Quickly now, quickly."

Only a few blocks through the market to their small flat. Oregano now mixed with spicy pepper powder and flowery teas.

The fragrance of home.

Just as they got to the door, a military car hummed down the street on the other corner from them. Asher turned the key, and they dashed inside.

Is this what life was to be like from now on, always glancing over their shoulders and scurrying like cockroaches when light was shined on them?

If so, how would they ever stand it?

CHAPTER SIX

The brilliant Greek sun hid its face this day, as it should. Today Samuel would be laid to rest in the huge Jewish cemetery where hundreds of thousands of their ancestors slept, including Mathilda's own father. Dark clouds filled the sky, threatening to weep for Samuel as Mathilda did.

As they trekked the fifteen minutes or so from their flat to the synagogue, Asher held her by the hand the entire way. Her words ran dry, so they didn't speak.

The service was a blur. Through her tears, she couldn't spot Asher on the other side of the room. By rote, she recited Psalms 49, 16, and 23. The *Tziduk Hadin,* a prayer of faith and of divine justice, was said.

The rabbi, not Rabbi Koretz who had traveled to Athens, led the memorial prayer. What he said didn't register with Mathilda. All was dark and silent in her world.

Then came the funeral procession. The congregation followed the hearse toward the cemetery, the parade of people behind it carrying food. Usually onlookers would throw candy and coins, but not today. Today they remained hidden in their homes and shops, afraid of the Germans who now lined the processional route.

Life rushed by them as they passed the *hammam*, the ancient Turkish bath, its many brick domes covering it, and entered a newer part of the city, one that had been touched by the 1917 fire and rebuilt.

When they arrived, the professional mourners were already

there, as they were every day. These women, all wearing *kofia* headdresses, two silk ribbons on top of each other that went over the head and tied under the chin, were paid to come to this place of eternal rest and weep and wail for all the lost souls. Their cries went to heaven, to Dio's ear. This allowed Mathilda to keep her sobs silent, her cheeks from becoming tearstained.

As a woman, Mathilda was not allowed to enter the cemetery. Instead, she stood with a small cluster of people gathered on the cemetery's edge, near where Samuel would soon be lowered into the ground.

Once the short service had concluded, the handful of people who had come to pay their last respects to Samuel dissipated. There hadn't been many of them as Samuel had never married or had children. That's why he said he loved Mathilda so much. She and her sisters were the children Dio had never blessed him with.

The rabbi touched Mathilda's elbow and whispered something in her ear, but the words didn't reach her brain. The world around her faded into a haze, and a scene from long ago broke brilliant in her mind.

She had been a small child, one who had just lost her father in a horrific manner. Their home was gone along with all their possessions. Papa had left some money in the bank, and Mama had gone to try to find a job and a place for them to live. The four of them couldn't stay with Mama's friends much longer. It was too crowded with so many crammed into a tiny flat.

Mathilda had wandered down the stairs and sat on the front stoop as she had most days in the weeks since they had come to stay here. Horse-drawn carts rumbled down the street, and a few motorcars whizzed by. Mostly it was the people who attracted her attention. Men in business suits hustled to their offices. The old men ambled toward the coffee shop on the corner where they would while away the hours playing checkers and sipping on the strong brew softened with cream.

Mathilda's burned and bandaged fingers itched to write what she saw, how life continued for some even as it ended for others, the acrid odor of burned wood and flesh mingling with coffee, oregano, and sea salt. She had no paper or pencil, however, so she wrote it in her mind, etched it deep in her heart, where it would remain forever.

Then from down the street came a small man who wore round spectacles and had a bloody apron wrapped around his waist. When Mathilda glanced at his face, though, a smile wreathed his mouth, and a pleasant twinkle lit his eyes.

He approached and reached into the bag in his hand and pulled out a piece of Greek delight candy dusted in powdered sugar. "This is for you. While I like bergamot flavor the best, you seemed to be a sour cherry girl to me."

Mathilda jumped to her feet. "That's my favorite." She took the proffered treat and nibbled the edge of the soft, jelly-like sweet. "*Gracyas.*"

"*Denada.* You're most welcome. Every day when I am on my way to get myself a cup of coffee, I see you sitting on this very step, gazing outward but looking inward."

To her eight-year-old self, his words were strange, but as she recalled them now, they made so much more sense because that is just what she did. So many thoughts and hopes and dreams swirled inside of her, both now and then.

"My name is Samuel." He reached out to shake her hand. She had never done so with anyone, but it was time for her to grow up. That's what Mama had said after Papa died, so she shook his hand with her bandaged one.

He said nothing about it.

Her fingertips touched his palm. His hand was warm and dry, and in that instant, a bond formed between the two of them. "I'm Mathilda, and I'd like to be your friend."

Samuel had chuckled, as smooth as the harbor on a windless

day. From that day on, they had been the best of friends, this strange duo. He had helped Mama get a job and had found them a flat near his butcher shop, the one Mathilda and Asher still occupied. When Mama had to work, Mathilda would slip over to Samuel's, and he would provide her the tools she needed to write.

When the other girls at school picked on her, he encouraged her. When she had a birthday, he celebrated with her. When she brought Asher to meet him, he gave them his blessing.

Now his light too had been snuffed from her life. Another loss, another grief to bear.

Mama would always shake her fists at heaven. "Ach, there is nothing but toil and trouble for our people in this life. Until the Messiah comes, we will suffer. That is our lot in this world."

Asher returned to Mathilda's side, bringing her back to the present. She knelt in the damp grass at the edge of the cemetery. "I shall miss you so very much, Samuel. You will never know all you meant to me. If only I could have told you. I should have told you, but now time has run out. You helped a frightened, lonely little girl find her way in the world. You taught her to be brave, and so I will be. I promise I won't give up until the very last breath leaves my body. You will not have died in vain."

She lifted her face toward the sky as the first raindrops splattered on her cheek. Or were those tears? It was impossible to tell. Her headscarf slipped, and she straightened it.

Then Asher helped her to her feet and held her in his tight embrace. She wept on his shoulder, but he never let her go. When her well of tears ran dry, he offered her his handkerchief, and she wiped her eyes.

"Let's go home. This has been too much for you. I'll try to find some nice music on the radio and brew you a cup of coffee before we aren't able to get any." Asher once again took her by the hand, and much as they had on their way to the synagogue, they traversed the city's streets without saying a word.

Just as Samuel had been good and kind to her, now Asher took his place, drying her hair with a towel when they arrived home rather damp from the rain, combing it through, relaxing her while she sipped her coffee. He knew just how much cream to put in.

"Te amo, my husband." She took the brush from him and turned toward him on the sofa. "Those words don't come easy for me, but that doesn't mean the feelings aren't there. In case anything ever happens to separate us, I want you to know how I feel. You are everything to me."

"Te amo, Mathilda; te amo. I can't replace Samuel in your life, but I promise I will always be here for you and I will always take care of you the best way I know how."

"I'm praying that we can always be together."

"If it is within my power to make that happen, I will."

"No matter how stubborn I am?"

"No matter what. There is nothing you can do that will ever make me love you less. You don't have to say the words. Your love radiates from you to all you touch. Samuel knew. He knew how you felt."

"With Mama and my sisters in America, you're all I have." She stroked his beard, so thick and dark. "Samuel taught me how to stand up for myself when the girls at school bullied me. He taught me how to fight. He isn't here anymore to do that. The torch has passed to me."

"Then you fight, and I will fight with you. You aren't alone."

Yet despite Asher's reassurance, her heart was empty.

She went to the bedroom, lifted the loose floorboards, and withdrew her journal. Today was a day she should commemorate. She positioned herself at the little table in front of the window, curtains drawn, and wrote:

Today we buried the most wonderful man other than Asher. Samuel is gone. Asher has been so good to me, comforting me and taking care of me, reassuring me that he will always be by my side. Still, there is a hole yet to be filled, but with what? We have no children, but we have agreed that this isn't the time to bring new life into such an uncertain world. If—when—the world returns to normal, then would be the time to have a baby.

I'd like that very much, to blend Asher and myself together into another whole human being. Often I imagine myself rocking my child, singing a lullaby and kissing the soft, downy head. But I want my child to have a good, happy, and safe life, somewhere they can live without fear and persecution.

Does such a place exist anywhere in the world?

Is that what is truly missing in my soul?

I believe there is more to it than that. All my life, I have dreamed of going to Israel, the Promised Land, to stand on Mount Nebo and look over it as Moses did. I would like to dip my feet into the Jordan River and walk the streets of Jerusalem, Dio's dwelling place.

If I manage to get there at some point, perhaps that would fill the void in my heart. Then I would feel more connected to Dio. Perhaps I would feel His presence and I would gain a measure of peace.

I sit here in front of the darkened window, only a small lamp on the desk illuminating my words. How distant all those dreams are. I can't even reach out and brush them with my fingertips. Deep inside I fear Samuel's death will be the first of many.

Maybe it's the fear that has carved out this space inside my soul. When the Nazis leave, the hole will close on its own, and I will be healed.

If only I knew what to do, how to fill my cup. Even my work, which brings me great joy, isn't enough. It should be fulfilling, but it's only frustrating. What I have been warning the people about for months has come to pass, and just as I predicted, we have sat by and allowed the Germans to occupy us.

So here I am, left no closer to an answer than I was at the beginning. Perhaps this emptiness is merely loneliness and aching for Samuel, a missing of Mama and my sisters in America. But I feel that it is so much more, so much deeper than that. I am searching in the darkness, but I have no answer.

I am empty.

CHAPTER SEVEN

I can't believe it. As I write this, I'm more than 30,000 feet in the air over Germany, and Greece is getting closer and closer on the map on the screen in front of me. Somehow I managed to sleep for several hours on the plane. I'm just ready to be there now. What will this adventure hold? I have no idea. But something deep inside tells me this trip will change me forever, in ways I never imagined.

—From the journal of Tessa Payton

As she made her way down the steps from the airplane to the tarmac, Tessa clutched her backpack's strap, more tired than she had ever been in her entire life. The hot Greek sun beat on her as she filed along with the other passengers to the waiting bus.

This was Thessaloniki. From all the reading she had done on the plane, she discovered it used to be called Salonika as well as Thessalonica, the city where Paul had preached and the people to whom he wrote the book of Thessalonians.

It was all a bit surreal, to actually be here where her grandmother and great-grandmother had been born, where generations of her family had lived. At least, that's what she had believed until a few weeks ago. Nothing was certain anymore.

The bus ride didn't take long, and as the airport wasn't large, it didn't take her much time to collect her one, very overstuffed, suitcase and find her way out of the airport. She had been through immigration in Athens a few hours before.

Now where was her driver? There was supposed to be

someone outside holding up a sign with her name on it, but though she searched the sea of people and papers, none of them was for her.

She forced herself to keep her breathing even. There was no need to panic. He had to be around here somewhere. She adjusted her backpack, found an out-of-the-way spot against the building, and pulled up the email on her phone.

Meet at terminal two.

Sure enough, there were two terminals, two separate buildings sort of in an L-shaped configuration. She returned to where she had been. That was terminal one. Okay, easy enough explanation as to why she couldn't locate her driver. But when she got to the other building, there was still no one with her sign.

She worked to get some internet and reach the taxi company, but she couldn't connect. It refused to go through. Now what? The email had said the driver would wait only so long and then she'd be stranded.

Great. This was her first time out of the country, and now she was going to be stuck at the airport with no way to get to her short-term apartment rental. Her chest tightened.

For what seemed like forever, she wandered back and forth between the terminals without success. He wasn't here. Perhaps some Good Samaritan would take pity on her and call a taxi. The city was too far away to walk.

Down the way, she spotted a group of people with luggage. That might be a good place to gather her thoughts and figure out her next step. As she rolled her bag along in that direction, a short, dark-haired man scurried toward her, a sign with her name clutched in his hand.

She raced toward him, the wheels on her luggage clacking on the sidewalk. "I'm Tessa Payton. I'm her." She pointed at the sign.

The man grinned and nodded. "Tessa Payton. I look all over for you but not find you. I call you but you don't answer."

"I can't get a cell signal. I didn't know where to look for you.

I'm glad we met."

"Come, come, we go now." He grabbed both her suitcase and her bag and hustled toward a parking lot.

She settled into the back seat of the black Mercedes, and they sped toward the city. At first it wasn't much different from the Pittsburgh suburbs Tessa called home, though maybe a little more spread out. Shopping malls and subdivisions lined both sides of what was the Greek answer to an interstate highway.

As they got closer to the heart of Thessaloniki, however, everything changed. The buildings stood shoulder to shoulder, packed one on top of the other, but they weren't tall like in Pittsburgh. Definitely not sleek or modern. Every five- or six-story apartment building boasted multiple balconies.

For this entire time, they had been traveling close to the harbor, but then the driver turned inland, and the streets narrowed. With cars parked on both sides, there was room for only one vehicle to get by at a time.

He stopped. "This is the address." He grabbed her bags from the trunk, placed them on the narrow sidewalk, and zoomed away.

To say that it took Tessa several minutes to get her bearings would be an understatement. She had to look up on her phone the directions for getting the key to the building and then figure out that she had to turn the key several times in the lock on the main door before it opened. The tiny elevator in the lobby was a no go for her. All she needed was a panic attack brought on by claustrophobia, so she lugged her bag up four flights of stairs and through two more doorways before she finally found herself inside the apartment.

Clean and cool. For the first time since Riley had dropped her off at the airport this morning—or was it yesterday morning?—Tessa took a deep breath and allowed her shoulders to relax.

Leaving her bag in the middle of the living room, she plopped on the gray sofa and closed her eyes. Fatigue pulled at every muscle, but she couldn't sleep. She was as buzzed as if she'd had ten cups of coffee.

After washing in the large shower, she slipped into some clean clothes, wrapped her hair in a towel, and sat cross-legged on the bed. From deep within her overstuffed backpack, she pulled out her journal. Ever since she'd been in sixth grade, she'd been keeping one. She hadn't even graduated college yet, but she already had a shelf full of them.

She wrote in purple ink:

What on earth am I doing here? I don't even know what day it is to title this entry. Everything is so different, from the language to the architecture to the toilet paper. Don't ask.

I thought this would be a fun adventure, but I'm having second thoughts. All I know is that I can't run home and admit to Mom and Jay that they were right and that I was crazy for wanting to come here. I may not find out anything about where I came from and who my ancestors were. I may not find out anything about what it means to be Jewish.

Then again, what if I do discover something? There are secrets in the family—there have to be. Otherwise my DNA would have more closely matched Riley's. She would have come up as my first cousin once removed or second cousin or something like that. But she didn't.

So someone along the way hid something. What was it? Who was it? Why did no one ever talk about us being Jewish?

I guess it's those questions that have driven me here. Or flown me. Forgive me if this rambles. I'm rather jet-lagged. Mom would always tell me curiosity would kill the cat. Maybe she even knows something she's refusing to tell me. I should have talked to her more.

I'm here now, and there's no going back. I've spent the

money and taken the trip. I'm scared about discovering the secret and scared about not discovering it. I'm scared to be in a foreign country all alone.

God, protect me and keep me safe. Help me to navigate here and to figure out how this culture operates. Help me to find what I've come so far to discover. And Lord, send me to just the right person to help me.

Tessa slept until ten the next morning, waking to a stream of sunlight pouring through the balcony door. Today was the day the rest of her life started. That may be a little melodramatic, but she couldn't help the tingling in her fingers and toes that told her something was going to change.

Thanks to great Wi-Fi in the apartment, she managed to locate a nearby coffee shop, get herself a cup, and successfully find her way back to the Airbnb. Maybe this wouldn't be so hard after all.

The coffee, stronger and more bitter than anything she'd ever had before, woke her up the rest of the way. While still at home, she had searched a little bit about the city and decided that the Jewish Museum was going to be the place to start. It wasn't far from the apartment.

About fifteen minutes later, she proudly stood in front of the building on a street that resembled many of the roads she'd traversed to get here. An iron grate covered the large arched doorway. Above it was a bunch of Greek letters that meant nothing to her, but in English there were the words *Jewish Museum of Thessaloniki.* An armed guard stood sentry outside but didn't stop her when she entered.

A middle-aged woman sat behind the counter and smiled when Tessa approached. She said something in Greek, then switched to English. "Hello."

"Hi. I'd like to see the museum. Do you speak English?"

"I do." She smiled again. "I need the passport, and you

give me your phone."

"My phone? Why?"

"No pictures allowed."

"Oh. I'm here to do some research into my family. Photographs would help."

"You come to know more about them? You are Jewish?"

"Yes. I just found out. I don't know much. I was hoping someone here could help me."

After the woman peered at Tessa's passport and handed it back to her and took her phone, she nodded. "This is good. You wait here. I will find someone to help you."

Several minutes passed in which Tessa wandered the exhibits in the entry area. Glass cases displayed various Jewish items including candlesticks and menorahs. Had some of her Jewish ancestors owned and used items such as these? What a strange thought, yet it drew her closer to those who came before and gave her a small glimpse into what their lives were like.

She hadn't quite finished examining all the displays before the woman returned with a young man, probably not too much older than herself, unruly dark curls crowning his head. His smile warmed his very cliché chocolate eyes. "Welcome. I am Giannis Matarasso. How can I help you?"

His English, though rather accented, was about the best she'd heard since her arrival. "I'm searching for information on my family."

"Yes, yes. So you tell me what you know."

She filled him in on everything she had learned in the past few weeks. "That's about all there is, and I don't know where to go from here, so that's why I came to Greece."

"Do you know the name of your grandmother or great-grandmother?"

"My grandmother was Edie Long. That was her married name. Her maiden name was Stavrou."

With a frown, his dimples disappeared. "That is not Jewish. Greek, yes. Jewish, no."

"My DNA test told me I was Sephardic Jew on my mother's side of the family." Though there was no one else in the museum at the time, she leaned closer to him and lowered her voice. "I think there are secrets my family never talked about. Yiayia was born here but came to America when she was small, soon after World War Two, so she remembers nothing about Greece. Mom said her yiayia never talked about the past."

"You want to find out what your family is hiding. Is that wise?"

It wasn't like Tessa hadn't given this any thought. "My great-grandmother passed away when I was young. Yiayia is also gone. What secrets are to be discovered won't hurt them."

"The history of the Jewish people in Thessaloniki, it is not easy."

Tessa nodded. From all she had read, that much was true. She may uncover some ugly things about her family, but nothing would diminish her love for Yiayia.

"If you are sure, then I will help you. But one thing you say is strange, that your yiayia left here after the Holocaust. Not many Jews survived that terrible time. My family is one of the few. What about yours? How can that be?"

Tessa had never thought about that. Of Thessaloniki's fifty thousand Jews, only one or two thousand had survived. So how had her great-grandmother and her yiayia made it?

CHAPTER EIGHT

What a terrible and utter tragedy has befallen our fair city of Salonika. One mere week ago, we were a bustling metropolis, humming and brimming with life. The sun streamed on our heads and favored us. Children went to school, men went to their jobs, and women went to the market.

Now we are a city once again occupied. It is nothing we have not known in our history, at one time or another belonging to the Romans, the Turks, and not so distantly, to the Greeks once more.

This time, however, it is different. For hundreds of years, we lived peaceably with the Turks. The Greeks were not so kind and accommodating, but we lived our lives with only the smallest traces of fear. Now the Germans have come, barbarians from the north who seek our blood.

A few days ago, this reporter stood on the street as the life was beaten from a kindly old butcher. Though many peered through the lacy curtains over their windows, no one stepped foot outside to lend him aid. The soldiers marched over his body, humiliating a gentle man even in death.

Shall we, like the Jews in Poland, in France, in the Low Countries, in the rest of Europe, sit back and do nothing while the Germans steal all we have and all we have become? No indeed. We once were a proud nation, marching through Canaan, destroying the evil people who occupied the Promised Land. Even in those days, we had few weapons and fewer trained men. Yet with Dio's help, we overcame.

And what of these days? Do we no longer depend on Dio to be our ever-present help? Is that the reason we refuse to fight those who would dispose of us?

Do not be lulled into complacency, for it will be our sure ruin. Let us rise up against our captors and not allow them to defeat us as so many others have. Acts of defiance and acts of courage are called for in such times as these.

—*From* The Salonika Jewish News *by Mathilda Nissim*

In the days after the Nazis occupied Salonika, life returned to some level of normalcy, if you could count the Germans patrolling the streets in their uniforms the color of Greek olives normal. Once evening fell, when the spice shop closed and the busy market street quieted, Mathilda got out her typewriter and several sheets of paper. She surrounded the typewriter with blankets to deaden the noise of the keys striking the platen and let her words flow.

She reported on other happenings from around the community, for life continued no matter who ruled them. Babies were born and old people passed away. There was crime, and there were celebrations.

Word had reached her that Rabbi Koretz had been arrested while he was in Athens. While not much liked by the Jews of Salonika, it was a shame that he was in prison for no good reason. There may be those who disagreed with her, but it was a major news story in their city, so Mathilda included it.

Soon she had her small paper completed and pulled the mimeograph sheets from the typewriter. So far, so good. No one had noticed the noises coming from their flat. Or at least they had said nothing to the authorities about it.

When the telephone rang, Mathilda startled, her pulse pounding in her ears. Was this what life was going to be like from now on, jumping at every little sound? Asher, who had been in the kitchen washing the dishes, answered, speaking low.

He called to her and handed her the receiver. She gave him a puzzled glance, but he only smiled.

"Buenos diyas."

"*Yassou.* Oh Mathilda, I'm so happy to hear your voice." Ioanna, one of Mathilda's oldest and dearest friends, chuckled a soft laugh.

"And I'm happy to hear yours, my sweet friend. How have you been?"

Though Jews and Christians in Salonika didn't often mix, Mathilda and Ioanna had met when they were children, when Mathilda's father had been killed in the 1917 fire and Ioanna's family had provided aid to the many displaced Jews.

Ioanna sighed. "So far, life isn't too much different except for the signs in German all over the place and men in uniform marching down the street. If possible, I try to avoid them."

"As do I." Mathilda settled on one of the metal kitchen chairs, prepared for a long chat with her friend.

"But my concern isn't so much for myself as it is for you."

"We're fine, but our hearts are heavy. On the day the Nazis arrived, they dragged Samuel from his shop and—" Tears choked off the rest of her sentence.

Ioanna sucked in a breath. "No, they didn't."

"I saw it myself. It was the most brutal thing I have ever witnessed, even worse than watching my father race into the fire to try to get others out. At least then, people cared about Papa. No one cared about Samuel. After the Germans beat him, they marched over his body. I was the only one to come from my flat to try to aid him."

"You could have been beaten yourself. How could you have done that?"

"How could I not? We can't sit by and watch this happen without acting."

"You're so much like your father in that way."

Would Papa be proud of her now and the stand she was taking?

If only she could know for sure. He did what he had to for others, even though it put his life at risk, so that is what she had to do as well. "Papa fought his battles. Now I fight mine." She rubbed the scar on her hand.

"You have my sympathies on Samuel's passing. How are you holding up?"

Mathilda swiped away a tear that trickled down her cheek. "I would be lying to say that I don't feel the loss, but at least he won't have to suffer what I fear we may be forced to suffer in the future."

"Do you believe that? So far, it's just another government we have to live under, like when my family came from Turkey at the beginning of the century. This isn't the first time land has been conquered, and I daresay it will not be the last."

"This feels different. I have no explanation for it, but deep in my bones lies this fear that I can't shake."

"You know I love you, my dear, dear friend. If there is anything I can do for you, please ring me and let me know. I'll be there in an instant. When is Samuel's wake?"

"You remember that we bury our dead as soon as possible. It was very sad. Asher was by my side, or I might not have survived. He stood beside me and supported me."

"I'm glad you had him. There's so much else I want to talk to you about, but I know we can't chat on the telephone forever. When can I see you?"

They set a date for lunch and said their goodbyes. For a time afterward, Mathilda sat on her chair, her legs pulled underneath her, and stared at the telephone receiver in her hand. How much longer would she enjoy the company of her friend? How long until Jews and Greeks would be forbidden to associate? It had been difficult before this. Soon it might be impossible.

Already there were subjects they couldn't discuss on the phone. Ioanna was likely to ask about Mathilda's newspaper and what would become of it. You never knew who might be listening to their conversation. Even when they weren't in public, it would not be perfectly safe.

After a few moments, Asher entered the room. He took the receiver from her and returned it to its cradle, then gathered her to himself and held her close. No tears flowed, no tremors shook her body. An icy-cold numbness filled her.

He warmed her with his presence, and she drew on that strength. Though the words she wrote were bold and called for daring, she possessed little of it herself. How easy it was to give in to fear and allow it to dominate you.

She would have to refuse it a foothold. After enjoying Asher's hug for several minutes, she broke free from it, instantly aching for his arms to be about her once more. "Gracyas, *mi alma*. My soul."

"What did Ioanna say to rattle you so?"

"Nothing she said but what she didn't say. We can't speak freely anymore, and though she has been my friend for many years and we have told each other all our secrets, can I trust her? If she asks me about the newspaper, can I tell her the truth?"

Asher mussed his slicked-back hair and made a turn around the room. "At this point, I think it's best that no one knows what you are doing. Si, there will be those in our community who will figure it out because they will read the paper, but for the most part, it is better that outsiders, those with the ability to harm us, not know."

"And the rabbi?"

"If and when he is released from prison, don't tell him. He'll find out, I am sure of it, but you will not admit to anything." His words were strained.

"You promised me I could continue to publish."

He blew out a breath. "I know I did, and I will keep my promise for now. But the danger is already increasing. Our rabbi is incarcerated."

"I'll be as careful as possible." She rubbed the goose bumps from her arms. The flat was warm, so how did she even get them? Not from a chill, that much was certain.

"Have you finished what you need to do?"

"I need to run off the copies now."

Asher pulled the equipment from its hiding spot and got to work beside her. There was no need for either of them to speak because they worked as one. The silence was a balm. Just having him near her was enough.

With a lift of his eyebrow, he told her he needed more paper. With an upward tilt of her mouth, she told him that she was happy with what she'd written. With nods, they told each other their job was done.

Still not speaking, they cleaned up and hid the equipment. The stack of papers was another challenge. For tonight Asher hid the newspapers behind the hutch that held the good Shabbat china. By the next issue, they would have to come up with a better spot.

An hour later, she lay in Asher's arms in bed, only a thin sliver of moonlight sliding through the slightly parted drapes. He snored, but for the three years they'd been married now, it had become the music that lulled her to sleep.

Except tonight. Slumber eluded her. Thoughts chased each other around her mind like children in a park. She slid from Asher's arms and out of bed, careful not to wake him. Once in the living room, she turned on a small lamp over her desk and withdrew her journal from its hiding spot.

My heart aches from missing Samuel. A thousand times a day, I catch myself thinking of things I should tell him or ask him, only to be jolted to reality by the memory of his brutal murder. I wrote to Mama and my sisters of his death, but I have no idea if the letter will ever reach them. The United States isn't involved in the war, so perhaps there is a chance. It was so difficult to find the words to tell them. At least they will have each other when they hear what happened. They won't be alone.

I don't remember how long it took for the pain from Papa's death to subside. In a way, I suppose it hasn't, and in other ways, it was never this sharp because I was a small child. Samuel stepped in and took care of us.

Don't get me wrong. Asher has been good to me, so very good to me. I couldn't ask for a better husband. He too has been through much in his life, losing his mother at such a young age and his father not long after. We are all each other has now. We must cling to one another, like Dio said at the beginning of the world, when he gave woman to man.

Ah, to have such a fresh place to live in, free from the trouble and strife of the day. To never have pain or sorrow. Is there such a place? Is there freedom beyond our measuring? To these questions, I have no answers. Perhaps the answers lie in the Promised Land. But the questions interrupt my sleep and keep me walking the floors at all hours of the night. How Asher can slumber away is beyond me.

Tomorrow I will distribute my first newspaper since the occupation. My stomach quivers with thoughts of how it will be received. There will be some, without a doubt, who will welcome it with open arms and who will be ready to fight for our people. There will be others who will chastise me for what I'm doing and call me crazy or foolish. I'm prepared for it all.

At least I hope I am.

CHAPTER NINE

As soon as dawn streaked the sky pink and orange, Mathilda rose from her bed, slipped on her dark blue dress with red buttons and a pair of shoes, and made her way down the street. None of the shops in the market were open yet. A few hours would pass before the streets would bustle with hawkers and buyers alike.

Overhead, birds chirped their morning greetings to one another. A few sparrows hopped on the cobblestones, pecking at crumbs left over from yesterday. One tipped his brown head and studied Mathilda as she carried a stack of papers in the rucksack slung over her shoulder. After a moment, the bird flitted away.

She had her usual customers, and she slipped her paper underneath their doors, the route familiar by now, each door unique. Some were of carved wood, while others were flat-paneled and painted a variety of colors. She wore her soft-soled shoes so as not to wake anyone as she made her way down the street or climbed the marble steps.

By the time she got toward the end of her route, the city was waking. Shopkeepers rolled open their metal doors to display their goods, fruits, or meats. *Avuelas,* their gray hair covered with kerchiefs, stepped outside to sweep their front stoops or to lean over their balcony railings to hang their laundry on the line.

She met a few people on the street, most of whom she recognized by sight if not by name. She offered a paper to one old, stooped woman who glanced at it and tossed it onto the ground.

Mathilda retrieved it and dusted it off.

Next was a young man, perhaps ten years younger than herself, who scurried down the street. Judging by the rucksack he carried, he must be on his way to school at the university. She stopped him and handed him a paper. "Please read it and consider acting. Don't allow the Germans to persecute us. Or worse."

He nodded. "I will. Gracyas." And he was on his way again.

Down the street, she spotted a group of German soldiers, the polished metal eagles on their hats gleaming in the early morning sunlight. Mathilda scooted around the corner and, holding her bag tight against her constricted chest, bought herself a coffee. It was a special treat, but the last thing that would be helpful would be for her to stand out to the Nazis. Worse yet for them to question what she was doing or for them to try to read her Ladino language paper.

The next time she came around the corner, the soldiers were gone, and she breathed out a sigh. She wandered through the market for several minutes to make sure they weren't skulking about somewhere, and when she was convinced they had left the area, she resumed handing out the papers. Some took them while others refused.

"What do you think you're doing?" The deep voice from behind her almost startled her right out of her skin.

"Levi Behar, didn't your mother teach you how rude it is to sneak up behind people? You could have given me a heart attack." The craggy older man had never liked their family, especially after Mama rejected his marriage proposal.

"Not a pretty little lady like you. I doubt you would stand for it. How is it that your husband continues to allow you to publish this trash? It was bad enough before the invasion. Now it will only get you, and perhaps others, in trouble. Go home and make your husband happy by giving him a child and taking care of his house."

Though the morning was already warm, Mathilda grew even warmer as she spun to face the man whose dark beard didn't quite cover his pock-scarred cheeks. "Never you mind about what my husband does and does not allow me to do. He knows my business full well."

"And if you keep it up, so will all the Germans. Do you ever think of anyone other than yourself?"

She drew in a breath to tell Levi just what she thought of him, but before she could, a woman with three children surrounding her approached them. "Mathilda, there you are. We have been looking all over for you."

Perla's oldest, just five, clung to Mathilda's legs. She slipped the remaining papers in her knapsack and ruffled each curly head. "How did you manage to find me?"

"We know you well enough. And the murmurs we have heard on the street this morning led us straight to you."

Her heart twisted a little bit. "People are talking about me?"

Perla nodded, a strand of dark hair coming loose from her headscarf. "Some of it is good, but some of it is unkind. People don't know whether you're brave or foolish, especially after what happened to Samuel."

"But you understand, right?" Mathilda clasped her friend's hand and squeezed it.

"I know that you do whatever you have to in order to protect those you love. And that you love with the fiercest love I have ever witnessed."

"*Tia*, Tia." Bechar, Perla's oldest, tugged at Mathilda's knapsack. That he called her auntie was so cute. "Do you have a sweet for me?"

Mathilda laughed. "You are already too sweet. Any more sugar, and you would melt when it rains."

"I would take that chance."

"Of course you would."

The other children clambered for treats from Mathilda until their mother hushed them all. "That's enough of bothering her. We must get going and finish our shopping before these little ones need their naps."

A collective groan rose from among the children. One day, if Dio allowed, she and Asher would have beautiful children of their own to love and to watch grow up. She would probably give them too many sweets and spoil them, but Perla was right. If she ever had a child, she would love that little one with every fiber of her being.

Perla leaned over and hugged Mathilda, even with children still clinging to her legs. "You be careful, promise me?"

"Of course. I always am."

"Don't get me wrong. I admire what you are doing and only wish I could be half as brave as you are. But life is not what it was a month ago and probably never will be the same again."

"I know." They all knew, though very few spoke of it.

"Since the time we were small, it was you, me, and Ioanna. I couldn't bear it if anything happened to any of us. We have to be careful and watch our steps before we fall into a pit we cannot escape."

With those words ringing in her ears, Mathilda released Perla and shooed her and her children away. "Go, go, and let me be on my way to buy you all a special treat. If you don't let go, I won't be able to move, and when you come to visit me, my cupboard will be bare."

She hadn't even finished her sentence when the three unlatched themselves and followed their mother toward their home a few streets over.

"You would be wise to listen to her." Levi's menacing face appeared in front of her again.

"I thought you had gone." Why couldn't he leave her family alone?

"Oh, I'm not that easy to get rid of. Mark my words, you will bring trouble, not only upon yourself, but also upon our entire community. If you continue in your ways and bring grief to our people, I will visit a special kind of vengeance on you. I will not be as patient and as understanding as your husband."

"Good day, *Señor* Behar." Mathilda spun in the opposite direction and pushed her way through the gathering crowds, her coffee spilling as she walked. Never mind. She couldn't allow Levi to see how he had shaken her. Not that she was afraid of him, but he fed the doubts that continued to rack her.

Perhaps all of them were right and she shouldn't continue to operate. It was a little bit of craziness to do so.

Yet within her fingers lay great power, the power of the word to convict, persuade, and call to action. Perhaps even the power to save life.

That is exactly what Mathilda was doing. Even if she saved only one life in the process, then all her hard work, the sacrifices she and Asher made, the scorn and ridicule she would have to endure, would be worth it.

CHAPTER TEN

I've never been one for museums, but this one in Thessaloniki was so interesting. When I saw the silver Shabbat pieces, I couldn't help but wonder if they might have been owned by my great-grandparents or even their parents or grandparents before them. Who were they? What were their lives like? I'm separated from my true identity as a Jewish person. I know nothing about the religion or the culture. That's why this experience is so incredible.

—From the journal of Tessa Payton

Giannis led the way from the Jewish museum's entrance into one of the exhibit halls, the black-and-white tile floor laid in one of those old-but-new-again patterns. As they made their way deeper inside, Tessa studied the carved marble slabs on either side of the room.

She stopped and stared at a picture of a woman dressed in a dark skirt, a white shirt, a dark shawl, and a dark head covering. Giannis returned toward her. She pointed at the picture. "What is this?"

"Ah yes. That is a professional mourner. At the old Jewish cemetery, women would be paid to go every day to cry for the dead."

"Every day?"

"Yes. The stones you see here are from that cemetery. It was destroyed by the Germans in 1943."

"Why?"

"They wanted to rid all traces of Jews from Salonika."

Salonika was Thessaloniki. Tessa had read about that before she came. "That's awful."

"Come. There is something I want you to see." Giannis led her to a large room. Huge black stone slabs covered each of the room's four walls, and names were inscribed on all of them, completely filling them.

A hush filled the room. Something kept her from speaking but burst her heart.

Giannis leaned close enough for her to catch a whiff of a musky scent. "All these were Jews killed by the Germans."

"Oh." She said nothing but stared at the names. Finally, she stepped forward and ran her fingers over the strange letters. There were so many names. So many. An entire roomful. Name after name, each one of them a flesh-and-blood person that was brutally murdered.

The heaviness of the room settled on her shoulders and bent her over. This was a small fraction of the men, women, and children the Nazis had destroyed. Just a small fraction. It boggled the mind. No matter how hard she tried, she couldn't get her brain around it.

For several minutes, Giannis stood beside her as she absorbed all of this into her soul. Was she related to any of the names here? "Are there any Stavrous?"

Her guide moved to where the Ss must be and scanned the wall. After a moment's search, he turned to her. "No. There aren't any here."

She shrugged. "Then what?"

"Like I said, that is not Jewish. It is strange that you say you are Sephardim."

"You do believe me, don't you?"

They stepped from the room, and he turned to her and stared straight into her eyes, as if attempting to peer into her soul. "Why did you come here?"

"All my life, I was told I was Greek and English, but then my DNA said I'm Jewish." She reached into her small purse and pulled out a copy of the paperwork she had received from the DNA company. "Here it is. I was told there was no mistake in the results. There is no doubt that I'm Jewish."

He rubbed his whiskered chin, then nodded. "I believe you. I shouldn't do this, but come with me." He led her toward the back and through a door. The words on the placard on the door must translate to EMPLOYEES ONLY.

Inside was a huge room filled with books, shelves stacked with them, and various people working at desks. "Wow, look at all of this."

At her proclamation, many of the men and women there peered at her from behind their computers.

"This is Tessa. She is from America and wants to learn more about her family. She has come all this way to search."

Many of them nodded, and they all got back to work. Phones rang and computer keys clicked. The perfume of strong, cream-laced coffee filled the room.

When they arrived at his desk toward the back, he pulled an extra chair next to it and motioned for Tessa to sit. He picked up his coffee and leaned back in his chair. "This is an adventure you are having."

She nodded, fiddling with the lanyard around her neck. "Do you think you can help me?"

"You must be ready. The story of the Jews in Thessaloniki, or Salonika as they called it at the time, is not happy. It is sometimes hard to hear. Sometimes it rips your heart right from your chest. You saw the names on the wall. They each represent a person. They are not just letters written on a piece of stone."

"I understand." Her gut twisted though. Perhaps what she would discover here wouldn't be sunshine and roses. But her great-grandparents and their daughters got out. They did have a happy ending, so she clung to that. Whatever they had kept hidden all these years, whatever had happened to them during those terrible days, somehow they had stayed alive. That was good. Right?

"I can help you with your family. You will be here a week?"

She leaned forward and sucked in a breath. "It will only take a week? I had planned to stay as long as I needed to. I've quit school and have money to support me for a while."

"Ah. That is good, actually. I was going to say that it might take a while to learn about them. I cannot say if it will be a week or a month or a year. I don't know if my boss will like this, but I will help you as much as I can."

"Thank you."

"In Ladino, that is gracyas."

"Ladino? That sounds more like Spanish."

"Ladino is the mix of Spanish and Hebrew the Salonikan Jews spoke. The language is not spoken so much anymore. I try to learn it and to speak it to keep it alive."

"Gracyas, then. I appreciate your help, though I don't want to get you in trouble."

"Helping a pretty lady like you, it is no trouble."

Maybe she should be taken aback by his words or cautious of him, but there was a warmth to his brown eyes, a gold that shimmered in them, a sincerity that eased her apprehension. "I want to learn what it was like living here during the war. What was their daily life like?"

"Have you learned how to get around the city? Do you have a SIM card for your phone?"

Was he purposely evading her question? She shook her head.

"Okay. Then first, before we start to figure out things, we will get you used to being in Greece. You have traveled before?"

Again, she shook her head.

He took a long drag of his coffee. "We have much work to do. I'll be right back." He grabbed his briefcase from the top of his desk, disappeared behind another door, and returned a few minutes later. "Now we can go."

They spent the rest of the morning together. First he took her to get her phone set up so she could use it easily around the city. He added apps so she could order take-out food and get a taxi. He showed her where the grocery store was. One of the employees was squeezing oranges into juice, so she picked up a bottle of that along with some meat, cheese, bread, and a few snacks she recognized from home.

Once she had put away her food in the tiny refrigerator and the cramped cabinets in her apartment, Giannis gave a single clap of his hands. "Now, we go eat."

They wound their way through the open-air market, the Kapani market as Giannis called it, and past several restaurants. At one a sandy-haired man with a mustache stepped in front of them, a menu in his hand. "You come eat here."

Giannis shook his head and said something in Greek to the man before they continued.

"Is that a bad place?"

"No. The food is very good, and the man is nice. You should eat there, but today I will show you another place."

They went farther, Tessa trying to orient herself and failing miserably. She had no idea where they were or how she would manage to find her way home later. At least now she had internet on her phone, so she could always pull up a map.

They turned a corner onto a cobblestone street, and nothing but restaurants met Tessa's eyes. For blocks on both sides of the road were places to eat. Right now, early in the afternoon, most of the seats were deserted. Tessa laughed. "Which one do you pick?"

He led her to a menu stand. "See if there is anything here you like."

Thankfully, though a third of the menu was in Greek and a third in what she assumed to be Russian, a third was also in English.

She perused one or two but wasn't all that hungry. Her stomach had yet to make the transition to Thessaloniki time. "Why don't you take me to your favorite."

Giannis nodded. "Okay then." They strolled for a couple of blocks before settling at an outdoor table under a tan umbrella. With few other patrons in the establishment, their waiter hustled to them with bread and water in hand.

Giannis ordered moussaka while she went the adventurous route with stuffed grape leaves and fried zucchini.

Once the waiter had taken away their menus and had left to put in their requests, Giannis leaned forward. "Tell me, why are you really here?"

"I already told you."

"Most people don't give up their lives to come to this place because of a DNA test."

She toed her sandal on the concrete patio and stared down the street rather than at his all-too-charming face. "I want to find out about my past. My family's past. Where I belong."

"You have no family?"

This was getting too personal to talk about with a man she'd met a few hours ago. "I do. A mom, stepdad, and stepsister. They're great." She kept her voice bright to avoid betraying her feelings about Jay and his daughter, Lily. "What about you?"

"A dad, my mom, and a sister. I'm sorry if I ask too much. I can be, how do you say it, nosy, but I guess that makes me a good researcher."

"Do you get many requests for people wanting to know about their families?"

He shook his head. "Not many. Few families survived. Those that did often did not want to talk about the terrible things that happened during the war. It was not a good time for our people. They suffered much."

"Maybe my family changed their name, their identity, so they would not be taken away. They could hide that way and stay safe."

"It is possible. That might make it hard to find them, but I will do what I can."

They chatted about Pittsburgh and Thessaloniki while they ate. The grape leaves stuffed with cheese and sprinkled with a generous amount of dill were quite good, and the fried zucchini with Greek yogurt was delicious.

The meal dragged on and on. She didn't want to be rude, but the time change was catching up with her, and a nap sounded like a slice of heaven. The waiter never came to clear their plates or bring them their bill. Though it was rude, she checked her watch and even stifled a yawn.

At last, about two hours in, Giannis waved over the waiter. When he left again, Tessa shook her head. "The food was good, but the service was kind of slow, especially for there being no one here."

Giannis drew his eyebrows into a V, then chuckled. "Oh, that is what I forgot to tell you. I have heard that American waiters bother you very much and hurry you out of the restaurant. Not here. We take our time with almost everything. We relax and enjoy ourselves, not always running around. You will not be bothered. You tell them when you are done."

"That's a good tip." It was kind of nice to sit in the shade while a warm breeze blew across her cheek, the sun just now peeking under the umbrella and kissing her shoulder.

Once they had settled the bill, Giannis walked her back to her apartment. At least she wouldn't have to struggle to find her way. They stood in the entry, and he pulled a stack of papers from his briefcase. "You wanted to know what life was like for Jewish people here during the war. This is a copy of the diary of an amazing woman who lived much and saw much. I translated it into English myself because I feel the work is important. Many people will like to read it. I think you will find it interesting."

"Thank you. Gracyas."

When he turned to leave, she scurried up the stairs and through the maze of doors until she collapsed on the sofa. Tired as she was, she opened the wire-bound book and dove into the story.

CHAPTER ELEVEN

July 2, 1942

What I had feared, what I had warned our people about, has come to pass. Little by little, the Germans have been chipping away at our freedom until there is not much left. We have allowed them to make us their prisoners without a single struggle against them. Like sheep to the slaughter, that is what we have been.

Now what are we to do? I am drained and exhausted. I have no appetite, and even the smell of food churns my stomach. Asher is afraid I will turn to skin and bones. In the end, all of us may be nothing but flesh-covered skeletons.

The oppression weighs heavy on my shoulders. Every day it grows more unbearable. Soon I will not be able to breathe. The Germans are siphoning the life from me, from all of us. Asher's eyes are hollower with each passing day. He is a shell of his former self. My heart breaks for my husband, but there is little I can do to comfort him.

We are broken. Can we ever be repaired?

—From the diary of Mathilda Nissim

Mathilda fingered the lace collar of her red floral dress as she sat at her typewriter working out the latest edition of her little paper. With the large Jewish newspapers shuttered, she was the only voice left in the city.

A city that had undergone radical changes since the Nazis had arrived, especially in the past few months. Life went on, but not as it had been. They were being carried away on a wave.

"Mathilda, this sock has a hole in it." Asher entered from the bedroom and held up one of his very last black socks.

She sighed at the sight. "When I finish here, I'll darn it for you." Even the thread for sewing up the holes was running low.

"Gracyas, my dear. What would I do without you?"

"And I without you?"

He placed a light kiss on her forehead. "Let's hope neither one of us will ever find out."

"What are you going to do today?" Though the sound was muffled, she clacked away on the typewriter without glancing away from him. Heavy bags hung from his eyes, and his frame was stooped.

"I'm working on the deal to sell the pharmacy to Ioanna's husband. We should have everything finalized in the next few days." He finger combed his dark curls. "Most of the time, I'm happy that Petrus will buy it and keep it for me, for when this is over. Days like this one are the hardest. It feels like I'm giving up everything I worked so hard to build. I'll go from an owner to an employee, but I need to do this before the Germans take it from me."

Who knew when that would be. Likely sooner rather than later. Mathilda left her work and went to her husband and squeezed his hands in hers. "I know how hard this is on you."

"What good am I? I can't provide for you the way I have been. That shouldn't be."

She stood on her tiptoes and kissed the end of his chin. "Together, we will survive this. Neither one of us is solely responsible for this family. We are partners."

"I'm a useless lump." He heaved the words out on a sigh.

"That is the furthest thing from the truth. The only reason this is happening is because of the Nazis. Because of who we are, not because of anything you've done or haven't done." She stroked the side of his face. "Not to mention that you help me so much with the paper."

He shook his head, his mouth downturned. "With cash running low and supplies almost impossible to get, you won't be able to run the paper much longer."

Not have her paper? Like the sun breaking over the horizon, she recognized how difficult it must be for Asher not to be in control of the pharmacy he had poured his life into. Mixing medications so that his patients could recover from their illnesses, even stay alive, was his passion. He loved nothing better.

That was how her little paper was to her. In the black-and-white words on the page, she could express herself, a difficult accomplishment for a woman who was expected to sit without a word beside her husband.

A few minutes later, wearing a holey sock, Asher left the apartment, closing the door with a soft click. Mathilda drew in a deep breath. She should do something special for him when he returned this evening, but what?

Before she managed to come up with a plan, a knock sounded at the door. Was that Asher? Why would he knock?

Or was it the Germans? Here she was, with all her equipment sitting out. As fast as she could move, she unwrapped the towels from the typewriter and lifted it to store it in the back of the wardrobe.

The knock came again, this time accompanied by a soft voice. "Mathilda, it's Ioanna."

Oh good. Ioanna knew what Mathilda was doing, so she had no need to hide the equipment. Then again, maybe it would be best to get it stuffed away before allowing anyone in. She finished putting everything away, pulling the shirts and dresses and coats into place and shutting the cupboard, and answered the door.

Ioanna stepped inside and drew Mathilda into a hug. "It's so good to see you, my friend."

"And it's good to see you as well. I wasn't expecting you."

"I know that you've been busy, but I wanted to make sure you and Asher were doing well. Especially today, when he'll sign the pharmacy to Petrus."

"We are as good as we can be, given the circumstances. Difficult as it is, Asher recognizes that he can't keep the store any longer. We are so grateful to you and Petrus for safekeeping it for us."

"When life returns to normal, it will be waiting for him. I promise you that. We'll take the best care of it we can. And Asher will be there to make sure everything is run the way he wants it to be. His name may no longer be on the ownership papers, but he will continue to be in control."

"For as long as that will last."

The women moved to the kitchen where Mathilda set the kettle on the stove to boil some water for tea. She knew Ioanna so well, she didn't have to ask if she wanted any. "You too have been suffering under the occupation."

"Not to the extent you have been, though there are some who have been collaborating with the Nazis to make their lives easier."

"Rabbi Koretz might fall into that category."

Ioanna wrinkled her brow.

"He goes along with each new order that comes from the Germans and tells us to just obey them, because if we do that, perhaps it will go well for us." Mathilda made a small turn about the tiny kitchen. "Does it look like life is going well? Can't he see that going along with the Nazis only brings us more misery?"

"And what would happen if he told you to defy the orders? What would the Nazis do then?"

Mathilda plopped into a chair and rubbed her throbbing temples. "I have heard horrible stories where many Jews are murdered for even one act of defiance."

"Do you think that he may possibly be trying to save your lives by telling you to obey? I know it's difficult, especially now that

Asher is signing away the business, but God is good and gracious. He will care for you."

The kettle whistled, and Mathilda rose and made tea. As she carried the cups to the table, Ioanna reached into her bag and pulled out bread, cheese, and olives. "These are for you."

"No, no, I can't accept that. It's too much." Though Petrus would pay Asher, restrictions on which shops Jews could enter and where they could buy food made it difficult for them to keep their bellies full. "You need it to feed yourself and Petrus."

"My husband has a job, and while food is rationed, we can afford to buy all we need."

"But you used your coupons for this."

"Don't worry about us. I promise, we'll be fine."

Once again, Mathilda made a hard landing on the chair. The yeasty odor of the bread tickled her nose and sent a wave of nausea racing through her. She ran to the bathroom and lost the little breakfast she'd eaten. After rinsing her mouth, she returned to her guest. "I apologize. The stress is making me sick to my stomach. Food is unappetizing."

Ioanna leaned forward and studied Mathilda. A slow smile spread across her oval face. "Right now, I can't eat much or stand the smell of food either. I'm getting sick every morning."

"Maybe there's something wrong with what we've been eating. Could the Germans be poisoning it?"

Ioanna laughed. "I know that my sickness is because I am going to have a baby." Her eyes twinkled in the sunlight streaming through the window.

Mathilda smiled and clapped her hands. "Oh really? Really? I'm so happy for you. How wonderful. That's the best news I could have received today."

"Thank you. Petrus and I can't wait for this new little life to come into the world. Each one is so precious and right now is a reminder of God's goodness and graciousness to us—that even in the hardest times of life, there is some joy."

"Joy is so much needed these days." And easier to come by if you weren't a Jew, not that Mathilda would deny her friend this amazing gift.

After a sip of her tea, Ioanna cocked her head, a light brown strand of hair slipping from the pin that held the roll in place. "I'm glad that you're happy. Do you think your sickness might be for the same reason?"

Mathilda furrowed her brow. Pregnant? No, she and Asher had been so careful. This was no time to bring a child into the world, especially with the new restrictions on Jews. Who knew what would happen to them? To any child they would bring into the world? "It's impossible."

Ioanna gazed at Mathilda and sighed.

"Well, not impossible." Could Mathilda have counted wrong? When she had thought it safe, perhaps it wasn't. "I don't want to have a baby. How could I do that to a child, to subject them to this awful, evil world?" It was one thing for Ioanna. Quite another for Mathilda.

Ioanna leaned forward and clasped Mathilda by the hands. "A child is always a blessing, no matter what. God's timing is perfect. There is a reason He has chosen to give you a child right now."

"Maybe I'm not expecting. You must be wrong." Mustn't she? If Dio was even a little merciful, He would spare her from having a baby now.

Ioanna listed all her symptoms and how the doctor was finally able to confirm that she was expecting. With each one, Mathilda's heart sank a little lower. "I have all of them." Her words were little more than a whisper.

Her friend, however, beamed. "Then I think we can say that you and I are both going to become mothers."

The lump in Mathilda's throat enlarged so that she had difficulty drawing in a breath. "What have we done? What have we done?"

"What do you mean? This is the most joyous news a woman could receive."

"You, si. Not me." Mathilda's stomach spasmed but not from a bout of nausea. "Though your child will also be born during a war, at least you aren't being persecuted. Your husband will own a business and, though limited, you have food on the table, while our freedoms are being stripped away at lighting speed. Your child has a future. Mine does not."

"Don't think that way. This war will end at some point, and you and Asher will have a beautiful little one to help you forget all of the difficult times. Just think. When you visit Palestine, you'll be able to take your son or your daughter with you. That will make it all the sweeter."

Ioanna knew and understood Mathilda's dream. But she could never understand the dilemma this coming child created. "Whatever you do, please tell no one. Not your husband and not mine."

"Why not?"

"When I am surer, then I will let him know. He's anxious to be a father, and I don't want to get his hopes up until I'm positive. We could both be wrong. Much as I love you, you aren't a doctor. I might have nothing more than the stomach flu."

Ioanna stood, then kissed Mathilda on the top of her head. "I will do as you request unless Asher asks me a direct question. But I know that you're with child. I can see the glow on your face. I pray you will find happiness and peace with this wonderful gift."

Mathilda would pray that Ioanna was wrong.

CHAPTER TWELVE

July 11, 1942

Though the Sabbath morning light had yet to shine through the window in the little flat above the spice shop, Asher and Mathilda were already up. While he packed his bag, she prepared him food that would last for a while.

Because neither of them knew how long he would be gone.

A few days ago, he had received a letter in the mail requiring him to report to Liberty Square so the Germans could register him for a work camp. The Nazis must have picked a Saturday on purpose, the holy day of the week. Today they should be gathering in worship, not gathering for whatever fate their occupiers had deemed suitable for them.

She fought to keep the tears at bay as she kneaded her flatbread. Even the yeastiness of it churned her stomach. Ioanna had to be right. With Asher going away for who knew how long, though, she would not burden him with the news right now.

He had to focus on staying alive, and she had to focus on doing her best to give him a bright, cheerful send-off so he wouldn't worry about her. The news of a coming child would only make him worry. She placed the bread in a warm spot on the back of the stove and went to the bedroom to see how he was coming with his packing.

He stood in the middle of the room, arms crossed against his chest, staring into the distance. She went to him and wrapped him in a hug from behind. "What are you thinking?"

"I'm praying that you won't miss me too much while I'm gone and that we will see each other again. That the Nazis won't ship you to a labor camp. I'm glad I'm the one going and they're leaving you alone for now."

Si, they were leaving the women in Salonika for the time being. How long that would last was anyone's guess. Days? Weeks? Months? "Are you sure you don't want to go into hiding? It's not too late. We can still find you a place. I'm sure Ioanna would be willing to help."

"She's going to have a child. I wouldn't want to do anything to put her or her family in jeopardy."

Exactly why Asher must not know that she was also expecting a baby. He would obey the authorities without question to ensure their safety, even though it would likely do just the opposite. "We could ask someone else then. I don't want you to go."

He turned in her embrace and drew her tight. "Don't worry. It's just for a short time. Poland isn't that far away."

"It's much too far away. Even down the street would be too much distance between the two of us."

"The time will go fast, and I'll be back before you know it. I promise you."

With a touch to his lips, she shushed him. "Don't make promises you can't keep."

"I have every intention of coming back to you, mi corasón. I will do this for us, to keep the peace, and then I will return."

"We shouldn't be allowing them to do this to us at all."

"You keep resisting with your words." He kissed her forehead, as soft and gentle as a spring rain. "If I know you are here doing the work you love, the work that is so important, then I will also be able to fight."

She stood on her tiptoes and kissed him on the mouth, adding every ounce of passion she had for him in that kiss, leaning into him, as if she could imprint the feel of his body against hers and never forget.

Breathless, he pulled away. "That will have to do. I should be going."

Though every fiber in her screamed to lock him in her hold and never let him go, she released him and checked his suitcase. "Have you packed enough warm clothes?"

"It's July, mi corasón."

"Poland will be very cold by the time you return." The Germans had said six months, but could they really take them at their word? More lies spewed from their lips than truth. If the belief they would soon be reunited helped them to endure this separation, then she wouldn't crack his egg.

"Por favor, don't concern yourself about me. Look at all I have to come home to. I'll do everything in my power to return to you and resume the happy life we have enjoyed these years."

If only Dio would hear their prayers and return their life to what it once was.

While Asher ate a little breakfast, she fried the bread and packed it, still warm, into his suitcase. Once he helped her dry the dishes, they set off toward Liberty Square. The early morning sun already blazed on their heads. Poor Asher, having to stand in it. Hopefully the registration and assignments would go fast. By the time they reached the gathering place, Mathilda was already sweating.

Germans armed with machine guns, their dogs baring their teeth and straining at their leashes, ringed the square. Mathilda and Asher stepped up to one of them.

"Papers."

Asher handed them over. The guard glanced between the identification and Asher, then returned his papers to him.

Asher turned toward Mathilda. "It's time for me to go."

"How can I let you? We're intertwined, two lives that are one.

Where you go, I will go; where you stay, I will stay."

Asher shook his head, a dribble of sweat trickling down the side of his face. "Not this time. And it's better this way because I won't have to worry about you."

She thumbed the moisture from his cheek. "But I will be frantic about you, wondering every minute of every day where you are and what is happening to you, when you'll return to me. If you return to me."

He touched a spot just above her left breast. "This is where I will be. In your heart, part of you forever. And I will return, no matter what it takes. Nothing but death will keep me from you."

"That's my fear." She could no longer hold back the tears but clung to him until the very last moment, kissing his face, his hands, whatever she could kiss.

Before she was even ready, the Nazis whisked Asher away, ripping away a piece of her. "Te amo, Asher. Te amo."

"Te amo," came his answer. Before too much time passed, he blended in with the crowd and she lost track of him.

Men packed the square, every inch of it, so there was not much space to move. Nowhere did she see any registration tables, though it was impossible for her to notice what might be in the middle of the packed crowd. With so many men, though, it would take a great deal of time to register them all.

She stood around the outside along with many of the other wives. A few of them whispered to each other, but most of them stood silent. Even the children they held on to were quiet.

After a tap on the shoulder, Perla appeared at her side. None of her little ones were with her. "I can't let him go." Her dark eyes were teary.

"I know." Mathilda rubbed the spot where her child grew. Only she and Ioanna knew her secret. Perhaps Ioanna was right, and it would be some kind of comfort to have a bit of Asher with her, even while he was so far away.

"What's going to happen to us?"

"We have to be strong. It's time for us to show the men we love that we will not break." She said this despite the way her own heart was shattering, already missing Asher. "We won't collapse. For their sakes, for the sakes of our children, we will be strong and not allow the Nazis to strip everything from us."

"They already have." Perla pulled a handkerchief from her black pocketbook and dabbed at the tears leaking from the corners of her eyes.

"No, they haven't. They haven't. You have your children. You aren't living on the streets. Focus on the good that is remaining in your life, but give them nothing else." Words Mathilda herself needed to heed.

"How can we fight back when our men haven't?"

That was a question Mathilda didn't have an answer for.

A German solider in a brown uniform stood in the middle of the group of men with a megaphone. He barked commands to the men, ordering them to do squats and push-ups, to stand on one foot, to meow like cats and quack like ducks. They were treating the men worse than animals.

Mathilda held herself back from charging into the group and demanding the soldiers stop this humiliation.

Another command went out, this time for the men to sing a children's song. Those who didn't cooperate were rewarded with a strike from the butt of one of the soldiers' guns. Mathilda winced with each crack to the head of an innocent man.

The sun beamed down harder, brighter, and hotter. Sweat rolled down her back and each side of her face.

Perla grabbed her by the upper arm. "Is something wrong? You're as white as a cloud."

"I'm fine." The world swam in front of her, but she wouldn't leave. If Asher had to endure these conditions, so would she.

A couple of shots rang out, echoing between the buildings. A woman elsewhere in the ring around the square screamed. Other women joined her. Mathilda had to swallow her own yell. She moved forward to get to Asher, to get the Nazis to stop this cruel and inhumane treatment. Again, Perla grabbed her. "What are you doing?"

"What we should have been doing all along. I'm pushing back. I won't allow them to do this to my husband and all the other men. You should keep them from doing this to David too. If we told them to stop—"

"They would shoot us all. Much as we may want to, there is nothing for us to do."

"There are more of us than there are of them." Thoughts whizzed in Mathilda's head.

"There is one difference. They have guns, and we are unarmed."

Another command came for another humiliating exercise. Mathilda turned to Perla. "I want to save my husband. I cannot bear to stand here and watch them treat him like a dog and then kill him."

Tears swam in Perla's eyes. "I know. I know. What trouble is this that Dio has wrought on us? For what sin is He punishing us?"

They held hands for a long time, even as the sun continued to shine its burning rays on them. They supported each other. At last, sweaty and wrung out, Mathilda released her grasp on Perla. "All I want to do is cry for what I'm losing, but I want to be strong for all the women here, to be an example of how we won't allow the Germans to break us."

"There's no shame in showing your true feelings. You are, after all, a human, just as we are."

"The Nazis might have a different idea."

Perla gave a single laugh. "That doesn't change the fact that we fear and are sad. You have nothing to be ashamed about if you weep."

"Well, I'll put on a brave face for the others and for the Germans to show them that, no matter what they do to us, we'll stand against them." But the beatings and the shootings continued, each one leaving a mark on Mathilda's heart.

Well into the afternoon, the humiliation continued. Finally, they called the men to line up to be registered. The queue was long and the Greek sun merciless, much like their captors. Men continued to faint from the heat. She had yet to pick Asher out of the crowd.

The men who were registered were led away toward the train station. Just when Mathilda could no longer stand the waiting, the heat, and the lack of food, Perla's husband came to her side and swept her off her feet, swinging her around as he hugged her.

Mathilda scanned the area for Asher. There was no sign of him. Though she stood as tall as she could, she couldn't catch the slightest glance of him. Where could he be?

She turned to David and interrupted his reunion with his wife. "Did you see Asher? Was he with you? Where is he?"

"Si, I did see him. In fact, we were together most of the day. We were separated when it came time for registration. I did see him heading in the direction of the trains."

Mathilda held in the scream that pleaded to be released from her throat. "Why did they take him and release you? Not that I'm not grateful that you're free, but why one and not the other?"

David shook his head. "We will all be going to Poland in the next few days. Right now, there aren't enough trains to take every one of the men to the labor camps. I must come back here every day until it's my turn. Maybe because he's going first, Asher will be home first."

Somehow Mathilda managed to get back to the flat above the spice shop. The silence inside was oppressive. Asher wouldn't be walking through the door anytime soon. She would eat supper alone tonight. She would sleep in bed alone tonight.

She poured herself a glass of water and wandered the empty rooms. How could she stand this? Would she make it until her husband returned home?

What if he never did?

CHAPTER THIRTEEN

There is so much I have to wrap my head around, and it's difficult. Though I love being here, I would have been just as happy to have my DNA test come back boring. No surprises, at least not to this extent. Then my life wouldn't be upended like it is. I should be working on the stuff I have to do for my internship, but I can't focus. Too many questions hound me. Will I ever have the answers? Do I even want them?

—From the diary of Tessa Payton

Tessa set her diary beside Mathilda's on the glass-and-wrought-iron table on the balcony. She stood and stretched her muscles. Across the street, in the only older building on this road that had withstood the 1917 fire, a woman hung her underwear over the intricately scrolled railing of her Juliet balcony. It was bad enough that Tessa had to do so on a line in the back. She could never air her panties on the street side.

She leaned over the railing and watched the activity below. Men and women hustled down the lane. A few cars maneuvered their way through the parked vehicles that clogged the road. At the hair salon next door, a woman in very high heels arrived for her appointment.

What must it have been like for Mathilda when Asher went away to the labor camp? How eerie it must have been to have the streets empty of men. Unimaginable. Though Tessa attempted to put herself in Mathilda's place, she couldn't.

The diary was very interesting, and it gave her a glimpse into what life was like for Jewish women in Thessaloniki during the war. Her family must have endured an awful lot. Did her great-grandfather go to one of those labor camps? Did he ever return?

Just thinking about it gave her a headache. But the pain in her head was nothing in comparison to what those poor people suffered.

Her poor people. She still had a difficult time wrapping her mind around the fact that her people were Jewish. Greek, yes. Mom made souvlaki and baklava for special occasions. She would say *"Opa!"* when Tessa fell when she was a child. Other than that, they weren't connected to this place anymore.

Would she ever be connected anywhere? Would she belong to anyone? Dad's parents were gone, and she had lost contact with the couple of cousins she had on his side of the family.

On Mom's side, other than Aunt Fran and Riley, there was no one else. Yiayia had been incoherent in her last days. She had never said a word about the past, even before the Alzheimer's set in.

But something about this place spoke to Tessa. Her soul was a little more at peace here. She basked in the sunshine, in the odors of spices and fruit and fish from the market not far from her apartment, in the friendliness of the people.

This was temporary, however. At some point, she would have to return to the States and resume her life there. If only she could have some resolution before she left.

Today was Saturday. Because she was Jewish, did that mean she should be at the synagogue now? Or should she continue going to church as she always did?

God, help me to know.

Was she speaking to the Jewish God or the Christian God?

That was far too many questions for so early in the morning. She finished her daily coffee with a pastry that she had picked up from the bakery yesterday. Covered in sesame seeds, it was delicious, though she had forgotten what it was called. When she had almost finished with a touch of makeup, her phone dinged.

Giannis was here. She grabbed her phone and purse, locked up, and bounded down the stairs. The elevator was still a little sketchy for her.

He greeted her with a smile. "Good morning. You look very nice."

She glanced at her white shorts and sleeveless red polka-dotted shirt. "Thanks." She hadn't even done anything with her hair but put it in a messy bun. It was too hot to have the length of it hanging down her back.

"Are you ready for today?"

"I'm looking forward to it so much, I had a hard time sleeping last night. Not many people get to say they've had a private tour of the city. I can't wait for you to show me around."

"I also have some information for you, but that will have to wait until the end of the tour." He held open the passenger door to his little red car, and she slid in.

The sun had already baked the black seats. They stung, almost burned, the back of her legs. "So where are you taking me?"

"Let's start at the top of the city." They wove through narrow streets that didn't always run straight. He shifted gears as they climbed until they reached a road that ran along a long wall with a tower at the end.

He parked in a spot near a small taverna, and they hiked the rest of the way. "This is the wall that the Ottomans built when they occupied the city in the 1400s."

"So it wasn't here when the apostle Paul was here?"

"No. Then it was a collection of five small neighborhoods with no walls. It was an important city at the time, a crossroads of commerce and trade, but it was nothing like it is now. Here. Climb up, and I'll show you what I mean."

She marched up the steps and turned around. The view was stunning. The city curved below her until it met the gulf. Light-colored buildings with red-tiled roofs stretched out almost as far as she could see. The height, the splendor, sent her reeling.

She must have wobbled, because the next thing she knew, Giannis had his arm around her. "Be careful. I don't want to chase you as you roll like a ball down the hill."

A sudden sense of being in the right place filled her, warmed her even more than the intense summer sun. The encounter was brief, only a few seconds, but it left her tingling even more than that view. "Thank you." She righted herself. "Just a tiny fear of heights."

He pointed out some of the important sights below them, sometimes brushing her arm as he reached out. Each time he did so, she had to catch her breath. His nearness did strange things to her, things she'd never experienced before.

Because she'd been here for a few days, she was able to orient herself. He showed her where the Jewish cemetery used to be, and the euphoria of the day wore off a little. Soon afterward, they climbed into the car and made their way back down the hill, stopping at a few churches along the way, including one purported to be on the spot where Paul escaped from the city.

As she stood in the ornate, gold-covered church covered with icons and frescoes, she shivered. The rituals performed here, like the kissing of the case containing relics, were empty. Giannis was explaining how the services here worked. With a touch to his arm, she stopped him. "Are you a Christian?"

He gazed at her, and his Adam's apple bobbed as he swallowed. "I am. This—the candles, the icons, the relics—is all outward. Being a Christian is an inward relationship that reflects itself on the outside."

"You aren't Jewish?"

"Half. My father is. His family was one of the thousand that returned here after the war. When Papa married a Christian woman and converted, his family would have nothing to do with him. That's what made me work to discover that side of who I am."

"Wow. I didn't think there was anyone in the world who could understand what I'm doing here, but I think you can."

"We are much alike in that way. Papa talks about being Jewish and taught us about Passover and Hanukkah, but he doesn't know much about the family's past or their time during the war."

God's presence was in this place, wasn't it? He had brought her the perfect person to work with when she walked into the Jewish Museum. But which God was it that did that for her? "Sometimes do you wonder whether Judaism is right or if Christianity is? How do you decide which one to follow when your heritage is one thing but you've been brought up a different way?"

He rubbed his square chin, a bit of dark stubble dusting it. Several moments ticked by while he stared at the frescoed ceiling. "I never really think about it much. I follow the religion my parents taught me and have been a Christian all my life. I love Jesus, and I always have."

"At some point, though, we all have to make a choice for ourselves, don't we?"

"I suppose we do. We have to decide if we will take what we have been taught and make it our own, if the faith of our fathers will be our faith also."

Another minute or two of silence passed before Giannis turned toward her and smiled. "Are you ready to keep going?"

"Lead the way."

Once they were farther into the heart of the city, Giannis parked his car, and they continued their tour on foot. He showed her more churches, an ancient Turkish bath, and a bunch of Roman ruins. Finally though, with sweat coating every square inch of her skin, Tessa had had enough. "You're a great guide, but I need a break. Can we find some shade and something cool to drink?"

"Your timing is perfect. We are close to Aristotle University, and many young people gather in this area. There are a lot of good places to eat and shop here." He pointed to a low wall in the pedestrian area, just two blocks from the sea. The trees were small but offered a little shade. "Sit there, and I will come back with something for you."

"I can come."

"You rest and let me do this for you."

Who was she to argue? No guy had ever treated her this well or been so concerned for her. Giannis was very different from anyone she'd ever met. She sat on the concrete wall as young people her age with backpacks hustled by, as well as women with young children and even a few couples hand in hand. It would be so easy to—

No. She was here for only a short time and couldn't leave with entanglements. A soft breeze blew a loose strand of hair in her face, and she brushed it away. The wind carried the scents of pizza and honey with it. In front of her, the bay sparkled in the sun, and around her swirled the Greek language. Then again, the sun, the history, and the food all beckoned her to stay. It would be difficult to go home.

Giannis arrived carrying two pastries and two cups of orange juice. She rushed to help him. "I told you I should have come along."

"It was no trouble. Sit down and enjoy."

She held up the triangular pastry, cream spilling from the top of it, the lower half of the creation covered in white-and-red-checked paper. "What is this?"

"It is called a *trigona* or triangular. The bakery here sells the best in all of Thessaloniki. Try it."

She bit into the confection, the smooth vanilla cream the perfect offset to the crispy, honey-soaked fried phyllo. "This is heaven."

They enjoyed their treats for several minutes. Then Tessa smacked her lips. "At the beginning of the day, you told me you had some information. I'm out of patience. What did you discover?"

He sipped the last of his fresh-squeezed orange juice from his cup. "I managed to locate several Stavrou families living in Salonika during the war. Do you have your great-grandmother's first name?"

Tessa shook her head. "Like I said, my yiayia never spoke much about the past, so I don't know my great-grandmother's name. All I know is that Yiayia was born here in 1943 and that they came to America a few years later. Yiayia's mom died soon after I was born. I could ask my mother, though I doubt she knows."

"You really did just jump on a plane and come here, didn't you?"

"I did." Tessa chuckled. "Maybe I should have researched more before I left, but other factors were driving me away from Pittsburgh. I was in a hurry to get out of there."

"Well, it may take us some more time, but I think we should be able to trace which Stavrou is your family."

"I'll call my mother tonight. Maybe she'll remember something." Though the thought of having to dial the number sent the delicious dessert churning in her stomach.

CHAPTER FOURTEEN

October 1942

I have sat by idly for far too long. I allowed the Nazis to take my husband away. Who knows if he's even still alive? Perhaps the emptiness in the pit of my stomach is a sign that he is no longer here on earth.

I pray that I am wrong.

All this time, however, I've been encouraging my people to action while I do nothing but continue to write and tell them what actions they should be taking. Have I dirtied my hands? Have I left the few comforts I still have and gone to the streets to resist those who invaded us?

Have I done one single thing to bring my husband home?

No. I am ashamed that I have not. So now it's time for me to rise from my inaction. It's time to fight with all I have left to save our men. We need them, all of them.

I need my husband. The loneliness is about to overwhelm me. I have Perla, who is in the same situation as I am, and I have Ioanna, who loves me like a sister, but it's not the same as having Asher. They come to talk to me, though it is getting very dangerous for Ioanna to do that. Perla is often busy with her children.

There is no one, though, to hold me close when I don't think I can stand any more of this. There is no one to share my bed with.

Worst of all, Asher is missing out on watching his child grow within me. I have been certain of this pregnancy for a while. Though it is not what we had planned, I am choosing to trust Dio in this situation, difficult as it is. Perhaps He has given me this little one to comfort me while Asher is away.

It is strange about the city. A large part of our hearts is missing, and all the women are downtrodden.

I continue to publish my small newspaper. Ioanna brings me paper when she comes, if she can, because getting it is now impossible. I can only print a few copies at a time, and then the ladies must pass it around. When I do write, I do my best to keep spirits up, to remind them that our sons, husbands, and brothers will soon be home.

Even as I type the words, though, I question if that will be the case. Some died before going to the camps. How many will perish there? The Germans can't be trusted, so there is always the doubt that our men will come back.

Oh, return to me, my love, my heart, my soul.

—From the diary of Mathilda Nissim

Mathilda paced the floor in front of both Perla and Ioanna. Inside her, the whisper-soft wings of her child fluttered against her stomach. Even that small consolation did little to cool the heat burning in her chest. "There has to be a way."

Perla, one child clinging to her leg and the other crying on her lap, shrugged. "What is there to be done? Our men have been gone for weeks now with no word from them."

Ioanna added, "I know you're desperate, Mathilda—"

She raised her hand, stopping her friends' words. Si, her heart ached for Asher. She should have told him about the miracle growing inside her. That was one regret she would never outlive. "We aren't going to give up. There has to be some action we can take that will force the Nazis to bring our men home."

"What do you propose?" Perla freed her hair from her youngest son's chubby fingers. Ioanna picked up the other child and bounced her on her knee, as much as she could with her own expanding waistline.

Mathilda drew in a deep breath. "What is it that the Germans love more than anything else?"

"Power." Ioanna didn't hesitate in her answer.

"No, I believe there is something they desire even more. Or perhaps this will be what will bring them the power they long for."

Perla huffed. "I hate guessing games. Just tell us."

"Money. They can't operate their war machine without great amounts of cash. With the Americans in the conflict now, it's only a matter of time before the Allies step foot on continental European soil. The Germans will require great amounts of money to be able to fight them on the ground."

"I think I see where you're going with this." Ioanna set down the little girl and allowed her to play with a few items from her pocketbook. "You want to offer a ransom for the return of your husbands."

"What other language do they speak?"

Perla shook her head. "Do you have any idea how much that will be? You're talking about millions upon millions of drachmas for the thousands of men they're holding. If any of them are still alive. Right now, most of us don't even have incomes."

"There are a few wealthy families who can contribute a great deal to the cause. And I invited Ioanna here because she has connections in the Christian world and might be able to raise some funds from them."

Perla clucked her tongue. "The Christians have never liked us. They're probably plenty happy that half of our population is gone."

Ioanna grabbed her precious tube of lipstick before the child could apply any to her lips. "I'm afraid Perla is right. Too many of the Christians may be apathetic to the plight of the Jews, though I can think of a couple of families who perhaps would be willing to contribute. There are a few good people left in the city."

With fatigue a common ailment these days, especially with the poor food, Mathilda sat on a chair facing her two friends. "I think it's our only option. What other choices do we have?"

Both women remained silent.

"Then I'm going to Rabbi Koretz to see what is to be done. Despite his earlier arrests, he remains on fairly good terms with the Nazis, so perhaps he can arrange a meeting with the Germans to see if they are receptive to the idea. Perla, will you come with me? I think it would help if we gathered as many women as possible."

"I'll go with you." Perla rocked her little one. "I doubt it will do much good though. Why would they want to negotiate with us when they already hold all the power?"

"Like I said, they're going to need money. They'll get it any way they can, including allowing some of the Jews to be released. I haven't heard a better plan."

They agreed to call on the rabbi in the morning, and Perla gathered her children together and left. Ioanna stayed behind. "Do you believe your scheme has a chance of working?"

"I have to have faith that it will. Without Asher, what do I have? I promised to fight for him, for all the men, and for all my people. Right now, I can't do anything other than take that chance, however small and difficult it will be."

"I understand you wanting Asher home and doing whatever it might take to get him here. You aren't alone in this."

Mathilda rubbed her belly. Si, she had this blessing to come, hard as it was to think about bringing a child into the world now. There was no stopping the birth of her own infant, nor would she if she could. "I have this baby and you and Perla, that's true."

"You also have God. He loves you and is taking care of you and of Asher. He has a perfect plan, and all the events of the past few years are within His control."

"That may be what you as a Christian think. I can't help but wonder if Dio has turned His back on His people yet again. He did so when He scattered us into exile. This is our punishment for whatever sin we may have committed. I haven't practiced the faith as I should have. This is my call to return to it."

"There is so much more to what is happening than that."

Mathilda waved her away. She had enough on her mind right now.

Ioanna reached into the canvas bag she had brought along. "Here is some bread for you. I managed to get some feta cheese and olives as well. You're looking peaked and pale. You have to take better care of yourself."

Ioanna, further along in her pregnancy and with limited but still better access to food than Mathilda, had round cheeks and was healthy and plump. Each glance in the mirror reminded Mathilda that she was not so fortunate. Every night she prayed that her child would remain strong and healthy and would be born vigorous for the challenges ahead.

"Gracyas, my dear friend. I don't know what I would do without you."

"I'll be praying for you. May God give you strength and peace. Remember, even in the darkest of times, when the dawn seems so far away, He is watching out for you."

By the time Mathilda finished her meager breakfast, cleaned her single plate, and completed several chores, it was almost midday. Perla had managed to secure someone to watch her children, so she came alone. It would do no good to visit the rabbi to speak to him with Perla's attention divided. Mathilda met her on the street.

Perla grasped the straps of her pocketbook so tightly her knuckles were white. "I hope this works, but I have a feeling this is a crazy mission doomed from the start."

"With that kind of thinking, it will be. We have to be positive and firm. We can't take no for an answer. If we allow them to dissuade us from pursuing this, we may never see our husbands again. Fight for David. Think of having him home again."

For herself, Mathilda could think of little else besides Asher's return. Daily reminders, like his clothes in the wardrobe or a note in his handwriting, only increased her longing for him and intensified her loneliness. The time had come to stop moping and to act. Isn't that what Papa would want? Isn't that what she had been calling the people of Salonika to do? How could she do less?

She rubbed the scars on her hands and wrapped her sweater tighter around herself as she and Perla huddled against a brisk wind. Summer and its intense heat had left the city. A promise of the winter to come was in the air. What more misery would that bring for her people? Already they had suffered through two harsh and miserable winters.

She pushed those thoughts aside as she and Perla arrived at Rabbi Koretz's residence. A housekeeper let them in and ushered them to a living area to await the rabbi's arrival.

He soon entered wearing a dark suit with a long coat, thick eyebrows crowning deep-set eyes. "Good morning, ladies. I must admit to my surprise at being told you were waiting to speak with me."

Perla nodded at Mathilda to do the talking. Since she had plenty to say, she had no problem being the spokeswoman. "We have come with a proposal for getting our men returned to us."

The rabbi nodded. "I've been in contact with Dr. Merten for a few months now, ever since the Germans forced me to be part of the Jewish council. I can tell you that he is in no mood for negotiations. The Germans are the ones in control. They have no need for anything from us."

"That's where you're wrong." Mathilda went on to outline her plan. "You see, this gives us a chance."

"You realize the sum will be substantial." Rabbi Koretz bore his gaze into her, almost daring her to answer his rebuttal.

"I believe every Jew within the city will be willing to give what they can, and there are several who can donate a great deal. We don't know if we will fail because we have yet to try. On behalf of all the women of Salonika, those wives, mothers, sisters, and daughters who are suffering greatly because of the loss of the city's men, I beg you to consider this. No, more than consider. I beg you and the council to act."

The middle-aged rabbi, often despised among his own kind because of his Austrian heritage, stroked his close-shaven beard peppered with gray. "You do make a persuasive argument, Señora Nissim. Then again, you were always the outspoken one with the progressive ideas."

"Not progressive." Well, maybe a little. "Just practical. How will the women and children who are left behind survive without the income the men provide? There's no chance at our survival without them. Already, children are hungry. The sick and elderly don't have access to medications to save their lives. The poor are poorer than ever, despite what we do to help. We are all suffering terribly, each and every one of us. If we don't try, we fail."

He eyed her small, rounded stomach. "It appears as though you have real incentive for your husband to return."

She rubbed her belly, as if to protect her child from whatever harm may be lurking. "I found out I was expecting just days before Asher was taken to the camp. He knows nothing about our coming child. He should be here, and our son or daughter deserves to have a father. That's only right."

Rabbi Koretz stroked his beard some more. At least he was thinking about her proposal.

Perla took the lull in the conversation as the opportunity to speak. "I have three small children at home, so I can't work because I have no one to look after them. That's four mouths I have to feed with not a drachma of income. We had a small amount of savings, but that's disappearing. What am I to do without my husband? We'll soon be out of money, out of food, and out of a home. Inaction will lead to destitution. It's your obligation to aid the women under your care."

If propriety had allowed, Mathilda would have applauded.

The rabbi nodded at each of them. "I admire your tenacity and willingness to do what you need to for your husbands, though I fear the way you go about it, Señora Nissim, may be your downfall. However, I do agree that something must be done about the situation. I'll speak to Dr. Merten on one condition."

Mathilda raised a single eyebrow.

"You will come with me."

Now I must appear before the German military administration counselor of the region along with Rabbi Koretz. While I am happy about this turn of events, that the rabbi is willing to act in getting our husbands returned to us, I am frightened to talk to a German. I don't speak the language, and I doubt he speaks either Greek or Ladino.

What am I to do? What am I to say? I pray that Dio will untie my tongue and give me the words. Better yet, that he would send someone else in my place, like he allowed Aaron to speak for Moses.

I fear, though, that I am more like Queen Esther, who gathered her courage and went to the king to plead for the lives of her people. That is what I must do. So I will put up my hair, wear my best clothes, and put on my nicest pair of shoes.

Like Esther asked of her people, I will fast before I go before Dr. Merten. Perhaps then Dio will have mercy on me and grant me success.

CHAPTER FIFTEEN

Though Greece is beautiful and I'm enjoying my time here more than I thought I would, I understand Mathilda's loneliness. Not only am I homesick for America and my family and friends there, but I also understand the feeling of not belonging. Of not having a place to call your own. Their lives were ripped out from underneath them. That's how I've felt for years.

When Dad died so suddenly, the foundation underneath me shifted. Imagine coming home from school, finding your mother cleaning out her closet, and having her tell you that there was an accident and Daddy won't be coming home. Ever. When I reflect on that time, it still steals my breath.

The worst part was her remarriage. I was cast aside in favor of Jay's daughter. She was the favorite. No one ever left her at a rest stop on a family vacation. They didn't even miss me for a good number of miles. Then I got yelled at for putting the entire trip behind schedule.

Would I have the courage Mathilda had, to go to the rabbi and talk about paying ransom to free her captured husband? I'd like to think I would, but I'm not sure. She had some faith, that much is clear. Praying and fasting are good things. I still don't know, though, which is the right God to be praying to.

—From the journal of Tessa Payton

Tessa's phone chose that moment to ring. She set down her pink pen and answered it. Mom was calling. Maybe she would be more inclined to answer questions today. "Hi."

"Hi, yourself. Other than a couple of texts, we haven't heard a word from you since you left," Mom huffed.

"I'm sorry. I've been fighting jet lag and trying to feel my way around the city and the culture, and I've been busy learning about the Jews and about our family."

"First of all, are you okay? You haven't run into any trouble?"

"I'm fine. I got some good advice from the person at the museum. He was very helpful when I needed to get my sea legs under me."

"That's good. I still worry about you being there by yourself."

"Don't. I really don't go out after dark, I'm always aware of my surroundings, and I keep my door locked. Actually, I might be safer here than in Pittsburgh."

Mom yawned. "Sorry. It's early here, but I was trying to catch you before you had dinner."

The conversation continued in this vein for a while. Mundane, day-to-day things. Jay got a raise at work, but not as much as he'd expected. His daughter, Lily, found a beautiful town house that she'd put a down payment on. So on and so forth.

"That's nice." Tessa kept Mathilda's journal open in front of her. "I'm enjoying it here quite a bit. The people are nice, the food is amazing, and I'm getting a fabulous tan."

"What have you discovered about the family?" Mom finally asked a question Tessa wanted to answer.

"Not much yet. There were no Stavrou family members who died in the Holocaust. That's not a Jewish name even."

"See. You wasted the money on that trip for nothing."

"Giannis is working to find out more about anyone by that name who was in the city at the time. What I need is your mother's first name. That would help in locating her family."

"It was Edie. Not anything very Greek. They might have changed it when they came to this country. That's about all I know."

"You don't have papers for her? Any of them?"

"Not anything before they arrived here."

"What about your great-grandmother's name?"

"I seem to remember my mother referring to her as Anna once or twice, so that's what I would say it was. I'm sorry I don't have more information than this. You were always the curious one. What matters to me is that I'm here and I'm who I am. I wish you would drop it and come home."

"But who you are today is shaped by what happened to your family in the past. Don't you wonder where some of our customs come from?"

"Sure. They came from my mom and hers before her. I don't tend to think much beyond that. Their lives must have been very different from ours."

"They were. They were persecuted and killed during the war in the most heinous ways you can think of. The diary I'm reading now of a woman named Mathilda tells about how her husband was taken to a labor camp, leaving her with no income and a child on the way."

"That is terrible. Many people suffered a great deal."

"I'll agree to that."

"I miss you, you know."

Sometimes Tessa wondered. "Yes. I miss you too. I can't wait to share with you everything I've learned about Greece and its people. And I hope to come home with answers about where we came from and what it means to be Jewish."

"I really don't think of myself like that. I was raised Christian, and that's what I am. That's what you are too."

"It doesn't make you think about which God is the true one? Or make you question how your faith plays into your life?"

"Not really. My faith is my faith, and I know it's the truth. Oh listen, Jay just came downstairs and is expecting breakfast. I'd better get going. Love you. Stay safe."

"Love you." Before Tessa could say more, Mom hung up.

She just didn't understand. None of them did. Riley might, but she had to be up early for her shift as a CNA at a nursing home. She was probably at work already. Maybe Tessa could catch her tomorrow morning, when it was evening there.

Even though the phone call with her mom had been more frustrating than anything, at least it was a voice from home. The loneliness pressed harder on Tessa's chest. Giannis had a meeting today, so he couldn't help her. Not that she expected him to be with her all day every day, but at least he was someone familiar in this strange city.

She couldn't stay in this small apartment any longer. She grabbed her phone and some money and headed out. Instead of turning left to go to the market, she turned right. Just a block away was a busy street lined with tavernas and coffee shops.

Since she had explored those before, she continued up the street to another main thoroughfare. She wandered the area until she wasn't exactly sure where she was. Once she was good and hot and tired, she stood underneath the canopy in front of a green-cross pharmacy and studied the area. Oh good, a juice bar.

Emblazoned above the front door was Σταύρου. Though she didn't know much Greek and the letters were very strange, she'd picked up enough to know that said Stavrou. Perhaps this was someone who was her family or knew her family.

As soon as the light turned, she crossed the street and headed straight for the bar, skirting tables sprouting orange umbrellas as she made her way inside. A young woman with light pink hair stood behind the counter. "Yassou."

"Hello." Answering in English, Tessa had found, was the easiest way to tell someone you didn't speak Greek.

"Hello." The girl's bright pink lips curled into a smile. "What can I get for you?"

"I'll have some orange juice." She'd never tasted better juice than here.

Once the girl brought her order and Tessa paid, she scanned the store. No one else was about. She leaned over the counter. "The name of this place, Stavrou. Is that who owns it?"

"Yes." The girl drew out the word.

"Are you a Stavrou?"

"Why do you ask these questions?"

"My grandmother's last name was Stavrou. I might be related to the people who own this."

The girl nodded. "I'm not Stavrou, but the owner is here, if you want to talk to him."

"Yes, I would, very much. Thank you."

Just a few minutes later, the girl returned with a man who was maybe in his later thirties, just a few lines radiating from his eyes. "You want to talk to me?"

All of a sudden, Tessa's mouth went dry, and her heart pounded so hard it might break her ribs. "Um." She sipped her juice and coughed when she swallowed it wrong. "Your last name is Stavrou?"

"Yes. I am the owner, Manos."

"My grandmother's maiden name was Stavrou. I'm trying to figure out if we're related."

"Oh." He didn't give anything away with his expression, but his single word was flat. Had she said the wrong thing?

She hadn't come all this way to be a quitter. "Her name was Edie."

"That is not a Greek name. She was born here or in America?" He pulled his eyebrows into a V.

"Here, though I understand she was very young when they immigrated soon after World War Two."

"I am not old enough to remember that."

Tessa sipped more of her juice, buying herself some time to work up courage for the next question. "Is there someone in your family who might remember?"

"I can ask. You give me your information, your phone number, and I will let you know what I find."

They exchanged numbers, and she gave him as much information as she had. As she left the building, she glanced over her shoulder at the sign once more. Was she close to discovering a puzzle piece? Would it be anything she wanted to discover?

She managed to find her way back to her apartment with ease and climbed the steps, her legs heavy. Her entire body was. Here she thought she was over jet lag. Maybe not.

She took a long, hot shower and heated some leftovers for dinner. No sooner had she sat down with her food and Mathilda's journal than her phone rang. It was Manos, the owner of the juice bar. She set everything aside and took the call.

"Yes, you asked if there is someone alive who might remember family who left for America. My grandfather is getting very old, but he was here then. He says he knows there were some who left when the war was over."

This was better and faster than Tessa had dared to hope. "Can I speak with him?"

"He will talk to you." They worked out the details for a meeting over the weekend, and he agreed that Giannis could accompany her.

By the time she hung up, her food was cold, but that didn't matter. At least she was on the right track to getting answers. Perhaps that would ease the loneliness that had dogged her for more than ten years.

She set Mathilda's journal aside and pulled out her own.

What was life like for you, Mathilda? I can't even imagine. Your husband was gone, you were expecting a baby, and the Nazis were persecuting you. I've researched the Holocaust in Greece and know that the outcome likely wasn't good.

Did you survive? I hope so, I really do. I didn't ask Giannis about that, and he didn't offer. Perhaps he wants me to discover the ending on my own. I'm almost afraid to know.

That's how I feel about this meeting with what might be my family. There had to be a reason that the Jewish side of me went by a Christian name. Maybe that's how they survived. Why would it be such a secret though? What if I'm only stirring up trouble?

I think I need a good night's sleep, and maybe I'll be able to put everything into perspective in the morning. I should be able to talk to Giannis. He's great at listening and great at helping me out.

Then again, I might be getting a little too attached to him. It's good that I was able to get out today and make a discovery on my own. I'm proud of that.

Good night, Mathilda. You lived a short distance but a long time removed from this place. I hope you survived. I really, really hope you survived.

CHAPTER SIXTEEN

Dio, if you are at all gracious, grant us success.

—From the diary of Mathilda Nissim

As she clipped along the streets leading toward the German headquarters near the White Tower, Mathilda couldn't distinguish if the fluttering in her midsection was the wakening of her baby or nerves about meeting with the Nazi commander. All day yesterday she had gone without food, praying for success for her mission. By evening she was faint, but she continued her prayers.

Throughout the night, she had beseeched Dio for His favor. Did He even listen anymore? Did He care? From all that had transpired in just the past few months, her answer would have to be no. Still, she wasn't about to take a chance and incur His wrath. So she fasted.

She took some food and drink this morning to fortify herself. The fluttering continued.

"Señora Nissim, please wait."

She turned as Rabbi Koretz hustled along the street toward her, his suit coat flapping behind him. She pulled her own coat tighter. "Good morning. I would have thought you would be there by now." The walk was long, on the other side of the city, on Macedonia Hill, once Anatolia College, now requisitioned by the occupiers.

"I forgot to wind my alarm clock last night. What a night to forget. So, as you see, I'm running behind, and I'm a bit disheveled.

Not a good impression to make."

"I think it will be our words and not our appearances that sway him to our side. Since you arranged this meeting, I have thought of little else, other than what I might say."

"You are prepared, then?"

"I will do whatever it takes to get my husband home." They arrived at Nazi headquarters, situated far from the water. She stopped on the step and turned toward Rabbi Koretz, then nodded at him. "Do you mind if I give you a hand with your appearance?"

"No. Do what you must."

She straightened the cap on his head and adjusted his suit coat and even slicked back a stray lock of hair. "Now you can feel confident when we speak to Dr. Merten." Though her words were firm, her limbs were anything but. She shook from head to toe.

They passed under one of the many arches across the front and crossed the portico. Rabbi Koretz opened the door for her, and she entered the well-appointed building. They located a secretary, a Greek collaborator, and told her about their appointment. The woman disappeared for a moment, and when she returned, she instructed them on how to find Dr. Merten's office.

He sat behind his desk piled high with papers and didn't bother to rise when they entered. He shot each of them an icy glare. "So, you have come with a request for me?"

Since they hadn't been invited to sit, both the rabbi and Mathilda stood. She clasped her hands together so Dr. Merten wouldn't see them shaking. Unlike what she had believed, he did speak passable Greek.

Rabbi Koretz stepped forward. "This woman, and many thousands like her, are without their husbands. They have no means to support themselves, and they and their children are going hungry."

Dr. Merten stroked his thin mustache. "What a pity. The men, however, are needed to work for the Reich. I am sorry, but that is the way it is. We all must sacrifice to see the establishment of the great German government."

"We cannot do without all of the men." If this were the soft sand of some of the Greek islands, Mathilda would have dug in her heels. "I refuse to leave until we come to some kind of understanding that will bring our fathers and husbands home to us." She did cross her arms over her chest.

Dr. Merten stroked his rounded chin. "My, what spunk you possess."

Rabbi Koretz cleared his throat. "Sir, if I may—"

"No, you may not. The lady has me intrigued. I will speak with her. What is it that you propose? I cannot allow my entire workforce to be taken from me without some sort of compensation."

Mathilda glanced at the rabbi. She had not been in the meeting where they discussed how much they were willing to pay to ransom Salonika's men. He mouthed the words to her, and she turned to Dr. Merten. "One billion drachmas." The immense price sent her staggering, and the rabbi caught her by the elbow and kept her upright.

The German laughed, no mirth reaching his steely blue eyes. "That is a paltry sum. I cannot speak to my superiors in Berlin about such a small price for such a large workforce. They are proving invaluable to us."

One billion drachmas was already a large sum. Raising that kind of money would be almost impossible. "Sir, we are poor people."

Another chilly chuckle from Dr. Merten. "That is the furthest thing from the truth. In reality, you are well-to-do people who have stolen jobs and opportunities from Aryans. But I like you, so I'll allow you to continue with what you were saying."

"We are poor people, especially now with no husbands or fathers to support us. That sum is already a large amount of money. We can't go higher."

"Why are you here, Frau Nissim?"

She shrunk back and cradled her small belly. She could barely force the words through her tight throat. "Because I want my husband back."

"You miss him, don't you?"

All she could do was nod.

"You would like him to be with you when your time to deliver your child arrives, isn't that so?"

Again, she nodded.

"What are you willing to give to make that happen?"

She swallowed hard. She had no authority to offer him more money. Once more, she turned to see what the rabbi had to say.

Dr. Merten pounded on his desk. "Focus on me." His loud words echoed in the room.

She shot her gaze in his direction.

"You speak to me and to no one else. I will only negotiate with you, a woman who would do anything to have the man she loves warming her bed once more."

Heat rose in Mathilda's face.

"Speak for your fellow wives and mothers, since that is what you say you are here to do. How much is the community willing to pay to get them back?"

Right now, she couldn't form a rational thought, much less speak a sentence that made sense. What might be a number that would satisfy the Germans but would be feasible for the community to raise? Why did this decision rest on her shoulders? The weight of it was about to collapse her knees.

She stared at her sturdy lace-up shoes for several minutes.

"Frau Nissim, are you going to speak, or have you suddenly gone mute?"

She stood with her back as straight as a row of grapes in the nearby vineyards. To make her words carry weight and sound confident, she stared Dr. Merten straight in the eyes. "One point five billion drachmas. That is our offer."

"Ha." The Nazi fiddled with a pen on his desk. "You are in no position to be bargaining. I will speak with my superiors and see what they have to say, but my recommendation to them will be two billion."

Two billion? They would be hard-pressed to come up with that amount. It would take contributions from everyone. Each member of the community would have to sacrifice in order to make this happen.

Then again, having their men home where they belonged was worth every missed meal.

Dr. Merten nodded toward the door. "That is all. I will call for you when I have an answer from Berlin. Good day."

On shaking legs, Mathilda made her way out of the office, the carpeting softening her footfalls, Rabbi Koretz beside her each step of the way. The receptionist mumbled a derogatory slur, but it was nothing Mathilda had not heard before.

She didn't draw a deep breath until they were outside on the street again. Then the air whooshed in and filled her lungs. She turned to the rather pale rabbi. "Did I do the right thing?"

He shrugged, his hat falling askew once more.

"I didn't know what to say. Maybe 1.5 billion was too much. How was I to know?"

The older man touched her arm. "You did just fine. I'm not sure I would have been able to say a single word. You are daring and brave, and I commend you for it. But do not put news of this out in that little paper of yours. Doing so may jeopardize the entire negotiation."

"I understand." At least he wasn't asking her to give it up. "Do you think we'll be able to raise such a large amount?"

Again, he shrugged. "Time will tell. With you at the helm, though, I would say that our chances are pretty good. You are a persuasive young woman, and I pray this venture succeeds."

They made their way toward the Jewish section of the city. Silence stretched between them, and at last Mathilda could hold it in no longer. "Do you believe Dio has abandoned us?"

He stopped and stared at her for a long minute. "He turned His face away from His people and took them into exile in Assyria and Babylon. Then He set the Romans over us, destroyed the temple, and scattered us to the farthest regions of the world. It would seem He has shown us His back once more." With that, he marched away, leaving Mathilda standing alone on the walkway.

It was amazing that no flies buzzed into her open mouth. He was the spiritual leader of all of Salonika's Jews, yet he believed Dio's presence had once again left His people. If that was the case, what hope was there?

None.

If that was the case, their ruin and destruction were sure.

She shivered and pulled her sweater tighter around her shoulders. Soon she wouldn't be able to button the bottom buttons. She rubbed the place where her child slept. This time there was no doubt that the fluttering was from her baby's movements.

"I am so sorry, little one, to have brought you into such a situation. What kind of world will you be born into? Will you be born at all?"

She meandered toward the harbor, her favorite place in the city besides the spice shop.

The wind whipped her face as she stared over the water. In the summer, it sparkled like all of the diamonds in the world had been scattered across its surface. Now, on such a dreary day, it was brown and black and churned, a menacing sight.

She shook away the rabbi's words. Not all hope had vanished. Dr. Merten had promised to talk to the higher-ups in Berlin. Perhaps her people could ransom the men and life could get back to what it had once been.

No, it would never be what it once was. Who knew how long the Nazis would be here? Even with the Americans now in the war, it had made precious little difference to their worsening circumstances. Even if Asher and the others returned, the Germans would think up new ways to torture and torment them. Just look at what they had done at the square.

Mathilda turned and shuffled her way toward her flat, shutting out the sights and sounds around her, focusing only on returning home to another day spent alone.

But a surprise awaited outside her flat. Ioanna stood, the wind whipping her skirts and brushing her hair across her cheeks, turning them a rosy shade of pink. In her hands, she held a woven basket that promised a loaf of fresh bread or a jar of olives.

Ioanna had taken the risk of ridicule and possibly even punishment from the Nazis by being seen coming to the home of a Jewess.

Mathilda let out a little squeal and rushed into her friend's arms. And there, she wept.

CHAPTER SEVENTEEN

October 13, 1942

Mathilda sat on her red-and-yellow embroidered sofa, staring out the window and across the street to another flat over an olive shop. Or what had been one. No more did the aroma of oregano and chilies perfume the air in her home. No more did crowds bustle down the street, bartering with those hawking their wares.

These days the market was almost empty and most of the shops were shuttered. There was little food to be had.

Ioanna kept Mathilda from losing her mind. She came by every other day or so with some food and reminded Mathilda to eat for the sake of the coming child. If not for that, who knew what state she might be in? There would come a time, however, when Ioanna wouldn't be able to help them. It was approaching, there was no doubt about it. Little by little, the Germans were tightening the noose around the Jews' necks.

The late afternoon sun slanted through the window and rested on Mathilda's lap. It warmed her and the chilly flat, and she soon dozed and dreamed of Asher knocking on the door and calling for her.

The knock, though, was real. Mathilda roused herself and went to open the door. There stood Rabbi Koretz, a grin stretching his beard-shadowed face. "I come bearing good news."

"They have agreed to our terms?"

"In a way, si. Three point five billion drachmas. But at least the men will be released and will return home."

"That much?" She couldn't comprehend such a number.

"That is what it is going to take to ransom them. Dr. Merten was quite firm. There is no negotiating that price."

"We will never be able to raise that amount of money."

"That is what I am counting on you for. You have such eloquence and this ability to sway people to your way of thinking. With your help and your determination, we can do this. I know you want your husband home more than anything."

"I do."

"Then I can count on you?"

"Of course, but there has to be a way that we can get the amount reduced."

"The committee agrees that the community will never be able to raise so much in a short amount of time. We are meeting tonight to formulate a plan to submit to Dr. Merten. A compromise, of sorts. Though it is out of the ordinary to have a woman present, because of these special circumstances, we will allow you to come. In fact, we would like for you to come."

"I'm not sure what I will be able to contribute, but I will be there. Are you meeting at the Matanoth?" Before the war, the beautiful yellow baroque building housed a soup kitchen for the community's poor. Now it was home to the Jewish committee the Nazis required them to set up.

"Si. We will see you at six o'clock this evening."

"In the meantime, I will get to work on raising the money, if that's at all possible."

"Don't even tell me what that means. You know my position."

"Then I will refrain from divulging what I'm going to do."

"Gracyas. I will see you tonight."

No sooner had the rabbi shut the door than Mathilda pulled out her typewriter from the compartment in the wardrobe. The words in her brain were already scrambling to be let out. With her machine wrapped in towels, she went to work, fast so she didn't forget what she wanted to say but careful not to make a mistake on the one sheet of paper she had.

> *Do you long for your husbands, brothers, sons, and fathers? We have an opportunity to bring them home where they belong. If we work together, we can soon have them in our arms.*
>
> *Dr. Merten has agreed to ransom our men for the sum of 3.5 billion drachmas. While it seems an exorbitant amount, we can raise it if we want them home before winter. It will mean more scrimping on our part, but think of what our men have endured and sacrificed for us. Can we not repay them for all they have given on our behalf?*
>
> *Details will come soon as to how you can donate to this ransom fund. Think of how our ancestors donated to build the temple. They gave all they had. That is what it will take from each of us to bring our husbands, brothers, sons, and fathers home.*

Once she had pulled her article from the typewriter, she reread it about three times. Even though she couldn't change the words, it needed to be perfect. A call to action for each and every woman in the community and even those beyond.

For too long, they had sat back and watched their freedoms drained from them. At long last, they could act. She clutched the precious paper to her chest and bounded down the stairs. The first person she met on the street was an older gentleman, one who had not been selected to go to Poland. She thrust the paper in front of him.

He skimmed it, then turned toward her. "I wish you would not get your hopes up. Those men aren't coming home."

That was one old man's opinion. She allowed several younger

women to read her words. They all shook their heads. "If only I could believe it was true," one said as she reined in a rambunctious toddler. "But that sum is astronomical. Even if Dio showered money from the sky, we will never be able to raise that amount. It's extortion, plain and simple."

The others murmured in agreement with her.

An hour later, Mathilda dragged herself home. The reaction hadn't been the positive one she had anticipated. She climbed the stairs and entered her flat, leaning against the door after she shut it.

"Oh, Asher, have I failed you?"

The small room in the Matanoth was crowded with men, some dressed in business suits and others, the more pious among them, attired in long, fringed, blue-striped prayer shawls.

Mathilda was the only woman. Her palms sweated as she took a seat among them. The weight of their stares pressed on her chest. She clasped her hands together to keep them from shaking and pasted a wobbly smile on her face.

Rabbi Koretz took over the meeting. "Señora Nissim is here at my request. As I have explained to you, she is the one who began this action to return the men of this city who have been stolen away to the labor camps. If what happened to them before they left is any indication of how they are being treated, then it is imperative that we get them home before the worst of the winter weather sets in."

One elderly man waved away the rabbi's words. "Enough with the prattle. All of this, we know already. Tell us what the Germans have said."

"Three point five billion. That is their price."

A rather loud murmur went up from the assembly. Rabbi Koretz called for quiet. "We cannot allow the men, the most vital members of our community, to rot while we sit by and do nothing to stop it. That is our job as the governing council."

Mathilda cleared her throat. "If I may, Rabbi?"

He nodded.

"We women are doing the best we can without our husbands and fathers here, but it isn't enough. We're hungry, tired, and lonely. And without them, we are vulnerable. The Germans could come at any time and harm us.

"We refused to fight back when they first arrived. We refused to fight back when they killed an old butcher, an innocent man. We refused to fight back when they assembled the men and humiliated them." She fisted her hands and drew herself straight and as tall as possible.

"We can no longer allow them to work our men to death while they take advantage of our women. How long will it be before we too are shipped away to God-knows-where? You cannot leave the community's women undefended and open to attack. We need our men to protect us."

Levi Behar eyed Mathilda up and down with such intensity that she squirmed. "You seem to be doing just fine on your own, Señora Nissim. Quite well, in fact. Independent, just like your mother."

She cradled her unborn child. "There is no doubt that we are capable of cooking meals and taking care of our children. But without the men, we will soon starve to death. Some already are despondent without their husbands. Children miss their fathers. This is not the time for us to be separated. This is the time for us to be united. No matter what the cost." She sat back, exhausted.

Rabbi Koretz flashed her a small smile. "Gracyas, Señora Nissim. I agree with you. Under such conditions, families must be together. We don't function well if half of us are missing. There has to be some way to compromise with the Germans."

"What about installment payments?" This was called out by a younger man missing a leg, probably not fit to be taken to the labor camp. Likely he had lost it fighting the Italians a few years before. "If we don't have to pay them all at once, it would buy us more time to raise the money. Perhaps they would even start letting some of the men go when we make each payment."

The idea was agreed to. So was asking the wealthier non-Jewish citizens of Salonika to help. Then the young man spoke again. "Aristotle University has been asking for ground to expand their campus, ground that is now the Jewish cemetery."

One older man with a prayer shawl pounded his fists together. "I won't even entertain the idea. That ground is sacred."

"If they gave us time to rebury our dead elsewhere, we could sell the land to them. That would bring a quick infusion of cash."

The debate spun around Mathilda. The thought of moving her ancestors' bodies. The graves had been there for hundreds of years. Ancestors she didn't even know were buried there.

The warmth of the room got to her, swirling her stomach and her head. She rushed from the meeting into the cool night air. What had her idea produced? How many would hate her because bringing the men home might mean the destruction of holy ground?

She only wanted Asher at her side. She longed for him to hold her close and to remind her that things were going to work out, that they would be together forever, just as they had promised when they married.

She had said that no cost was too high, but perhaps she had been wrong. This might be the line they would refuse to cross. And so they should.

She was a strong woman but not this strong. As she stumbled her way home, she had a difficult time drawing a breath. Around her, the sounds of life continued. Glasses tinkling as people at the tavernas got ready for dinner. Children laughing as they played on the balconies. Music floating from a flat high above her.

Her world, however, had ended.

And then her child stirred within her.

No, it wasn't over. Couldn't be. She had a very important job to do whether she had Asher by her side or not. Dio, for whatever reason, had chosen this time to give her a child. It was her responsibility to bring this little one into the world and to do everything within her power to protect him or her.

"Si, my little one. I promise to be the best mother to you. If I have to be, though I pray it won't be the case, I will be both mother and father. Whatever I have to do for you, I will do."

CHAPTER EIGHTEEN

Drizzle dampened Mathilda's coat and sent a shiver coursing through her as she huddled with a horde of mourners sheltering underneath black umbrellas. Tears streaked down her cheeks as German bulldozers lined up at the edge of the cemetery. The wails of the professional mourners filled the air.

There hadn't been time. Not enough time to move the hundreds of thousands of bodies that were supposed to find eternal rest in this plot of ground. Within days of the agreement with the council, the Nazis were here to raze the marble graves.

These were no simple markers. These were elaborate above-ground sepulchers with carved headstones. Some had occupied these spots for hundreds of years.

How could the Germans do this to them? Then again, they would have been foolish to expect anything different from their occupiers.

Some had been able to move their departed to another cemetery on the western side of the city, but Mathilda had not been able to make arrangements for any of her family members or for Samuel. That's what ripped her heart from her chest. In a matter of moments, their graves would be desecrated. She shivered to think about what the Germans would do with the bones.

Perla was beside her, none of her children with her today. She drew Mathilda into a side hug and squeezed. "We will be fine." Her voice cracked on the last word.

"This is my fault."

"Our men will come home. That is the most important thing. You were very brave to go to the Germans and to secure their release. All the women I have spoken to have told me how proud they are of you and how thankful they are to you."

"We have no guarantee that any of them will return. The Germans aren't to be trusted, yet I put my faith in them and their word."

Perla released her and turned to face her. "What is wrong with you? Of everyone I know, you are the most optimistic, always finding the good amid heartache and trial."

"Maybe this is what expecting has done to me. Or perhaps the occupation has just worn me down and made me cynical."

"Don't lose heart. Asher and David will return. Remember Esther."

Esther. She had been wise. King Artaxerxes had allowed the Jews to arm themselves to fend off their enemies. This time they had no means of defending themselves.

Dr. Merten saluted, and the engines on the heavy machinery roared to life. This was it. Mathilda locked her jaw and forced herself to keep her attention on the scene unfolding in front of her. As the first bulldozers hit the first marble monument, she touched her chest.

While the dead were disturbed, the new life within her stirred. The mourners' wailing increased in pitch and volume until the sound reverberated in her head. For as long as she could, she stood and observed the destruction taking place in front of her.

The crunch of breaking stones crushed her heart and sickened her stomach. The Germans yanked the bones from the ground and piled them in stacks throughout the cemetery.

Were Papa's and Samuel's among them? All her other loved ones? She spun away. "I can't look any longer."

Perla looped her arm through Mathilda's. "Neither can I. I need to get back and prepare for David's homecoming. I've been saving my money to buy food for a special dinner for him. And I want to give the house a good cleaning, like for Passover. It will be another exodus of men from exile returning home."

"Si. What is done is done."

"No one blames you."

"The best course of action is to move forward and anticipate Asher's arrival."

"And what a surprise he will have."

This brought a small smile to Mathilda's lips. "That he will. He will not expect that I am going to have a child."

"See, you have so much to look forward to. Even with the hardships we are facing, there is joy."

"This is why I love you so much, *mi amiga*. I'm not the optimistic one. You are."

"We pick each other up. That's what true friendship is."

"For now, let's put today's awful events out of our hearts and minds and keep our focus forward facing."

The rest of the damp walk home, they chatted about what they would do when their husbands arrived from the labor camps, and Mathilda's spirits buoyed. Dwelling on the past only brought pain. Turning your attention to the future brought hope, so that's what she would do.

By the time she and Perla parted and she arrived at her building, she was exhausted. The coming baby drained her energy, and she needed more rest than ever before. She would dive into cleaning after a nap and a warm drink.

She unlocked the door on the street and climbed the stairs to their little flat. As she turned the corner to the door, there stood a man, almost as large and as hairy as a bear she once saw in the circus. She clutched her racing heart. "Levi, you startled me. What are you doing here?"

He approached her, tottering on the way. Once he was within a meter of her, the odor of anise-flavored ouzo overpowered her. "I have something to say to you." He gazed at her belly.

She pulled her sweater tighter around herself. "I have nothing to say to you." When she attempted to push past him, he grabbed her by the upper arm, his thick fingers digging into her soft flesh.

Bread crumbs littered his unkempt beard, and his leathery skin fell in folds down his face, large bags underneath his eyes. Why would he ever think her neat-as-a-pin mother would be interested in him? "That's too bad because you're going to have to listen to me."

She switched the keys to her free hand. If he tried anything, she could stab him in the eye. She labored to keep her breathing steady and her face neutral. Better not to let him see her fear.

"Your condition is becoming obvious."

"Si, I am going to have a baby. Asher will be very surprised when he comes home. I knew about the child before he left, but I was waiting for the right time to tell him. Then the Nazis took him away."

His downturned mouth sagged farther. "Or perhaps the child is not your husband's."

"How could you say such a thing? Of course the child is his."

"Then why not tell him before he left?"

"I wasn't sure of my condition. It was only a suspicion, and I didn't want to get his hopes up. Also, I wanted him to concentrate on himself, on coming home to me. He didn't need another worry to burden him."

"What a defense you raise." His dark eyes bored into her soul, and she tore her gaze from him and toward the door beyond.

"It's nothing but the truth. Por favor, let me go. I'm begging you. You're hurting me."

"I am not inclined to release you. You sicken me with the way you strut about town, thinking you can tell all of us what to do, putting out that paper that sets us all in danger's path. You are your mother's daughter. Don't you think the Nazis will figure out who is writing this and punish us all for your actions?"

She had thought about it long and hard and had consulted with

Asher. "It's the right thing to do. We can't allow them to control us. If we do, they win."

He squeezed all the tighter, his fetid breath hot on her chilly cheek. "You need to learn your place as a woman. Go back to cooking and caring for your home and your husband. You've been plenty busy."

She bit her tongue to hold back the reply that begged for release.

"Ah, so now you have nothing to say. How interesting. You know that I'm right. If only you had held your tongue instead of going to Rabbi Koretz and arranging for the release of the city's men."

"The women need their husbands. The children need their fathers. There are too few to take care of us in the way you say we need to be cared for. When I first thought of paying a ransom, I had no idea that the council would sell the cemetery to raise the money." Her voice caught, betraying her.

"Because of you, our ancestors no longer rest in peace. The Germans disturbed their spirits." His roar echoed in the small hallway. "It's because of you. The blame is entirely on your shoulders. I hope they haunt you day and night until you lose your mind."

He pressed her against the wall and choked her, his hand so large he could reach almost all the way around her neck.

With all her might, she shoved him, creating the smallest bit of space between them. But it was enough for her to reach up and stab him with her key. The first try, she only managed to poke him on his flabby cheek. On her second attempt, she hit her target. He released her, grabbing his eye, and staggered backward, howling.

For good measure, she stomped on his foot before rushing to her door, unlocking it as fast as she could, stumbling inside, and locking it once more. She raced toward the telephone, lifting the receiver to her ear.

She paused. Who could she call? The police department was now controlled by the Nazis. There were no men who could come.

She didn't dare phone Perla. But maybe Ioanna's husband could help. For a moment, she waited. Levi still huffed outside her door. With shaking fingers, she asked for Ioanna's number.

As soon as her friend answered, Mathilda swallowed the scream that clogged her throat. "Could Petrus come here? I need him."

"Yes. Why do you need him?"

"Levi is here and is causing trouble. The door is locked but. . ."

A muffled sound came over the line next, as if Ioanna was covering the receiver and speaking to Petrus. A moment later, she was back with Mathilda. "He'll be there soon. How are you holding up?"

They had to watch what they said. Anyone could be listening on the line. If Mathilda had to make a bet on it, she would bet that the Germans heard every word she spoke. "This has been a difficult day, but I'm fine and so is the baby."

"I heard what happened. I'm so sorry."

Mathilda had to swallow hard once more. Over the telephone, she couldn't say what she longed to tell her friend, to hear a comforting word. "At least Asher will be home soon. That's what I have to hang on to with all my strength."

"And you possess a great deal of that. I wish it hadn't come to this point."

"There's nothing more to be done now. We move on from here. That's all we can do."

"You said you are feeling well, that the baby is fine?"

"Yes, the little one is growing and moving just as he should be." They continued to speak of mundane, everyday life matters, as if the world around Mathilda wasn't crumbling, as if her heart wasn't shattered into a thousand little pieces. What would she have left to give her husband when he walked through their door?

About fifteen minutes later, a voice came from outside her flat. "Petrus is here."

"Good. Good."

"Thank you for keeping me calm."

"I never want to see you harmed. Petrus will handle the situation and make sure you're safe. Let's talk soon."

Mathilda hung up and went to the door, pressing against it to hear what was going on in the hall.

"Why do you come to interfere in our affairs?" Levi's words were still slurred enough to lead Mathilda to believe that he had stashed a bottle of ouzo in his coat.

"This has nothing to do with whether anyone is Jewish or Christian but with the safety of a woman who is expecting a child. You can have no good reason to be here." Petrus' voice was calm yet firm.

"She's a whore, sleeping around with what men are left, finding comfort in their arms, carrying one of their children. Since she was a child, she has flouted the way we conduct life here. You may allow women to rule you, but in this community, we do not abide it."

"That's between Mathilda and Asher and has nothing to do with you. You need to leave. Now."

"What will you do if I don't? Call the police? The only one who would get in trouble is you, for defending a Jewess. You're the one who should walk away."

"I won't go until I am certain that Mrs. Nissim is safe."

"Seems that you're in for a long wait."

A scuffle ensued, soles swishing on the floor like a soft-shoe dance. "You will leave." Petrus' words were louder.

"Let me go." Levi's command rang in Mathilda's ears. She cracked open the door and peeked out just as he landed a fist on Petrus' nose. Blood spurted everywhere.

She flung the door open and scurried between the two men, Levi's fist raised. "That's enough. Will you assault me as well? Do you realize what you've done? You could be taken away for good if Petrus calls the Germans on you. A Jew attacking a Christian is a serious offense."

Still holding his bloody nose, Petrus stared at Levi. "I will give you to the count of three to be out of here. Otherwise I will do just what Mrs. Nissim has said. You won't live to see many more days if I place that call."

With that threat hanging in the air, Levi hurried down the stairs, the street door slamming behind him. Mathilda leaned against the wall, her legs too shaky to continue holding her upright. "Thank you from the bottom of my heart. He wasn't going to go away. What would I have done without you? Let me take care of your nose." She stood, returned to the flat, and went to collect bandages and ice.

Petrus couldn't stay here until Asher returned though. What would she do if Levi came back? Would she allow him to silence her?

Never.

She pulled out her diary and got busy writing.

Other than the day when Asher was taken from me, or perhaps when Papa died saving me from the fire, this has to have been the worst day of my life. There is a saying: "Jewish gravestones are fairer than royal palaces." And because of my actions, hundreds of thousands of stones have been desecrated and demolished.

Dio, hear my cry for mercy. Do not turn your face from me nor hide your goodness from me. Have compassion on my soul.

I have been selfish in wanting to have Asher home as my time to deliver this child, Your blessing, draws near. In doing so, I have destroyed what once was holy. Our land now belongs to our enemies, and they will not use it for sacred purposes.

I know that this is not my burden alone that I bear. The council agreed to my suggestion and took the money, but it was my pleas that swayed them. If I had not fought so hard to secure the release of the men, we would still have a cemetery.

Yet I have to ask myself if it is the living or the dead who are more important.

CHAPTER NINETEEN

Mathilda's words ring in my head. Are the living or the dead more important? The answer should be clear to me. Of course it's the living. There is nothing more to be done for the dead. Then why am I here in a foreign country, chasing the stories of those who have long since passed away?

—From the diary of Tessa Payton

Tessa set her frappé on the little table where she sat at the coffee shop overlooking Thessaloniki's harbor. She had been here only a couple of weeks, but in some ways this city was home. She drew in a lungful of salty air and released it slowly.

Mathilda had mentioned the importance of gravestones in the Jewish culture. Perhaps that was something she should ask Giannis about. He would arrive at her apartment in a little while to take her to meet with the Stavrou patriarch.

She wiped her hands on her skirt, the moisture dampening her palms not coming from the warmth of the sun. Today might be the day she got her answers. Maybe she would discover who she was and where she came from.

That must be what drove this quest. How could she move forward with her life if she didn't understand the events that had shaped who she was? Why would Mom continue to hold back information? What could it be? Why wouldn't she tell her anything?

Ever since she'd been young, Tessa had hated secrets of any

kind. She hated having them, and she hated being told them. Not that she couldn't keep her mouth shut, but just that withholding information bothered her. Call it her Christian upbringing or her conscience or whatever, but she couldn't stand them.

She picked up her coffee cup and strolled back toward her apartment. The city already brimmed with life, even at this early hour. Though many people walked to their jobs, cars were parked on both sides of the street, even on the divided roadway. A few of the old men had already set up their black-and-red checkerboards on the café tables on the walks and sat with cigarettes hanging out of their mouths, contemplating their next moves while laughing with each other.

The neighbors, now familiar with her morning routine, shouted to her from their balconies. "*Kaliméra*." They still chuckled at her poor attempt to answer them in Greek.

Next door to her building, the hair salon owner was opening for the day. "Kaliméra."

"Kaliméra."

The thirty-something woman with purple streaks in her hair and big, round glasses glanced at the sky before returning her attention to Tessa. "It will be a good day, will it not?"

"I hope so."

"Why such a sad face?"

"I'm not sad. Just nervous. Today I meet with someone who might know my family."

"That is good, no?"

"Yes and no." Tessa sighed. "In a way, I'm afraid of what I'll find out."

Nadina smiled, her pierced lip curving upward into a crescent. She held up a brown paper bag. "I got *koulouri*. Come in, and we will talk about it. My first person doesn't come for an hour."

"I hate to take you away from your work. And I don't have coffee for you." Then again, she was a sucker for the round, sesame-covered bread, similar to a bagel.

"I will make my own frappé. Come, come."

Tessa glanced at her watch. Thirty minutes until Giannis was due to arrive. She shrugged. "Sure. Thank you."

Once Nadina had the coffee brewing, they both settled into leather barber chairs turned away from the mirrors that lined the wall and the counters covered with combs and scissors and razors. Nadina handed her a koulouri. "So now you tell me why you are afraid of your family."

Maybe a virtual stranger was a better person to share her feelings with. There was no way she would spill Tessa's secret to anyone. She bit the pastry and relaxed against the back of the vinyl chair. "I might learn things that would hurt me or the people I love. Isn't that why you keep a secret? So you don't cause harm to another person?"

"Sometimes to protect them."

"Exactly. Protect them from getting hurt. Maybe that's why my mom and my yiayia have been keeping this from me my entire life and why Mom was so opposed to me coming here. What if the information I get today isn't good news? It could change my life. How could I ever live with it?"

"Maybe what you learn will be good news. You cannot always think about the bad."

Tessa managed to chuckle. "I have been accused of being a pessimist, that's true."

"When the time comes, you will know how to deal with it. You will know what to tell people, what to tell your children someday."

"So you mean that the secret might have to become a secret again?"

"If that was for the best."

Tessa swung her leg, the tips of her sandals brushing the shiny tile floor. "Just what I hate most in the world."

"Then don't do it. Go home and keep living your life." Nadina brushed a violet-colored strand of hair from her eyes. "But there must be a reason you are here."

"I never thought through what all this would mean. I hopped on a plane and came here without a second thought. Impulsive, Mom would say, but that's who I am."

"Then you will let me make your hair pink? You would look good."

"No!" The shriek burst from Tessa's lips as she covered her head in defense. "My mother would kill me. Even though she can't see me right now, I guarantee that she would find out some way or other. Mom may be able to hide things from me, but I can't ever hide anything from her. It's like this sixth sense she has."

"If you change your mind, you know where to find me."

"Right next door." Tessa finished the pastry and wiped the crumbs from her fingers. "Thank you for all your help. I appreciate it."

"I like you for a neighbor. I wish you would stay."

"Me too. As long as you don't touch my hair."

Nadina was still chuckling as Tessa left the shop and made her way next door. Giannis was already waiting for her, leaning against the sun-kissed white brick of the building, his golden skin in contrast to the light paint.

"Oh no. Am I late? I just was chatting with Nadina."

"No, I am early. This is not usual for me, but I wanted to be on time to see Mr. Stavrou."

Just the mention of the name was like a starting pistol to Tessa's heart. For a moment, she had forgotten what the day held. Nadina had done her job well. "Then it's a good thing I didn't allow Nadina to dye my hair pink."

Giannis' mouth dropped into an O.

"She was teasing me." Tessa withdrew the key from her pocket and opened the door, which Giannis held for her. "At least I think she was."

"You had me scared."

"Me too." They rode the elevator to her floor, the dim bulb the only light. The car was small, and his arm brushed her bare one as they stood side by side. A tingle raced up from her fingers to her shoulder, and she sucked in an involuntary breath.

Giannis turned toward her. "Are you okay?"

All she could do was nod.

The ride ended, though she couldn't say if that was a good thing or not. She led the way to the apartment, bright sunshine spilling across the gray floors. "Just let me double-check that I'm presentable, and I'll be ready to go."

"You already look beautiful."

She stared into his brown eyes for a long moment, her mouth dry, until she forced herself to break contact. "Thank you." She threw the empty coffee cup into the garbage can and closed the door behind her.

She leaned against the sink and gazed at her reflection in the mirror. Before this got out of hand, she had to get ahold of herself. An entanglement with Giannis is not what she needed at this moment. In a few days or weeks, a month or two at the most, she'd be gone, back to living her life in the States, fighting with her stepdad and. . .

Who knew where her relationship with her mom would stand after today.

Okay. Time to pull herself together. She brushed out her hair and applied a little pale pink lipstick. Riley had always commented that she hardly needed any makeup with her beautiful skin. Now they knew where that came from.

She stepped into the living room where Giannis had made himself comfortable on the contemporary gray sofa. He stood when she entered. "Are you ready?"

She nodded, then shook her head. All the good that Nadina had done for her was erased in that second. "I'm not sure. What if

I don't like what I discover? Then again, it might be worse not to find out anything at all. I'd still be in this state of limbo, and we'd be no further along than we are now. Than I am now."

"You will never know until you try, right? Isn't that what you told yourself when you got on that plane in America?"

"Yes, you're right. But then it was a vague notion, not a concrete reality. This is different. This could be my birth family."

"Then I say it is time we go and meet them."

She flashed him a more confident smile than she felt, and he led the way to the road. Once there, he took her by the hand, his palm warm against hers. They wound their way through the streets, some of them paved, some of them cobblestone, until they came to a street and a building very much like Tessa's.

"Ready?" Giannis hovered over the row of buzzers, all the residents' names in Greek. Good thing he was with her, though she could recognize the Stavrou name.

She nodded. "It's now or never."

After a few minutes, the buzzer went off, and they entered, climbing a few flights of stairs. Manos answered the door. He towered over Giannis, not an easy feat, and surveyed them with his green eyes. For a minute or two, he spoke to Giannis in Greek.

Tessa shifted her feet. Was he turning them away?

No. A moment later, he ushered them inside. "Hello." He shook Tessa's hand. "Good to see you again."

"It's nice to see you too. Thank you for allowing me to come."

"I was not surprised to hear about a possible relative coming from America. When *Pappoús* was younger, he talked about his family so far away. I hope he can help you. Today is not his best day. His memory comes and goes."

"So did my yiayia's before she passed away. It's hard to watch."

"That it is." Manos ushered them into the apartment, this one not as updated as her rental. Gold-hued tiles covered the floor. The rooms were dark and small, but more light came into the living room from the balcony doors. A shriveled old man sat on a faded avocado-green armchair in front of a 1980s-era television.

He turned, his dark green eyes sparking. "Tell them to go away. I don't want to talk to anyone today."

CHAPTER TWENTY

Early November 1942

Thank goodness, Levi has not returned to bother me after his run-in with Petrus the other week. The threat to have the Germans called on him must be keeping him at bay. With not much reason to go out other than to shop for the few groceries my coupons and money will allow me to purchase, there is little chance of running into him on the street.

Ioanna brought a loaf of bread yesterday, wrapped in a sheet of paper. How I cherish her visits. She and Perla come often. Without them, I'm not sure I could function. Each day is more of a struggle.

—From the diary of Mathilda Nissim

Ioanna had once again come to visit Mathilda. Between her and Perla, Mathilda kept busy, and her mind stayed occupied. After she and Ioanna had enjoyed a good conversation about their coming children and Ioanna had returned home to prepare supper for Petrus, Mathilda had unwrapped another loaf of bread with the greatest of care. It was difficult to say if the food or the paper was the most important item.

She attempted to smooth the creases from the sheet, though some remained. Once she had it as flat as possible, she brushed the crumbs from it. One corner was ragged, but it was paper, a commodity she was no longer able to procure. If she wasn't going to allow Levi to intimidate her, this was what she had to do. She rubbed her belly and spoke to her child. "I hope you understand someday that everything I do, I do for you. To make this world a better place for you to live. To give you the best life I can. To keep you from all harm."

Before getting to her work, she parted the lace curtains that hung across the living room window and looked over the market. She reached for the memory of the odor of cinnamon, oregano, and chili that had once perfumed the air. Little meat was available, and even if there were an abundant supply, no one had the money to purchase it. A few women attempted to keep their husbands' shops open, but most of them sat cold and dark.

Mathilda hugged herself to ward off the chill that ran from her heart to the tips of her toes. Dull gray clouds hung in the sky and pressed on her chest. Mama would have called it a foreboding, a dark spirit. Never had Mathilda met anyone as superstitious as her mother.

Oh, Mama. To have her nearby. Instead, an ocean separated them. America now fought in the war, but from what Mathilda understood, life had changed little for those living in that country. They had rationing but not hunger. Some gave their lives, but the Jews lived without fear of being rounded up.

She and Asher should have gone. What then? Who would have helped those left behind? Someone had to stay and do what they could for those who were being persecuted here.

Then again, how much help had she really been? It was because of her, because of her actions, that the cemetery was no more. The Jews here had lost their important connection to the past. She'd deprived them of it.

A stooped woman, her hair gray, her clothes tattered, a holey shawl slipping from her shoulder, pushed a pram down the bumpy cobblestone street. The wheels squeaked and echoed off the empty storefronts. From what Mathilda could tell, there was nothing but rags and garbage in the pram. Junk to most, treasure to her.

Many were suffering now, none more than those who were poor before the invasion. The council did what they could, but with the food shortages, they had been forced to shut down the soup kitchens. *Dio, what will happen to us?*

At the speed of a train, she cut two slices of bread, soaked them in the last of her olive oil, and hurried to the street. "Avuela, wait."

The old woman turned and flashed a gap-toothed grin. "What do you want, child who is to have a child?"

Mathilda slowed to catch her breath. The baby took up more space every day. "I have some bread for you. It's nothing much, but I thought you might like it."

The woman swung the pram around and headed in Mathilda's direction. When she approached, Mathilda held out the bread, and the woman snatched it from her hand. She gobbled it, licking the oil from her fingers when the bread was gone as if loath to waste a single crumb.

She readjusted her old black shawl around her shoulders. "May Dio bless you for your gift. Because of your act of kindness, you will receive a blessing today, an unexpected surprise." She glanced at the heavens. "Enjoy this from above and savor it, much as I have savored this offering from you." She reached up and touched Mathilda's cheeks, her hands cold. She kissed each side of Mathilda's face with her chapped lips.

A moment later, she disappeared around a corner, the squeak of her pram fading away.

For a while, Mathilda stood in the near-empty street. Had what happened been a dream or a vision, or had it been real? She glanced at her hands and rubbed the sheen of oil left on her fingers. A yeasty aroma arose from them. No, it had been very real, as real as the movement of the child in her belly.

And what about this blessing the woman had pronounced? What did that mean? Her child kicked. Perhaps the blessing was that of her baby. Certainly one to be cherished and savored.

Though she often longed for time to move forward so she could hold this infant, she should enjoy each moment she had. The time would come, as it always did. When it arrived, she would impress upon her heart each minute of that as well.

At last she returned to the warm cocoon of her flat. Where she had been chilled not so long ago, she was now swaddled and protected. Already the benefit of whatever the blessing was to be washed over her.

She too ate a piece of bread, though without the oil, not that she minded the sacrifice. Hadn't her forebearers been sent into exile in part because of their lack of care for and attention to the widows and orphans? Ioanna had been generous to her. What good would it be if she were not generous with others?

Once she satisfied the edge of her hunger, she returned her attention to the lone sheet of paper occupying the table. She now had something of interest to write about, something other than the desecration of the cemetery. People didn't need to hear the incident rehashed. They knew the details already.

With the greatest of care, she rolled the paper around the barrel of her typewriter. The blanket around it softened the sound of the keys striking the paper. Her words flowed for a paragraph or two before footsteps sounded on the stairs. Was Levi returning? Her heart fluttered in her chest. No, perhaps it was Perla or Ioanna come to visit.

What if it was the Nazis? They couldn't discover the typewriter, but she had no time to hide it before they would pound on the door.

She ran to her wardrobe in the bedroom and pulled out all the clothes she could, then scurried to the dining room and threw them on top of the typewriter. It was the best she could do on short notice. The Germans would search through the pile, no doubt, and find what they wanted, but it would buy her time to think up an excuse.

Oh, the paper inside. What she'd been typing. They couldn't see that. The little letters inked onto the page combined to form words that would send her away for sure. She stood frozen on the spot, no thoughts in her head, just staring at the pile of dark blue, red, and green clothes that hid a secret that could well cost her her life.

The knob turned, but whoever was out there couldn't open the door because she had locked it. She might as well have been made of stone. She couldn't move.

A knock. What would she say? How could she convince them not to arrest her?

Another knock. She hardly dared to breathe.

Another knock.

"Mathilda? Open the door, mi corasón. It's me."

The voice held a familiar timbre, songlike, melodic, soothing. The deep rumbling of it had lulled her to sleep and calmed her when troubled.

The stone crumbled from her limbs, and she raced to the door and flung it open. "Asher? Is that you? Is that truly you?" She flung herself into his arms, almost knocking him over.

He chuckled and kissed the top of her head. "Why don't we go in and sit down?"

She rubbed his cheek, so very bony and hollow. Though she released him from the hug, she kept hold of him by his hand and led him inside, where she once again locked the door.

Once seated, she gazed at him. The eyes were Asher's brown eyes. That's about all that was Asher. In the three months or so since he'd been gone, he had wasted away until his saggy skin hung on his bones. "Oh mi alma, what have they done to you?"

He shook his head. "May you never find out. What's important is that I am home and with you once more where I belong. No matter what, I'll never allow them to separate us from each other again. That is my solemn vow."

"Let me get you some bread. Ioanna brought a fresh loaf this morning. I gave two pieces to a poor old woman and had one myself, but the rest of the loaf is for you. You'll need it to regain your strength." She stood to make her way to the kitchen.

He caught her by the hand and spun her to face him. His eyes, so deep set, widened, and his mouth with its cracked lips fell open. "Mi corasón, what is this?" He touched the place where their child grew.

A lump choked off her airway, and she could do nothing more than nod.

"When did you find out? How long until the child comes?"

She swallowed and inhaled. "I suspected before you left but wanted to wait until the perfect time to tell you, to make it special. A moment we could share with this child. Then you went away before I had the chance."

He pressed his cheek against her belly and wrapped her in an embrace. "A child. We are to have a child."

"It's not the best time."

"When Dio decrees that the time is right, that's the best time. There's a reason and a purpose for this child's coming now. We have to trust."

Tears pooled in the corners of her eyes and blurred her vision. "How can you trust in Dio who doesn't prevent the evil happening to us? This can't be His perfect plan. A child should come into a world where they know calm and peace and security."

"Just trust. What else can we do? We can't grumble about the gift given us. Better circumstances would have been nice, but we'll take each day as it comes and do the best we can for our child."

"I love our little one already. Our babe was such a comfort to me while you were gone. Here I am, prattling about my troubles when you have been through so much worse. Did they hurt you or harm you?"

He shook his head. "I can't speak of what went on in the camp. It's better that you don't know and that I don't relive the memories. I have nightmares. That will be enough for you to deal with. But what about that promised bread?"

She scurried to the kitchen and sliced off two large chunks. Though she shook the bottle as hard as possible, it yielded no more oil. She had no butter or lard. This was the best she could give him. While she brewed a weak cup of tea, she brought him his plate and sat beside him.

The Asher she had known had disappeared. His eyes no longer sparkled. Instead, they were the eyes of a man who had experienced much trouble. As he reached for the bread, his hands trembled, his fingers work roughened. One was crooked, as if it had been broken and not set properly.

What had those monsters done to him?

She leaned against his shoulder and closed her eyes. He was dirty and needed a bath, but never mind that. He was beside her. On a whim, the Nazis could take him away again. Or her. She had to cherish each moment she had with him.

CHAPTER TWENTY-ONE

Monday, February 8, 1943

Every day the Germans close the walls around us tighter. Each day, it seems, there are more restrictions. For the sake of my coming child, I have to be careful. Though it eats away at all that I have fought for to this point, I must not do anything against the German laws and put my little one in danger.

Asher supports me. He is a good man. When I manage to get a piece of paper to type on, he takes it out for me, to the streets that used to teem with women on market day, and passes it around to those who will read it. Many who used to scoff at the words I wrote now realize that I had good cause to be concerned.

If we had resisted when we had the chance, would it have made a difference?

There is no changing the past, I suppose. For now, all we can do is keep body and soul together for today. We will worry about tomorrow when tomorrow arrives.

If it arrives.

—From the diary of Mathilda Nissim

Mathilda's hands shook as she struggled to make the entry into her journal. The nib of her pencil was shrinking each day, as were the number of pages left in which to scribble her thoughts. More than once she had toyed with the idea of setting the journal aside and picking it up once all this craziness ended.

But the child who was very soon to come needed to know what life had been like, what kind of world he or she had been born into. This drove Mathilda along, an unseen wave on the ocean pushing her toward shore when her limbs shook with exhaustion.

She picked up the pencil and gazed at her belly. More than one expectant mother at synagogue had laughed about how she hadn't been able to see her feet anymore in the closing days of her pregnancy. That wasn't the case for Mathilda. This child would be small. *Dio, may that be all that is wrong with my baby.* Asher gave her much of his food, telling her she should be getting twice as much as him because she was feeding twice as many people.

How she loved him for his sacrifice, though she often feigned fullness and returned some of his offering to him. Without him, she and their child would be lost. All three of them had to survive.

She blew on her hands to warm them, then stared out the window for a moment, the sky gray with weeping clouds, as if they mourned for the condition of the world. Would they ever know sunshine again? Would blue skies smile on them once more?

What had happened to her? Not that long ago, she had been upbeat, optimistic, without a care in the world. She had allowed the presence of the occupiers to cancel her joy.

She shook her head. If she allowed them to do that, they would win. They would succeed. For as long as there had been Jews, they had been persecuted and had been driven from one place to another. Just over four hundred years ago, the king and queen of Spain had forced them from that land to this one. If Mathilda's ancestors had behaved the way she was behaving, what would have become of them?

From now on, she would do everything in her power to recapture that bright-sided outlook she had once possessed. It would be good for her and Asher and their unborn child, if nothing else.

She peered to the alley below, the space between the buildings where the scrawny feral cats roamed and where women hung their washing. A man shuffled down the broken pavement, his head bowed, his shoulders weighted. His fedora was battered. Whoever this man was, he must be very old.

This time, however, she had no bread to share with him.

Then he glanced in her direction. Asher? She sucked in her breath. When had he aged so much? He waved at her and gave her a crooked half smile.

She met him at the door a few minutes later, where he handed her his hat. He needed a new one, but there was to be none of that. He drew her close to himself, his warm breath cascading down the back of her neck. Many long moments passed as they huddled together in the front entrance, the door still opened to the hall.

He clung to her as a drowning man would cling to a piece of driftwood.

She whispered into his ear. "What is it, mi alma?"

"I can hardly bear to say the words."

"They must be said." Whatever troubled his heart, he had to share with her at some point. Better to lance the wound now than to allow it to fester.

"There's a new notice today."

That was hardly a unique occurrence.

"The Nuremberg Laws are being enacted. We have to wear yellow stars inside and outside, on all our clothing. It's a good thing I signed over the business to Petrus, or I would have lost it."

"A yellow star isn't so bad. We'll be marked, but our accents already set us apart, so that won't be anything new. And your business is safe until this craziness is over."

He stiffened in her arms.

"What? What is it? There's more, isn't there?"

"They're moving us into ghettos."

She gasped. "What does that exactly mean?"

"That within the next few weeks, we'll be herded into certain areas of the city to live. There won't be enough room for all fifty thousand of us. We need to find a place as soon as possible and decide what we want to take and what to leave behind."

"Where?"

The question wasn't clear, but Asher understood what she was asking. "There are two zones. One around the Jewish Hospital, the other in the Baron Hirsch Quarter."

"Baron Hirsch? Asher, it's so. . ." She bit back the words about it being poor and run down. The lowly couldn't help their humble estates. Mama had taught her to never look down on those who didn't have much in this life. But to think about bringing her child into the world in such a place was beyond Mathilda's capabilities.

"Yes. The other zone is larger, so we have a good chance of getting a place there if we don't waste too much time. Mi corasón, I wish I could spare you from this. And I might have. We had the chance to follow your mother and sisters to America, but I was stubborn and wanted to remain here, where my ancestors were buried, where I had made a life for myself."

She stroked his stubble-covered cheek. "You couldn't have known. None of us could have. I agreed with your decision and didn't argue with you. We did what we believed to be right at the time. We can't live in a land where we made different choices. That's a place where only crazy people live. What we have to do now is face what is to come with our heads held high. We can't allow them to rob us of our dignity."

He kissed her forehead. "That is precisely what they intend to do."

"Then we won't give them the satisfaction. You and I must show the rest how Dio's chosen people behave. This isn't our first exodus, and I doubt it will be our last."

He squeezed her tighter, until he almost pressed the air from her chest. For her part, she clung to him. Su alma. Her soul. Together they would weather this storm and tell their son or daughter how they had never given up nor given in to their captors.

She broke her hold on him, and he released her. She hung his coat on the hook by the door and led him all the way inside. "I'll make dinner. Ioanna brought some soup the other day, and we can have that before we start packing. There's so much to do in a short amount of time."

Soon she had heated the thin broth Ioanna had managed to spare and carried the two steaming bowls to the table. As was their custom, Asher ate with his left hand and Mathilda with her right. That allowed them to hold hands across the table as they dined, no matter how rich or poor the fare.

"Do you remember the first time we had a meal in this flat?" Mathilda slurped a bit of the salty broth.

Asher chuckled. "You prepared chicken, as I recall. It was, well, interesting."

"Si, it was. I had no idea how long a chicken needed to bake. All I could remember was Mama saying that you should never serve a half-baked chicken as it could make your guests sick. The last thing I wanted was to make you sick on the first day of our marriage."

"There wasn't any harm in that." Warmth now filled Asher's eyes, a warmth that had been missing from Mathilda's life for many months.

"You'll never be able to say that my cooking killed you."

"I'm happy to report that it has gotten better with time."

"We should pretend. Pretend that this is a great banquet. A feast. What would you like?"

Asher bit his lip, then spooned broth into his mouth. "Lamb. That's one thing you never got wrong. That smoked lamb you made with the gravy was the best meal I have ever had. And then you served honey cake with that, remember? I can still taste the sweetness of it. Like your lips." He leaned across the table in an attempt to steal a kiss.

"No, no, no." She waved him away with her spoon, giggling for the first time in weeks. Months. "It's my turn now. What I would like for my feast is a piece of *bakaliaros* that you catch fresh from the pier. I would fry it with plenty of lemons and olive oil and garlic."

"Then you can forget about the kiss." Asher sat back in his seat, a pretend scowl on his face.

"Good. Then I can enjoy my feast in peace."

But they chatted throughout the rest of their meager meal, the outside world forgotten for the moment, the walls of their little home protecting them from the terrors that waited just outside their door. For now, this was a place of respite, of peace, of pleasure.

Asher helped her wash their two bowls, two spoons, and one pot. Then he brought in a few crates from the alley. They packed some kitchen items in one crate. She went to the bedroom and pulled all the clothes and diapers that waited in two of the drawers and placed them into her suitcase along with a few of the dresses that Ioanna had brought her.

Dear, sweet Ioanna. Mathilda would have to get word to her when they knew where they were going. She stroked her belly. They should be sharing their pregnancies together, like they would have before the invasion. Now Mathilda may not see Ioanna for a long time. Tears gathered in the corners of her eyes. Life wasn't supposed to be like this.

And what a good friend Perla was. Maybe they'd be able to live close to each other, possibly in the same building. That would be one blessing that might come of all this. To have her friend nearby, to see the children daily, for Asher to have David to chat with, that would be good.

They put aside their packing for the night. There would be plenty of that in the coming days. First thing in the morning, Asher would strike out to locate a new flat for them. As the clouds parted and stars sprinkled the sky, Asher and Mathilda sat on the floor, her back against his chest.

She sighed. "I remember when you carried me across the threshold as we started our life together. I loved you so much that day. I thought I could never love you more, but when I woke up the next morning, I did. And I have loved you more each day since, until my heart almost bursts."

He stroked her curls. "My love will continue for you until all eternity and beyond. Never doubt that, Mathilda, no matter what happens. I will live in your heart."

"What kind of nonsense are you talking?" She turned to face him. "You're talking as if we will die tomorrow."

"We're never promised another day." He rubbed her belly, and the child responded to his father's touch.

"Then don't talk at all."

"We have to be realistic. There's a good chance that this won't end well."

"Can we not spoil our last few nights in this place, por favor? I want our all memories here to be good ones. To leave behind a pleasant aroma."

"We aren't leaving the memories behind. Forever we will carry them in our hearts. Do you remember what we pledged on our wedding day?"

"Wherever you go, I will go. Wherever you stay, I will stay. Your God will be my God, and your people my people."

"I make that pledge to you again, mi corasón, my Mathilda."

"Wherever you go, I will go, Asher. I promise."

Long into that dark night, though, as her husband slept beside her, his breaths deep and even, she couldn't keep the wonderings at bay no matter how hard she worked to be positive.

Tomorrow was so uncertain. This could be one of the last nights she would spend in Asher's arms.

CHAPTER TWENTY-TWO

The more I read about Mathilda, the more impressed I am with her. It took all the courage I had and then some to board a plane and travel to Greece. Her trip was shorter, just halfway across the city, but in many ways it was longer. I arrived to an air-conditioned apartment decorated in the latest style. She went to an ill-equipped, run-down ghetto. While she was pregnant.

She was afraid. So was everyone. What the Germans were doing to the Jews was no secret. She left almost everything behind. The clock they got for a wedding gift. The dining room table where she and Asher ate their meals. Their photo album. They only managed to bring with them a few of the pictures they took out. I can almost see the black-and-white photographs on the paper pages with those little corners. An album much like Yiayia had.

What did my great-grandparents feel about all of this? I hope they were able to go to the bigger ghetto, not Baron Hirsch. Not that it mattered. A ghetto is a ghetto. I hope they were able to be with friends, like Asher and Mathilda were with David and Perla and their kids. They must have been so scared. Terrified, really. I can't imagine, yet it isn't that far removed.

Were they even in the ghetto? Maybe they were partisans living in the mountains. Maybe they'd gone into hiding. Come to think of it, I think Yiayia was born during the war, so they must not have been here.

All I want to know is the sort of people I come from.

—From the diary of Tessa Payton

Giannis scraped back the chair across the table from Tessa when he returned from the restroom. "I see you are reading Mathilda's journal instead of the menu." Dimples appeared in both cheeks as he grinned.

"I decided a while ago that I'm going to have the fried zucchini." She lifted her face to the sea breeze that blew in from the harbor, cooling her warm skin. Even though their sidewalk table was under an umbrella, a small trickle of sweat dripped from her temple.

"You and your fried zucchini. I never have met someone who likes it so much."

"And I don't usually like zucchini. At least I feel somewhat healthy when I eat it." Mom always pestered her about how she was eating at school and how she never ate enough. Mom's prying eyes didn't quite reach across the Atlantic, thank goodness.

"So what part are you reading now?" Giannis sat back and sipped his water.

"They had to leave for the ghetto."

"I can take you there, if you want."

"Since it doesn't look like we're going to get answers from Mr. Stavrou, I guess that would be something to do. All along the way, it's felt like I've run into nothing but blockades and barriers. No one wants to tell me anything. Why is that?"

"What is the saying in English? You have to cut Mr. Stavrou some. . ."

"Slack. Cut him some slack."

"Yes, that is it. He is an old man. You must remember that the war here was difficult on everyone. Not only were the Jews mistreated, but so were the Greeks. Many went hungry during those first cold winters. They lived with the fear that if they did something wrong, the Germans would take them away just like the Jews. Those memories are hard to bear and even harder to speak about. Mr. Stavrou may not remember much. It's even possible that his parents may never have told him about it."

"I understand that. I do. But I've come all this way for answers, answers that he has. Manos told us that sometimes he gets confused, so maybe there will be a better day we can go, one when he is more lucid and more likely to be able to talk to us."

"Maybe. You can ask Manos. What will it hurt?"

So while they waited for their orders, Tessa texted him and asked if he would keep in touch and let her know if there was a better day that she might come and speak to his grandfather.

In the meantime, her phone dinged with a text from Mom: WHEN ARE YOU COMING HOME? I THINK YOU'VE SPENT ENOUGH TIME CHASING AFTER THE WIND THERE. WE MISS YOU, AND WE NEED YOU HERE.

Sure they missed her. Missed her like the time they missed her piano recital, all because they supposedly lost track of time while at Lily's soccer game. She could see Jay not paying attention to the time. What hurt the most was that Mom did too.

She forced herself to breathe in and out and to keep the panic attack at bay.

"Are you okay?" Giannis touched her hand.

She nodded, still focused on her breathing. She'd only been ten when that had happened, just two years after Dad's death. Mom had moved on—moved on enough that she could leave Tessa by the wayside along with Daddy's memories. To Jay, Tessa was disposable. His own daughter was much better and more important to him.

"Tessa?" Giannis' voice was soft. He rubbed her fingers.

She drew in several more breaths, and the vice around her chest loosened. The buzzing in her head eased, and her vision cleared enough to chase away those awful memories. "I'm fine now, thank you."

"Was it bad news?"

"No. Sometimes I get panic attacks. Something Mom said almost triggered one, but I'm learning how to deal with them. Thank you for your concern."

"Do you want to tell me?" His eyes were as soft as his words and his touch.

This man cared. He saw her for who she was and was concerned for her well-being. That hadn't happened in a very long time, and it warmed a long-chilled spot in her heart. "No." She forced a chuckle. "I guess I understand now why Mr. Stavrou didn't want to talk to me. Some memories are very painful and very real, even many years later."

"Tell me why you study psychology."

"Because I like to know how and why people think and behave the way they do. The human mind is interesting to me. I hope to help people who have lived through trauma to be able to heal. The brain is amazing in its ability to overcome so much."

"It has helped you with your panic attacks?"

"Yes." Time for a change in subject before she poured her heart out to Giannis. Again. "Do you think you'll work at the museum forever?"

He tipped his head. "That is a very good question. Maybe I will. They are building a bigger museum, and it will be exciting to be part of that." He waved the waiter over to their table and, she presumed, asked for the check. Once they had paid, he held out his hand to her. "Come with me. I will show you why I keep working to help the world understand about the Jews."

They strolled along the waterfront, but not in the direction Tessa usually went, the area where the restaurants and shops were, especially the place that sold roasted nuts and popcorn. Giannis took them away from the busy tourist area, past the ferry station that transported visitors to some of the islands in the Aegean Sea.

After several blocks, the landscape changed from tightly packed older buildings to more scattered ones. The road turned into a highway lined by office buildings. They moved inland from the harbor.

Though the water she'd had at the restaurant had refreshed her, she was already very warm again. This was nothing like Pittsburgh weather, not even on the hottest of days. "How much farther?"

"Not too long now. I can start to see it up there on the left." He pointed to a wall.

Tessa squinted and made out some black-and-white figures, but her distance vision wasn't perfect, even with contacts. "What is that?"

"You will see."

They went a few blocks more, sweaty palms pressed together. And then they stood in front of it. Painted en masse on the wall were black-and-white figures, just their heads and shoulders. They all wore striped clothing and striped hats on their heads. Their eyes were big black dots, and their open mouths were downturned.

"This is graffiti about the Holocaust."

Giannis nodded. "Not too far from here is the ghetto where my great-grandfather lived with his first wife, close to the train station where they left for Auschwitz. His wife was murdered there when they arrived in the spring of 1943. He survived. One of the few."

She gazed at him and squeezed his hand. "I'm so sorry."

"No. If not for that, I would not be here."

"That's true." She returned her attention to the art in front of them. In several places, blue swastikas had been painted over the horrified faces. "Look at what someone did." How could they defile such a powerful picture of persecution?

"Some wish that none of the Jews had ever returned to Thessaloniki. Anti-Semitism is still very real here. The problem didn't start with the Nazis, and it didn't leave with them. I want to teach the next generation that we are not to be hated or feared, but that we are people, much the same way they are. That we love, we laugh, we hurt."

"Do you think it's possible that our ancestors knew each other?"

"The community was quite large at that time. About fifty thousand Jews lived here, so while it is possible, it isn't very likely."

"Wouldn't that have been something though?"

"It would have been. And maybe they did."

"Maybe." She stood for several more minutes, drinking in the sight before her. The horror of it, not only in the depiction of what happened to the Jews but also in the blatant hatred scrawled across it still today. If she had flowers with her, she would have laid them at the site in memory of those fifty thousand people who lost their lives.

She hadn't reached the end of the journal to know if Mathilda was one of them.

At last she had seen enough. "You said the ghetto is nearby. Can we go visit it?"

"If you'd like. There isn't much left to it."

And he was right. There was nothing more than a few scattered, empty, decaying buildings and grass and weeds that had grown high. All that was left to testify to where Thessaloniki's Jews had spent their final days.

What must it have been like to live here? The conditions, if they were anything like the ghettos Tessa had learned about in history, were awful. Crowded. Unsanitary. Disease ridden. Starvation and fear must have been their constant companions.

"How large was the ghetto?"

"There were two here. This is actually the smaller one. The one on the east side of town was larger, though as this one emptied, others were brought here because it was closer to the train station."

"For people here today to just forget what happened in this place is terrible."

"The wall is a way to remember."

"But they have desecrated that. It makes me pause. There was a shooting at a synagogue in Pittsburgh where I live just a few months ago. Eleven people were killed. My mom was in the area, for whatever reason, and witnessed it. Thankfully, she wasn't hurt. So bad things still happen to the Jews even today."

"Wait a minute." Giannis grabbed her by the upper arm, halting her as she was about to step over a crumbled slab of concrete. "Your mother was at a synagogue? Why?"

As if she were playing freeze tag, Tessa stood rooted to the spot. "I don't know. I never really stopped to think about it. She called me to tell me but didn't share many details. Just said she'd been in the area when it happened. But that wasn't near our house or anything we usually went to." Could it be?

"I think—"

"I think Mom knows. Our being Jewish wasn't a surprise to her. Somehow or other, she knew. Perhaps her mother or grandmother told her at some point." How could she lie to Tessa like this? She hadn't wanted her to come here. Was that because she knew what the big secret was and didn't want Tessa to discover it?

All along, she'd suspected that Mom wasn't letting on about everything she knew. That she was holding back.

This information only drove Tessa forward. She would discover whatever it was that her family didn't want her to know.

And why they didn't want her to know it.

CHAPTER TWENTY-THREE

We are here. Though Asher tried as much as he could, he wasn't able to secure us a spot in the bigger ghetto. He apologizes to me every day. He was heartbroken that our child would be born in Baron Hirsch. Though I tried to console him, it was in vain.

—From the diary of Mathilda Nissim

The shabby walls with their peeling paper barely kept out the cold wind that howled outside the tiny flat. Mathilda drew her thick black sweater closer around her, though the bulge of her belly didn't allow it to close all the way. She wore three pairs of socks, yet the chill seeped through the knitted material and froze her toes.

To keep warm, she strode around the perimeter of the small area they shared with Perla and her family. The two bedrooms weren't nearly enough space, so some of the children slept in the living room.

Perla stopped chopping the onion Ioanna had brought and gave Mathilda a hard glare. "Something is troubling you. What is it?"

"I don't know. I just can't sit still, although this baby is getting heavier and I'm so tired. I've tried to keep busy by making a little bed for the baby, and I've folded and refolded the clothes and diapers about ten times."

Ioanna, who had taken a great chance by coming here, nodded. "That means you'll have the baby soon. When you do, you'll long for a chance to sit and do nothing." She rocked her own daughter, only a few weeks old.

Mathilda went to her and stroked the child's light, downy hair. How unfair that this child, because of the blood that flowed in her veins, had a safe, sunny home. While none of them had much to eat, even in the few weeks since Katina's birth, she had filled out, her cheeks round and her hands dimpled.

Not that she wished Katina had to endure the same conditions they did. But it wasn't right that just because her child was born of two Jewish parents, he or she was condemned to this.

Perla's two youngest picked that time to race from the bedroom, through the cramped living space, and back into the bedroom, shrieking in delight the entire time. "See, Ioanna is right about wanting time alone."

"I understand."

Ioanna held her infant to her shoulder and patted her back. "I felt the same way the day Katina was born. How have you been feeling?"

"Some back pain and false labor. That's what Perla said."

"I had it with all of mine. You'll know when the real time comes."

A scratching sounded from behind the stove. Mathilda shuddered. Mice. They and the rats were everywhere. Perla had thought to bring a trap, but it wasn't enough. Their droppings were all over the place. The two friends cleaned up the best they could, but it was difficult. Sanitation here was poor at best.

"I only wish I could have given birth to this child in my own bed in my own home where I was comfortable and it was clean. That the baby could have a crib and a safe place to lay his or her head. A chance to grow and thrive."

Ioanna placed Katina on the floor in the pile of blankets she had brought, some of which would be staying, and pulled Mathilda into an embrace. "I promise you, my dear friend, I will do all in my power to make sure that your child is as strong and healthy as mine. Whatever you need, let me know. I'll do all I can to help you."

Mathilda squeezed her hard. "Thank you."

"You're a fighter. Keep it up and don't allow the Germans to break your spirit. That's what they want. When they accomplish that, they'll have victory. Don't give them the upper hand."

Mathilda gritted her teeth. Ioanna was right, after all. "Where is the paper the bread was wrapped in?"

Perla handed it to her. "There's the Mathilda I know and love. I'm excited that it's time for another paper. What you write is always inspiring."

"Gracyas, mi amiga." She glanced at both of her friends. "You give me the courage to keep doing what I've been doing."

The typewriter and her diary were the two items Mathilda had insisted they bring with them. She was going without so much, but not this. Ioanna assisted her in pulling it out of the false back of the armoire and setting it up.

Ioanna wiped her hands on her skirt. "Before you start, may I pray with you?"

Mathilda quirked an eyebrow. Throughout their friendship, she had known Ioanna was a Christian, and though she talked about Jesus, she had never asked to pray with Mathilda. At this point, what could it hurt? She nodded. Perla ceased her chopping, and even the children in the bedroom fell quiet.

"Dear Lord, be with Mathilda and grant her the words that will inspire her people to persevere to the end. You are mighty and powerful. You have saved Your people from their sins and have promised them eternal life with You. I pray that You will shine Your light on them and make Your presence known to them. Give them the peace that passes all understanding. I ask this in Jesus' name. Amen."

Mathilda opened her eyes and stared at the ceiling. A peace that passes all understanding. Oh, what joy it would be to possess such a thing. Certainly not something that could be attained here. Not in the middle of a war where her people were being persecuted and many, many of them were dying.

Where she herself might die.

She sighed and shook away the thought. She sat at the typewriter and allowed the words to flow from her fingers to the page.

To the Jews now confined to the ghettos of Salonika, do not lose heart. We have been forced into these deplorable conditions, crammed together like cattle in a barn. If we allow ourselves to feel such a way, we give the Germans the upper hand and allow them to control us. Maintain your dignity. Hold your heads high when you walk the streets, and do not shuffle your feet.

We are a people with a proud heritage and a long history of surviving much persecution. We will survive this also and come out stronger and better for it. The Nazis believe they can break us like a trainer breaks an untamed horse. Do not give them that satisfaction. Be brave. Be strong. Be courageous.

There was so much more she longed to say, but the size of the paper constrained her. She couldn't fit anymore. It would have to be enough.

When she reached to pull the paper from the barrel, a sharp pain ripped through her midsection. She gasped, and the paper floated to the floor.

Ioanna and Perla were by her side in an instant. "What is it?" Ioanna's voice was soft and calm.

She gripped Perla's hand. "Such a pain." She drew in a deep breath and closed her eyes until the aching subsided. "This false labor is getting worse."

A look passed between the two mothers that Mathilda couldn't decipher. "What?"

"This may not be false labor."

"Oh." Wait. Her baby might be born today? She would get to meet her little one, kiss his face, hold him close. She smiled until another pain gripped her. She turned to Ioanna. "Asher. Get Asher. He went out to find food."

Ioanna touched her shoulder. "You have plenty of time until you need him. A man has no place at a birth. Petrus didn't even want to be in the flat."

"I want Asher near me. He deserves to be here when his child enters the world."

"I understand. When I get back, you'll almost be a mother. Just think about that. Keep that in your mind when this gets hard." Ioanna dashed off.

When the next contraction hit, a small moan escaped Mathilda's lips. Bechar came into the room and pulled on her apron. "Mama, what's wrong with tia?"

"Go downstairs by Señora Pinto. Take your brother and sister and stay there until Papa or I come to get you. Do you hear me?"

The little one, eyes wide, nodded. "Tia is having her baby. You made that sound lots right before Abram was born. I remember."

Perla patted the child's head. "Scoot. Now."

A troop of tiny soldiers marched through the room and out the door, slamming it behind them.

"Keep it quiet up there." Señora Pinto hollered from below them for the fifteenth time that day. Wouldn't she be surprised when all of Perla's children showed up at her door in a minute.

Perla helped Mathilda to her feet. "It would do you good to walk a little bit to help things move along. Your waters haven't broken yet, have they?"

"No. I just hope that Asher makes it here on time."

"Don't worry. First babies take a long time to come. He'll be here with time to spare. He will be bored before the child is born."

The hours ticked by, waves of pain marking the time. At some point, her waters broke, and Perla tucked her into bed. The door opened and closed a few times. Ioanna entered the room. Asher must be home.

"Tell him to come here." Mathilda smoothed her hair. "I want to talk to him."

Ioanna shook her head. "You can talk to him later. Right now, you need to focus on giving birth to a healthy baby."

More pain came. She thrashed to try to escape it and tangled herself in the sheets. Heat radiated from her. Ioanna remained on one side while Perla acted as midwife. She'd given birth enough to know what to do.

Mathilda turned to Ioanna. "How much longer? When will I see my baby?"

"You're doing so well. Keep it up. It only seems like a long time. Once you have your child in your arms, this will be a distant memory."

"But I'm so tired."

"I know, I know." Ioanna wiped the sweat from Mathilda's brow. "There's no stopping now though. Not when you're so close. Keep taking deep breaths." She glanced in Perla's direction.

The time, however, stretched out forever, as if the hands of the clock had gotten stuck. The contractions didn't end. Mathilda's strength waned. She wouldn't be able to go on much longer. "Asher. Asher."

Ioanna leaned over her. "Hush now, hush. You will see him very soon. And your child. Just hang on. Just hang on."

More time. More pain. Ioanna disappeared for a while.

Perla continued to encourage her.

"Where did Ioanna go?"

"Keep up your good work. You're doing a wonderful job."

What other choice did Mathilda have? There was no stopping what was happening with her body. All she could do was to work with it and bring this baby into the world. The sooner, the better.

A man entered the room, but it wasn't Asher. He was familiar.

Si, he was the doctor. "What's wrong with me?"

He took over from Perla and examined Mathilda. Then he, Perla, and Ioanna huddled in the corner and whispered. Mathilda clutched the bedsheets and bit back a cry. Why wouldn't anyone say anything to her? Why wouldn't they allow her to see Asher?

"Please, somebody, talk to me." She screamed, or at least she tried to scream, but none of them paid any attention to her. Instead, when they returned to her bedside, the doctor took charge.

"Push, now, Señora Nissim. Push with all your might."

"I don't have the energy."

"Do you want to see your child? Do you want to live? If so, then you must do what I say."

She would do anything for her child, anything at all. Though it came at a time she and Asher hadn't planned, this little one was a blessing from Dio. She gritted her teeth, bore down, and pushed as hard as she could, over and over, while Perla pressed on her abdomen.

With one final bout of agony, one last push, the pain was over.

CHAPTER TWENTY-FOUR

How could a bond between mother and daughter, forged through nine months of pregnancy and many hours of labor, through nursing and sleepless nights, ever be broken? Yet that connection is all too often shattered. Once it's lost, can it ever be repaired?

—From the diary of Tessa Payton

Tessa gazed up from her journal and clutched her chest as she sat on a bench near the Stavrou's juice bar. Last night she'd read about poor, poor Mathilda. In a building in the area that Giannis showed her the other day, near where the trains left for Auschwitz, she gave birth to a little girl. How awful for her.

She couldn't imagine what it must have been like for Mathilda and how scared she must have been. At least the child, Achima, had lived. Or had survived her first night, anyway.

Cars, almost all of them smaller than American SUVs and trucks, zipped down the street in front of her. People passed in front of her, off to the store or to school or to a job. Here, where so much horror had happened only eighty years ago, life was normal. How could such things have happened in such an idyllic place?

How could it still be happening?

She had picked up her pen to continue writing, when her phone rang. Great. Mom. Tessa hadn't quite decided what to say to her about, well, everything. They needed to talk, but maybe now wasn't the best time. Giannis was going to pick her up soon to have dinner. He was supposed to have contacted the Stavrou family again today, and she itched to find out if he'd been able to arrange another meeting.

After a minute, the ringing stopped, only to start once again. Tessa sighed and answered the phone. "Mom? What is it?"

"I was just calling to find out how you were. Where are you?"

"Still in Thessaloniki, sitting in the shade."

Tessa had to plug one ear to hear Mom over the noise. "When are you coming home? Isn't it time to give up this ridiculousness and get back to school? Forget about all of this and get back to your life."

"It's hard for me to talk right now because I'm not home. But I do want to talk to you."

"We can do that when you come back to Pittsburgh. I can book your ticket right now, and you can be here by the end of the week."

"You knew all along, didn't you, Mom?" Tessa held her breath. Several cars moved in front of her and stopped to allow pedestrians to cross the street. "Please, don't lie to me. Why wouldn't you tell me?"

"You're young."

"I'm not as young as you like to make me out to be and not as naive either. If I can come all the way here on my own, then I think I can handle whatever it is you have to say. And I know the truth already."

"You what?"

"You kept it a secret from me that we're Jewish. Did everyone know except for me?" Several people on the walk turned to stare at her. They probably spoke enough English to know what she was saying, but who cared?

"I—I—I can't talk about this right now. Jay is going to be home soon."

"And he and Lily have always been more important than me, for whatever reason."

"That's not true. You're my daughter, my flesh and blood. I

love you very much and have always tried to do the best I could for you." Mom's voice was shaky.

"Then why would you lie to me? Why keep this information from me? Do you know our Jewish last name? And why would you bring a man like Jay into our lives after Dad died?"

The pause on the other end of the line was so long that Tessa checked her connection.

"Tessa, you just have to trust me enough to stop asking questions that don't have answers. Enough to come home and end this quest of yours. Enough to believe that everything I have done in my life has been for you. I would do anything for you. Absolutely anything. You won't understand that until you're a mother yourself."

I would do anything for you. Words so similar to what Mathilda wrote in her journal when Achima was born. It was true that she wasn't a mother and probably didn't fully understand that kind of love. Mathilda's journal gave her a little bit of insight into it, but she truly didn't know.

But was lying to your child what was right for them? What was best for them? "All this time, Mom, I could have been discovering who I was, and you kept my heritage from me."

"You don't know what you're talking about. I'll let you know when I have your ticket booked. I think it's easiest for you to go through Athens, but I'll see what's available."

"Haven't you been listening to a single thing I've been saying? I'm an adult, and I'm not coming home. If you buy that ticket for me, you're only going to be wasting your money."

"I'm begging you, Tessa."

"And I'm begging you. I don't mean to be disrespectful, but unless you can give me a good reason to stop my search, I'm not going to."

"You will only. . ." Static filled the line, then silence.

"Mom? Mom, are you there? Hello?"

Nothing.

Beep, beep. The honk of a scooter drew Tessa's attention. Giannis had made it to pick her up. Because he was sitting in traffic, she had no choice but to take the helmet he presented to her, put it on, and go with him to an early dinner. She might be a crazy college student who ordered pizza at 2:00 a.m., but she was also an American who liked her meals on a regular schedule. He thought she was insane for wanting to eat at six, but he was the loony one for not having dinner until eight or nine.

They drove up the hill that Thessaloniki was built on, a hill that curved away from the harbor and gave a spectacular view of the city and water below. Across the street from the old city wall was a taverna, where Giannis parked.

She handed him her helmet and shook her hair free. Matted hair just wasn't her look.

"This isn't the fanciest place in the city, but it has very good food and very good music. You will like it, I am sure."

The evening was beautiful, and up a little higher in elevation, it was cooler, so they sat outside.

She half-heartedly ordered something, then stared over the light beige buildings crowded together that made up the city, the sky above them still a brilliant blue.

"Something is the matter." Giannis passed her the bread the waiter had brought, but she waved it away.

"I read some more of Mathilda's journal. She had a daughter."

"I know."

"I keep forgetting that you know how this story ends but you won't tell me anything."

"If you want to know, you must read faster." There went those dimples in his cheeks.

"I just feel bad for her, having to give birth to such a little baby in conditions like she did." She pulled out the diary from the bag she carried almost everywhere she went. "Listen to this:

"What a twenty-four hours it has been. How my life has been changed by two events that happened almost simultaneously. The first was that my daughter was born last night. I am a mother and have never been happier to take on any title. Achima is her name. It means God will judge. Si, He will judge what the Nazis have done to us.

"The birth was long and difficult. For a time, the doctor and Ioanna and Perla didn't think I would live. Achima wasn't coming. There was no option of taking me to the hospital for a Cesarean, so there was nothing they could do. Instead, they continued to encourage me.

"Even before she was born, I was willing to do anything for Achima, including giving my life. I cared nothing for myself, only that she would be born strong and healthy.

"Her first cries were so weak and pitiful, and I cried along with her. She is tiny and frail, my sweet Achima. I wasn't able to do enough for her while I carried her. She hasn't had the easiest start to her life. As I held her the first time, though, I whispered a promise to her. I promised to do everything I could for her, to give her all I could of life, as little as that may be.

"I can almost picture Mathilda in that area and see what she saw. Almost. I really can't wrap my mind around what it must have been like to live there."

"It was pretty terrible."

"She said two things changed for her that day, one of them being Achima's birth. Am I saying her name right?"

He corrected her pronunciation, or at least tried to.

"I didn't get to the rest of it before Mom called."

"Oh." He raised one eyebrow.

"I know. I almost didn't answer, and now I wish I hadn't."

"I take it the call didn't go well."

"No. She's insisting that I come home, going so far as threatening to buy a ticket for me for the end of the week. But I'm not going anywhere until I have the answers I need."

"Will she tell you why she wants you home?"

"All she says is that I'm young and I don't really understand. I wish she'd just tell me and get it over with."

"So she does know something."

"She does. And I suspect she has for a while, which makes this all the worse. I only want her to trust me, but that seems impossible. Somewhere along the way, I did something to lose her favor, but I have no idea what it was."

"Are you sure? A mother's love is very powerful. I have seen it in my own mother and now in some of my friends and their children."

Tessa nodded and sipped her water. "She did say one very strange thing. It was something along the lines that everything she did, she did for me. Those are almost the exact words Mathilda wrote about Achima shortly after her birth. She said she would do anything for her child."

"You know what? You need to take a break from all of this. This weekend my parents and my sister and I are going to our vacation place in Nea Kallikratia. It's not far from here, maybe thirty minutes, and it's on the gulf. The weather is cooler, and there is a beach. Why don't you come with me?"

"Oh, I hate to impose." Though a beach and water and sun would be glorious.

"Trust me, they are excited to meet you. It will do you some good to get away. Many from Thessaloniki go to Halkadiki for the weekend. It's a peninsula. The beaches get better farther down, but Nea Kallikratia is a very nice little town."

"If you're sure your family won't mind."

"Not at all. That's a plan, then."

"Oh, I almost forgot. Did you hear anything from the Stavrou family?"

The waiter brought their food, and Giannis dropped a french fry in his mouth. "I did. The grandfather hasn't been well, so Manos asked us to wait. When the grandfather has a good day and is up to seeing people, Manos will give us a call. He has tried to talk to him a little bit, but so far he hasn't told him anything much. Just that he had a family member that went to America a long time ago."

Tessa sighed. "Maybe there's another way we could investigate it."

"Maybe. I can try to look up some of the records from that time and see if we come up with anything."

"Thank you. That would be great. So much of this is hard because it's all Greek to me." She chuckled, though Giannis didn't so much as crack a smile.

"What is so funny?"

"Oh yeah, I guess that wouldn't translate. In English, when we don't understand something, if it's really confusing, we say it's all Greek to us. Because Greek is. . . Never mind. I guess you have to be an American to get that joke."

Her phone picked that moment to ping with a message. Before she even picked it up, her stomach sank.

Sure enough. A text from Mom: You're booked on American Airlines returning from Athens to JFK on Saturday morning leaving at 11 a.m. I'll have your flights to Athens and to Pittsburgh booked soon.

CHAPTER TWENTY-FIVE

How can it be the best day of your life and the worst day of your life all in one?

—From the diary of Mathilda Nissim

Rain dripped through the roof and into the tin cans Mathilda and Perla had set up around the flat. The steady *plink, plink, plink* almost drove Mathilda crazy. Perla and Ioanna had helped her sit up and get Achima to nurse. She was struggling a little, but the baby was getting a bit of nutrition.

She needed it. Mathilda stroked her little hand, her fingernails so tiny. How could a living human be so small? Every part of Achima was miniature, from her soft little lips to her tiny toes. Mathilda kissed the top of her downy head. "I love you, Achima. You are my heart. Just grow and be strong. That's all I ask of you. Live."

If anything happened to her daughter, Mathilda would be broken, unable to be fixed. Irreparably damaged. Nothing Perla or Ioanna had said had prepared her for the intense, almost overwhelming love she had for this child. All she wanted for Achima was the best, happiest, safest life.

Ping, ping, ping. The rain continued unabated. A gust blew through the cracked window, and with shaking hands, Mathilda pulled the blanket tighter around her daughter. If only she could cocoon her and always keep her close to her heart.

Achima's eyes fluttered shut, and she stopped nursing. Ioanna, who had been nursing her own daughter, put Katina in a basket she had brought from home and took Achima from Mathilda and placed her in the little bed Mathilda had fixed for her. She ached when the weight of her daughter was lifted from her.

Asher still hadn't returned. He had missed the birth of his daughter, her first bath, the first hint of a smile that had flitted across her face.

Ioanna sat on the bed beside Mathilda and took her by the hand. "I know you're worried about your husband."

"Wouldn't you be? Baron Hirsch isn't all that large. He couldn't have disappeared into thin. . ." Oh, but he could. So many disappeared these days, leaving behind no trace, like they never existed. What if he was one of them?

Dio, may it not be so.

Yet the depth of her soul, the piece of her heart reserved only for Asher, was cold.

That premonition of evil Mama always talked about washed over her.

"When I went searching for Asher and couldn't locate him, I was frantic to get back to you, so I stopped at home and asked Petrus to go out and look for him."

"Since he has yet to arrive, I'm assuming that means Petrus was not able to find him."

"Please, don't worry. Achima will pick up on your concern, and it will make her fussy. You have to stay calm for her sake."

The cold in the pit of her heart spread throughout the rest of Mathilda's body. "So you also believe that he might be—"

"Rushing to judgment will only cause you more worry. None of us knows what happened. He might be outside the ghetto working somewhere."

Mathilda pointed to the dark sky outside the dingy window. "It's evening. He should be back here because we are forbidden to be outside of the ghetto walls after sunset."

"Right now, focus on Achima. That's all you can do. She needs you. And she needs you to get some rest. You've had a difficult delivery, and you need to heal."

Si, Mathilda was beyond exhausted. Never in her life had her eyes been so gritty, her arms so difficult to raise, her head so filled with buzzing. "Sleep does sound good. If I can manage it."

"Your body will demand it and take over. That's its way of helping you to heal."

Mathilda rested against the pillows and allowed the dreams to overtake her.

She and Asher were in the mountains outside the city. They hiked hand in hand, talking about little things.

Asher helped her climb over a large rock. "Do you remember the day we met?"

"How can I ever forget? I was at the university studying writing and journalism. On my way home, I stopped at your pharmacy to pick up something for Mama. I couldn't tell you what it was, but I do recall it was for Mama. And there you were, behind the counter in your white coat, the most handsome man I had ever met, your eyes the kindest I had ever seen."

"I noticed you right away as well. How could it be that on my first day on the job, the prettiest girl in all of Salonika walked into my pharmacy?"

"You gave me whatever it was I needed for Mama. I just wanted to keep you talking because you had the most wonderful deep voice I had ever heard."

"Ah." Asher chuckled as he steadied Mathilda on the uneven trail. "So you kept me talking so I would ask you if you wanted to have a soda with me when I finished?"

"No, I loved the sound of you speaking. But when you asked me for a date, I was the happiest woman in the world. You didn't notice my scars. Or if you did, they didn't bother you."

They reached a level spot on the path, and Asher drew her close to himself. She fit perfectly in his arms. She was never happier than when she was close to him like this. "What have I done to deserve a man like you?"

He kissed her, hard, passionately, until they were both breathless. "Mathilda, I love you more than I love my own life. Gracyas, gracyas for being the best wife a man could ever ask for. I am unworthy of you. Every day I only want to prove that I deserve you."

She kissed him again, their bodies, united in marriage, pressed against each other. "Mi alma, I am the one who is undeserving. You are so good to me, so kind and gentle. You have a soft heart, so willing to help others. That is one of the things I love the most about you."

They hiked for a while more until they came to the top of the mountain. Greece was spread out before them. Mountains, ancient cities, the bluest of blue seas. The place she loved with the man she loved.

She reached for his hand, to be near him while they surveyed this wondrous sight. All she managed to grasp was air. Where was he? Where had he gone?

Crying. Crying. Somewhere in the distance, someone wept. Was it her?

She bolted upright in bed. The crying came from her infant daughter, her thin arms and legs waving in the air as she wailed, her face reddening.

Mathilda sat on the edge of the bed and picked up Achima. "Hush now, little one. Mama is here, and Papa will be home soon."

Achima's crying trailed off, and her fingers tangled in a strand of Mathilda's hair, and she hung on.

"What a good little girl. You're strong and determined. That will help you in this life." She rocked her daughter and sang a little tune to her, one that she made up, one that had no words other than the words of her heart.

At the front door, a knock came. Perhaps that was Asher. He must have forgotten his key. Not that the lock on the door here worked, but it was the rational explanation that popped into Mathilda's head.

Holding Achima close, she hurried from the bedroom, her legs as flimsy as that of a newborn foal, only to find Petrus standing in the front hall, water dripping from the brim of his fedora. He took off his hat and his coat and shook the water from them.

"Where is Asher? Did you find him?"

"Can we have a seat? Ioanna, bring Mathilda a blanket."

Goodness, she had run from the bedroom in her nightclothes, forgetting about Ioanna being here, not giving it a second thought. Only now did a chill shake her entire body. She took the blanket and wrapped it around herself and Achima. "What is it?"

"I searched everywhere I could think to look and asked everyone about Asher." He cleared his throat.

Mathilda sat as stiff as a board. She didn't move when Ioanna came and took Achima.

"Finally, I heard from a few people that he had been moving around, circulating one of your papers."

She nodded. "He was good to me that way, especially the past few weeks when he didn't have much to do and it was difficult for me to get out."

"While he was handing it to an older man, the Gestapo rounded the corner and grabbed the paper. They proceeded to beat the old man, and Asher intervened."

How like her beloved to step in to defend the helpless.

"Mathilda, do you understand what I'm saying?"

She bit her lower lip. Her stomach knew, the way it twisted into knots, but her head refused to bring the thought to mind. "I'm not sure."

Except that she was.

"The blows the Germans delivered to Asher were severe. They beat him with the butts of their rifles. I'm sorry, Mathilda. I'm so sorry, but your husband is dead."

Dead.

Dead.

The word repeated itself over and over in her head, but it held little meaning. Because Asher being dead was incomprehensible. He had just become a father. He had so been looking forward to meeting his baby and watching his child grow up. To being more than just a couple. To being a family.

Like a punch in the stomach, it hit her. "He's dead?" She whispered the question.

Ioanna was by her side, pulling her into a hug, though she could barely sit up. "I am sorry beyond words, my dear friend."

"No!" Mathilda's wail was loud enough to wake Achima and Katina and send them both into their own fits of crying. "No! Not Asher. Not mi alma."

Ioanna held her and allowed her to weep and mourn.

How could it be? Surely this was a mistake. Surely he would walk through the door any minute now, ready to hold his newborn daughter, ready to love her. They would be the family they had always dreamed of being.

This was all her fault. He had asked her not to produce the paper once the Germans invaded, but she had insisted. Had wanted her own way. So she went ahead and did whatever it was that she thought best without listening to him.

If only she had listened to him, he would be here right now, not dead somewhere.

"Where is his body?" She turned her teary gaze on Petrus.

"They've taken him away."

"He must have a proper burial." Though it was also her fault that they had no cemetery in which to bury him.

"He will, don't worry. You aren't strong enough to go anywhere right now. In fact, let me and Ioanna help you back to bed."

The stares of Perla's children fell on her as she shuffled her way to the room she and Asher had shared. Forever, his side of the bed would remain empty. Cold. How was she supposed to go on?

She was broken.

Perla brought Achima to her. "I think she wants to eat."

Mathilda stared into Achima's face. In it, there was a likeness to Asher, especially around Achima's mouth and in her eyes. She was the continuation of Asher. His daughter, the one to carry on in his absence.

She brought her infant to her breast and allowed her tears to splash on her daughter's cheek as she fed. "It's all up to me now, isn't it? Up to me to take care of you and keep you safe and give you the best life possible. I will do whatever I can to make that a reality for you. Whatever it takes."

CHAPTER TWENTY-SIX

The days passed in a blur for Mathilda. With Perla and her family sharing the same cramped living quarters and with Achima demanding much of her time, she didn't have a chance to grieve. Only when she lay in her bed at night, Achima slumbering in her little drawer bed on the floor beside her, did Mathilda allow the tears to flow.

She clutched her pillow to drown out the sounds of her mourning so she didn't disturb Perla and David and the children. She was as empty as the streets during a rainstorm. Hollow, never to be filled again. If not for Achima, she would care nothing for living.

Asher had been her life, her only love. They had known each other for a long time, from synagogue and living in the same neighborhood, though they didn't speak to each other until that day in the pharmacy. Despite her scars, he was kind to her, never noticed them, never brought them up. He loved her with his whole heart anyway, even though she came to him broken.

They spent as much time together as they could. And though they were husband and wife, one flesh bound together by Dio, Asher gave her a measure of independence and encouraged her in all her endeavors.

A part of her had been cut off, cut away, and the pain was as sharp and as real as if she'd had an arm or leg amputated. There were times throughout the day that she had a difficult time catching her breath because the impact of the loss hit her so hard.

The nights were the worst, by far. Just when she dozed, Achima cried to be fed. Poor thing. Mathilda's milk had come in, but it wasn't as rich as it should be to give her daughter all she needed, so she cried often in hunger. Nursing did little to satisfy her.

The children were going crazy, forced to be cooped up in a tiny flat with each other, no space to run, few toys to play with. One day when the weather was fine, Perla took the children outside to explore the ghetto. Not that there was much to see or do, but it got them out of the flat and gave them some fresh air. If nothing else, they could chase each other up and down the streets.

Ioanna came soon after they left. She pulled off her sweater and set it on a chair before coming to sit beside Mathilda. She smoothed back Mathilda's tangled hair. "Let me brush it for you. It soothes me when I need comforting."

"Where is Katina?"

"Petrus has the day off. I fed Katina before I came and put her down for a nap, so I have a few hours before I need to be home. It's a good thing Petrus likes to care for his daughter and spend time with her."

"How did you get in here?"

"Cigarettes. The guards like them, and Petrus is giving them up."

The all-too-familiar tears pooled in the corner of Mathilda's eyes, and she swiped them away. "Thank him for me."

Ioanna got Mathilda's brush and ran it through her curls, the bristles massaging her scalp. Some of the tension in her shoulders relaxed. "What am I supposed to do without him?"

"What would he want you to do?" Ioanna worked on untangling a stubborn knot. "What would he tell you?"

Oh, her heart knew the answer. But for her mind to fully absorb it was too much at this point. "He would tell me to keep living and keep doing what I was doing. But what I was doing cost him his life." She choked on a sob.

Ioanna kept brushing while Mathilda wiped away yet another round of tears. "He knew the risks and still he took them. Why do you think that was?"

Mathilda shrugged and tucked her handkerchief in the sleeve of her sweater. "Maybe because he didn't want me to take the chance."

"That was part of it for sure. He also did it because he loved you and believed in you and your work. Though Asher was a man of few words and often left his thoughts unspoken, his actions showed how much he believed in the cause you trumpeted."

"He asked me not to continue writing the paper, but I did it anyway. He told me he would support me, but I should have listened to him. I should have done as he asked. If I had been an obedient wife, Asher would be beside me. He would have gotten to hold his daughter and watch her grow into a fine young woman. I stole that from him."

Ioanna stopped brushing and wrapped Mathilda in a hug from behind. "He willingly gave that. You can't live your life with regrets. You touched people and made them think. A few resisted."

"Just a few, and they ended up losing their lives as well. Resistance was not the way to go. I should have preached compliance."

"Do you think that would have saved lives?"

"Maybe. I don't know."

They sat together on the couch for a while, Ioanna's hug warm and comforting. Thoughts swirled through Mathilda's head like leaves in a whirlwind. "What happens to us when we die?"

"Do you want me to tell you what I believe or what you want to hear?"

"What I need is the truth. At any time, any one of us could be taken, beaten, and shot for little reason or no reason at all. So I don't need a false hope. I. . ." She rubbed her aching temples. "I need surety and certainty in an unsure and uncertain world."

"Your Messiah has already come." Ioanna went to her pocketbook and pulled out a little Bible. "The prophet Micah said he would be born in Jerusalem, and he was. The prophet Isaiah said he would die a painful death for our sins, and he did." She went on to show Mathilda passages from what she called the Old Testament that were fulfilled by Jesus in the New Testament.

"But I am a good person. I used to go to the synagogue every Sabbath when I could, and I kept a kosher home."

"That's not good enough. You can't do enough good deeds to wipe away all your sin. For a human, that's impossible. There needs to be a blood sacrifice for atonement."

"The temple is gone, though. It has been for almost nineteen hundred years. We still celebrate Yom Kippur, but we can't sacrifice as we once did. Perhaps someday we'll be able to return to the Holy Land and rebuild our temple."

"There is no need of that when Jesus has already paid for your sins. He died on the cross so that we might be washed clean. He was the perfect Lamb that only had to be sacrificed once to wipe out all of our wrongdoings. All that is left is for you to believe, and you will be guaranteed eternal life with him." Ioanna shared with Mathilda some more passages that showed how Jesus fulfilled all the laws' requirements.

"It can't be that easy. There must be something I have to do."

"Faith. And that comes from the Holy Spirit. You need nothing more."

"But what about what the rabbis say, that Jesus was just a man, that his body was stolen from the tomb by his followers, that we are still awaiting our Messiah? How can you answer that?"

"The people and the Pharisees and teachers were waiting for a political savior, someone to free them from Rome's tyranny."

"Or from Germany's tyranny."

Ioanna shrugged her eyebrows. "He has already come though. The Father didn't send him to overthrow governments but to save people from their sins and grant them eternal life. Oh, how much better it is to have freedom in Christ and suffering on earth than to have freedom in this world and suffering for eternity."

Achima picked that moment to whimper, then whine, then wail. Mathilda held her daughter close and walked the room with her, jiggling her as she went along. When she wouldn't settle down, she tried nursing, though it hadn't been that long since she'd eaten, and Mathilda didn't know how much she could give her child.

When Achima still cried even after nursing, Mathilda's own tears fell. "I can't even provide for my daughter. What am I going to do? How can I keep her safe?" She nuzzled Achima's neck, wetting it as she wept. They wept together for all they no longer had.

Ioanna took Achima. "Do you mind if I try to get her to nurse? Maybe it will satisfy her for a while. I only wish I could do more."

Everything in Mathilda screamed that she should be the one to give her daughter the sustenance she needed. That she should be the one to take care of her. This wasn't right. This wasn't how life was meant to be.

But Achima's cries tore through her, and at last she nodded. Ioanna got Achima settled, and she quieted as she ate, the soft sounds of her sucking still grating at Mathilda. Why couldn't she be the one to do this for her child? The Germans had taken her home, her husband, and now her ability to feed her baby. None of it was right. None.

When Achima was satisfied, Ioanna handed her back to Mathilda to burp. At least she could do that.

Ioanna leaned forward, her lips pursed, her eyes without their usual glimmer. "I'd like to talk to you about something, and I hope I don't offend you in the process. Life is dangerous for Achima and for you. I fear for both of you. I've heard of Christians taking in Jewish children and passing them off as their own, and I would be willing to do that for Achima."

"How would you get her out? We're not allowed to leave the ghetto at all."

"If I put her in a basket, the guards might search it and find her.

But she's so tiny, I can put her under my coat. They'll either believe me to be overweight or pregnant. You see that I have enough milk for both Achima and Katina."

Ioanna twisted her hands in her lap. "I would treat them just the same and do everything in my power to keep her alive. More than that, to help her thrive. When this madness comes to an end, I'll hand her back to you. I'll tell her about you and how much you love her so that she'll already know you in her heart."

"And what about me? What am I supposed to do? Is there a way for both of us to go into hiding?"

"Maybe. I would have to be very careful and speak to some people I know, but there might be a way to hide you in the mountains."

Mathilda bit her lip to keep from crying yet again. She shook her head. "If you would ask and try to find a way for both of us to go into hiding, then I would consider it, but I can't let Achima go. Not now. I need her more than anything. I have just lost my husband. If I lost Achima too, I would shatter like a mirror, a thousand shards of glass on the floor."

"For Achima's sake, won't you reconsider?"

"No." A wave of heat shot through Mathilda, and she came to her feet. "No! No! You're asking the impossible, to give up my daughter, the last piece of my soul that remains, the only good in my life. I could never do it. She's an extension of me and part of Asher. No matter what, she'll stay with me."

Ioanna held her hand and caressed her cheek. "Getting angry will only upset Achima. It was a thought I had in my head, nothing more. I understand that I've offered you an impossible choice. I know that. But the Germans may not allow me to come inside much longer. Each time, they question me more, and I'm forced to make up more excuses. Think on it. In the meantime, I will search for a spot for both of you."

Ioanna left then, a soft click of the door filling the empty flat.

Still holding Achima, Mathilda went to her bedroom and slammed the door behind her.

She would never give up her daughter, no matter what.

Never.

Never.

CHAPTER TWENTY-SEVEN

Sometimes it feels like I'm chasing my tail, running in an endless circle, never reaching my goal. I have this desperate need to discover where I belong, who I am. There's also this wall that various people have constructed to keep me from making that discovery.

—From the diary of Tessa Payton

"Hi, Mom. I just wanted to let you know that I canceled the ticket for Saturday and put the refund money into my account. I'll pay you back. Please don't worry about me. I will come home, I promise. This trip was never meant to be a permanent move, only a fact-finding mission. I love you very much, and we'll talk soon. I have to go."

Tessa pressed the END button on the voice mail message and gazed at the building rising four or five stories above her. The same one she and Giannis had visited just a few days before. Here they were again. This time Manos assured them that his grandfather would speak to them. He had been confused, Manos had said, but today was a good day.

Giannis rounded the corner, and a smile broke out on his face, his dimples deepening. If Riley were here, she would tease Tessa endlessly about how she had a thing for guys with dimples.

The idea brought her up short. Did she have a thing for Giannis? She didn't have time for analysis as he approached her and kissed her on the cheek. Then again, with the way he sent the pulse in her wrist throbbing. . .

"Are you ready to talk to him?"

The silky smoothness of his voice calmed her. "Yes. I've been praying that he remains lucid enough for us to get some information from him."

"Yes, I pray for that same result." He pressed the button for the Stavrou's apartment, and just like the other day, they made their way upstairs where Manos greeted them.

"Pappoús is very happy that you are here."

"Really? He didn't want to have anything to do with me the other day."

"That was my fault. I should have phoned and told you it wasn't the best time, but I was hoping once we got him talking, he would be better. Sometimes he is. When you were here beforc, that wasn't the case."

"I'm glad he's agreed to talk to me now. I really want to understand more about my family, if you're even my family at all."

"Come inside. My mother has baked a loaf of chocolate bread for you."

Tessa turned to Giannis and shrugged. This was much more promising than earlier in the week.

The old man occupied the same chair as he had before, the same program running on the TV. Sunlight streamed through the balcony door, whitening his hair more than it already was.

"Come in, come in." He waved at Giannis and Tessa, his hand gnarled but his English quite good.

"Thank you so much for agreeing to speak to me."

"I love to talk about my family. That is what my grandson says you want to hear."

"Yes, very much so."

"Sit over there." Mr. Stavrou pointed to a green sofa opposite him, one that had likely been in that same location for many years, judging by how sun-faded it was.

Giannis and Tessa settled on the rather comfortable couch

while Manos offered them each a slice of moist, chocolaty bread.

Mr. Stavrou sat back in his chair and closed his eyes. "Ah, my family. I grew up in Thessaloniki and have no desire to live anywhere else. My father worked at an accounting office, and my mother stayed home with her four children. We rode our bicycles in the street and swam in the water and helped Mama in the kitchen."

He sighed at the happy memories. "It was a good childhood. All through my life, there has been political instability in the country, but Mama and Papa kept us from that nasty business. They made life as happy for us as they could."

"Do you know anything about any relatives that went to America soon after the war?"

Mr. Stavrou's eyes flapped open, and he stared hard at Tessa. "I wasn't born until after the war."

"Yes, I know that."

"How old do you think I am?"

"I didn't mean any insult. I'm sorry if it sounded that way. I just wondered if your mother talked about a relative that went to America."

"I'll have you know that I am still a young man. I can do almost everything you can. You come here and think you can call me old."

Tessa gripped the couch cushion and stared at Giannis for help. What had she said or done to upset Mr. Stavrou?

For a few moments, both Giannis and Manos spoke to Mr. Stavrou in Greek. The words flew back and forth, and so did the glares that the older man shot Tessa. Her throat burned. She could never forgive herself if she had blown this chance at discovering more about her family.

A good five minutes passed before Mr. Stavrou was calm once more. Giannis leaned over to whisper in Tessa's ear. "Let me do the talking from now on."

"What did I do?"

"Later. Tell me what you want to know."

"Just what I asked him."

He nodded and redirected his attention to Mr. Stavrou. At last he nodded at Tessa. "My family loves Greece. This is an ancient land, a place that has nurtured us for thousands of years. I cannot imagine living anywhere else. But many people did leave after the German occupation and more during the civil war and the junta."

Tessa elbowed Giannis, and he spoke again in Greek.

Mr. Stavrou nodded. "There was one family member. My uncle. They called him nothing but my uncle, so I don't know his name. He left and went away, and I think it was to America. Papa didn't like to talk about him. I cannot say if he was angry with him for leaving or if he missed him or why he told me nothing about him."

"Do you know if he had any children?" Tessa couldn't help the question that spilled from her lips.

This time Mr. Stavrou didn't take any offense. "That would mean I would have had cousins. Because we talked about him so little, I never thought about it. I might have cousins in America." He turned to Manos. "Can you imagine that? All this time?"

Mr. Stavrou cackled. Then all of a sudden he sobered and leaned forward. "I have a secret to tell you."

This was it. Tessa worked to draw even breaths, and Giannis held her rather sweaty hand. "What is it?"

"We have twins in our family."

Tessa's shoulders slumped. That was the secret? Impossible. There had to be more to it. "Twins?"

"Yes, two babies at one time. Mama always hoped, and so did I, that I would have twins. Two boys that I could play football with, two girls if I got really lucky. My wife could push them in the pram, and the entire city would coo over my sweet babies. They would all talk about what good parents we were."

Mr. Stavrou's lucidity must be waning. "I'm sure you were a very good father. Twins would be nice. Did your uncle have twins?"

"Uncle?" He furrowed his already wrinkled forehead.

"Your father's brother."

"Bah. He is dead. They all are dead. They tried to save them, but they are all dead." Then he broke down in sobs.

Manos went to comfort his grandfather while Tessa sat at the edge of the worn sofa.

"I think he might have had enough for today." Giannis, still holding her hand, brought her to her feet. He spoke in Greek to Manos for a while.

"I'm sorry if I upset your grandfather."

Manos shook his head. "He gets like this sometimes. Though he says he is not old, he is, and this happens. Please, don't think you did anything wrong. Like I said, sometimes he makes sense, sometimes he doesn't."

"What about your mother or father?"

"My father passed away a few years ago, and my mother probably wouldn't know anything about this. She was never very interested in family history. I will ask her though. I would very much like it if you were a cousin."

"I would like that too. And thank you for your time. You have my email and my other information if you find out anything else?"

"Yes. If Pappoús says something that makes sense, I will let you know."

"I appreciate it."

A few minutes later, Giannis and Tessa found themselves out on the street once more. "Thank you for your help back there."

"I only wish we could have gotten more information for you. I hope you aren't too disappointed."

"A little. Especially after I told my mom that I canceled the ticket. She isn't going to be happy with me, but I'm not ready to go home yet."

"Come with me." He led her to the end of the street where there was a café. They each got an iced coffee and settled at one of the tables lining the street, small cars of all colors whipping by.

"Why do you not want to go home? Not that I don't want you here, but I was wondering. Maybe I am too nosy."

"Not at all." She sipped the strong coffee laced with plenty of cream and relaxed against the back of the wrought-iron chair. "My dad died, and my stepfather has always been rather cold toward me. He definitely favored his biological daughter. Sure, he said he loved me, but he didn't show it very much."

"So things are not good at home?"

"My mom is overbearing." There she went again, blurting out words before giving them any thought. What was wrong with her today?

"What do you mean by *overbearing*? I don't know that word."

"She. . ." How could she phrase this so Giannis would understand but that she wouldn't throw Mom under the bus entirely? "She likes to know every detail of my life, and she wants to plan out every detail of my life. What I'm going to study in school. Where I'm going to school. How often I come home. What job I'm going to get."

"Then it was a big deal when you suddenly left to come here."

"It's the first time I did anything really big in my life without her permission. Like I can breathe a little here. If I go home, I'm afraid I'll suffocate."

"Tell me about your dad."

"He worked a great deal, so he wasn't home too much. When he was, he was a great father. He played dolls with me, though sometimes he just stared out the window, and he watched movies with me. While I would get pop, he drank his beer. He had lots of business trips, and I missed him when he was gone.

"Then one day, Mom sat me down and told me he was dead. She moved on so fast. Packed up his stuff and got rid of it. Got remarried. And now I find out that she knew we're Jewish but for some reason refused to tell me, and now she won't tell me more. I don't recognize the woman I knew when I was a little girl."

"We all change over our lives. My father used to be a very quiet person. When he got a job as a salesman, he changed. He knows how to talk to people now, and that includes me. I didn't know him very well when I was growing up, but I know him better now. Like we are friends."

"That's an understandable change. I just don't understand Mom, and I guess I never will." She stared across the street to where a group of old men sat under an umbrella, a checkerboard in front of them, smoke billowing from their cigarettes. "Are there other families named Stavrou we could try to find?"

"I can look for you. But, Tessa?"

She dragged her attention to him.

"I thought I would never have a good relationship with my father, but God can do great things. Don't give up on your mother."

That was hard when Tessa didn't even know where to start.

CHAPTER TWENTY-EIGHT

I love my sweet, beautiful daughter more than I ever thought I could. At first when I learned I was to become a mother, I was reluctant to bring a child into such a crazy, mixed-up world. How could Dio present me with such a gift at such a time?

And then my child grew and moved within my womb. What a feeling that day when the first flutters tickled me, unlike anything I had ever experienced. In that moment, I knew I loved this child more than my own life. And that this child, whenever it entered the world, was the greatest blessing from on high.

From that point on, I cherished each moment I had with this little one safe inside of me, in a place where I could protect her and keep her from all harm. Every day, I sang to my child. Asher talked to my belly, telling his child of all the things they would do together. He would teach the little one the ways of Dio, would bring home plenty of sweets from the pharmacy, and would sit and gaze at the night sky, pointing out the constellations and why they are named the way they are.

Around me, the world continued to deteriorate. New laws, new restrictions, new homes. We did the best we could to keep the flat clean and sanitary, but with seven people crowded into two rooms, a building that was dilapidated before we arrived, and horrendously small pipes, it was almost impossible. My fear of bringing a child into such a world returned with a vengeance.

This time the feeling was different. It wasn't one of questioning the pregnancy itself. Instead, it was one of how I would protect my child once she entered the world. How was I to keep her strong and healthy? How was I to ensure the Germans wouldn't harm her? How was I to help her grow into a loving and compassionate person in a world where such qualities are in shorter supply than bread?

Those first pains came upon me, and I was terrified and excited. Both emotions roiled inside me and fought for control. I pushed both of them aside and concentrated on birthing my baby. How I wished Mama could have been here. She would have kept me calm and focused. She always had that way about her.

More than Mama, though, I wished for Asher to be by my side. The time for him to arrive at home had long since passed. Worry crept in, but Ioanna and Perla told me not to concern myself with Asher.

He should have been there. He should have witnessed his daughter entering the world. He should have held her, kissed her, bathed her. But he never heard her cries or her coos or her laughter.

Because he is gone. Mi alma. My beloved, the one my heart calls my own, is gone, nevermore to return.

He will miss Achima's first steps. He will miss teaching her about the stars. He will miss her getting married, setting up a home, having children of her own.

How can I bear this heartache? What hope is there left? We should have fought back harder against the Germans. Then again, there might have been many more deaths. Hunger, cold, illness, dying. They hem me in. They are my constant companions.

For Achima, only for Achima, I have to go on. She needs me more than ever. I now must be both mother and father to her. She is so very, very tiny, and my milk isn't enough to sustain her. Instead of growing round and plump, dimples in her hands, chunks in her cheeks, she grows thinner by the day. Her arms and legs are like little twigs that might snap off at any moment.

She cries so much because she is as hungry as the rest of us. Though I have no appetite, I eat what I can find and what I can choke down. Perla and David share a little with me, but they have three mouths beside their own to feed. Everyone has empty bellies. What we do eat goes right through us because of lack of sanitation.

My daughter's cries are pitiful, like the mewling of a kitten. And I am helpless. To whom do I cry out anymore? Dio ignores my pleas, my begging for His mercy. He has turned a deaf ear to me and to our people.

Where is His love? Where is His goodness? I cannot see it anymore. No one here can. There is nothing but desolation and despair. Emptiness and loneliness. Heartache and misery.

Hear me, Dio, hear me.
I cry to You, though You remain silent.
In Your heavens, You sit and turn Your face away.
You withhold your mercy to Your people.

How long will you be deaf to Your people's wailing?
How long will You close Your eyes to their suffering?
You have promised good to us, but we see none of it.
You have snatched it from our hands.

Where can we go? Who will listen to us?
When our forefathers forsook You,
You sent them into exile.
We, however, have not forsaken You.

We have walked in Your commands and kept your
decrees.
We observe Your Sabbaths.
We care for the poor, the widows, and the orphans.
We are careful to do all You require of us.

Lift this heavy burden from our shoulders.
Look kindly on Your people once more.
Make Your face to shine upon us and be gracious to us.

Before we are wiped from the face of the earth and the
land remembers us no more, show us your goodness.

Then the nations will know that You are Dio alone and
there is none besides You.
They will see Your goodness and compassion toward Your
people.
All the people will come to You,
and You will receive the praise You are due forevermore.

And now, Dio, what am I to do about this request from Ioanna? Would it be better for me to allow her to find a place for Achima to live, to hide from these evil men? Every fiber of my being screams at me, but I am torn in half. Part of me says si, to allow my daughter to be from underneath the watchful eye of those who seek her life. The other part of me cannot bear the thought.

How could I give up my very own flesh and blood, heart of my heart? That is inconceivable. She is mine. My child. I carried her. I birthed her. I gave her life. We are connected in a way that a woman who doesn't have a child would never understand. It is a cord that cannot be broken.

But Ioanna has a child. Surely she must recognize how impossible her request is, what she is asking of me. I am grateful for her friendship and companionship, how she has stood by me these dark days. She would know how it would rip my heart from my very body to have to give Achima to a different mother, no matter how temporary it would be.

It would be temporary, wouldn't it? I can't believe it would be anything other than that. One day very soon, this war will come to an end, and if I did send my child to safety, I would get her back. Wouldn't I?

No, no, no. I cannot risk never seeing my Achima again. Looking in her deep, dark eyes with their long, feather-like lashes. Listening to her coo. Watching her swing her tiny fists and pucker her little red mouth. If I could never be with her again, I would be like a piece of pottery smashed on the ground, nothing more than dust.

My daughter needs me. In these dark times, a child needs her mother more than ever. I wish I had mine. I will not deprive Achima of hers. I do not bear these scars on my body for nothing. They remind me of my strength and of Papa's great sacrifice for me. The ultimate act of love Papa showed. He thought more of me than he did of himself. He did whatever it took to protect me.

Now I have been staring out the window into the darkness for a full thirty minutes, pondering what I have written. He thought more of me than he did of himself. He did whatever it took to protect me.

Papa wasn't selfish. He ran into those flames and grabbed me from them without a second thought for his own safety. He did not go home and think long and hard about what his decision would be and what consequences it might have for him. He did not even take the time to stop and pray for the success of his mission.

He ran into the flames. He saved me at the cost of his own life.

Now I sit here holding Achima in my arms as I write. She isn't fussy but just awake and wanting to be with her mama, and her mama wants her to be here. This is how it should be, how it always should be. There should never have to be this wrestling with having to give your child away, even for her own safety. If only we could stay like this forever.

I peer into her eyes, and I see Asher through and through. There is no doubt that she is his child. Levi will have to eat his words. Through her, Asher lives and breathes and stays by my side. In losing her, I would lose him as well. That is unthinkable.

I will have to reiterate to Ioanna that unless Achima and I both go into hiding together, neither one of us will go. There is no way my damaged heart could continue to beat without my little Achima, my precious, precious gift from Dio. How can I give up such a gift, given at the perfect time?

No, I believe it is Dio's will that Achima should be with me to comfort me in these very dark days and very long nights when my bed is empty and my soul is cold. There is a reason He gave her to me when He did. I will not turn my back on such a gift.

Achima and I will be together, come what may. If the time comes when Ioanna finds a place for both of us, then we will go there if we can. It will be difficult to get me out of the ghetto, much more difficult than getting Achima out alone, but it can be done. There will have to be a way.

That is how I will direct my prayers, that Dio will guide Ioanna to find a place for us to hide where Achima and I can both go, and that He will make it possible for us to leave Baron Hirsch without being caught. He is great, and He is mighty, and He can do wondrous and miraculous things. If He can lead a people from Egypt, He can lead a woman and a child from a ghetto.

Achima has fallen asleep once more. Sleep well, my little one. Enjoy your happy, peaceful dreams, dreams of a world where there is no hatred and no evil. A world where people are not hunted for the blood that flows through their veins. A world where brothers love brothers and do not betray them.

May God bless you and keep you all of your days. May you grow strong and proud. May you always know happiness and love. May you be a helper and a blessing and a comfort to all those around you and all those you touch. And may Dio grant you long life, that you may live to see your children's children.

—From the diary of Mathilda Nissim

CHAPTER TWENTY-NINE

I think that Achima can sleep through anything." Perla grinned, then sipped her very weak coffee substitute, even as her children ran circles around her in the cramped kitchen.

"You may be right." Mathilda also brought the bitter brew to her lips. Ioanna had been good enough to bring the ersatz coffee, just enough for a few cups for each of them. On Passover, they ate bitter herbs to remind them of the hard times the people suffered in their captivity in Egypt. Perhaps this bitter brew that was supposed to resemble coffee would forever remind them of the oppression they suffered under the Nazis.

A knock came at the door, and both women glanced at it. Mathilda quirked an eyebrow. "Are you expecting anyone?"

Perla shook her head.

A knock at the door. A sound each Jew dreaded. A brown-shirted German could stand on the other side, and who knew what that meant for those living inside.

Another knock. Even the children quieted. Though the rule was unspoken, they weren't naive to what was happening.

Mathilda rose from her chair as slowly as possible and made her way to the door. Once she opened it, she almost sagged against the frame. "Rabbi. To what do we owe this pleasure?"

"May I come in?"

"Of course. Can I get you some coffee?"

"No, thank you." His long beard bobbed as he spoke. He settled himself on the lumpy couch and cleared his throat. "I wanted you to be among the first to know that I've been informed that deportations will begin in the next day or two."

Goosebumps broke out all over Mathilda's arms, and not from the chill that clung to the flat. This day was a day that was inevitable. Everyone talked about it ceaselessly. But now that it was here, the reality of it struck her in the gut. "Where are we going?" She asked the question even though everyone knew the answer.

"Poland. They are allowing the Jewish Council to select who will travel on which transport and have promised that we are only being relocated for our safety. They'll even exchange our money for zlotys to help us get settled."

Mathilda thumped into the seat across from the rabbi, then slid to the edge of it. "You don't believe them, do you?"

He shrugged. "I'd like to, so I guess that I do. Dr. Merten has given me his assurances."

"Bah. Their assurances have meant little to us so far. Bit by bit, day by day, they tighten the noose around our necks. At first we could come and go from this place. We only had to wear the stars when we went outside. Now we can't cross the ghetto's boundaries. Armed guards watch and keep us prisoners. We have to wear the stars at all times, even indoors.

"To this point, the Nazis have not proven to be true to their word. Why would I begin to trust them now? Don't you remember what they did to the cemetery? I don't know where they intend on taking us. Perhaps it is to Poland. But I can assure you that they don't mean to resettle us there. We've all heard the rumors."

"Exactly what they are. Nothing but rumors. Empty words on the wind."

"The only ones blowing empty words are the Germans. You are a fool if you believe them."

From the kitchen, Perla gasped. Si, it was bold to talk in such a manner to the rabbi, but he needed to wake up and see sense. All he was doing was helping the Nazis with their dirty work. The work of ridding themselves of the Jews.

It was so ironic, it was almost laughable. Almost.

"And you are a fool to think that you can do anything to change what is going to happen. Do you think when we left Spain four hundred fifty years ago that anyone fought back? No, we did as we were told and have made a good life for ourselves."

"I fear there is no life waiting for us."

The rabbi stroked his beard and cleared his throat again. "At any rate, I came to inform you of the beginning of the transports."

The beginning of the end.

Rabbi Koretz nodded in her direction. "In deference to you, to the help you have been to us, I wanted to ask you if you want to go on the first transport or wait until later."

That chill deep inside her bones intensified. She closed her eyes to picture what that might mean for her and Achima. Very possibly separation. Very likely death.

She shook her head. "I have yet to fully recover from a difficult birth, and Achima is so tiny. She needs to gain some strength. We'll wait."

Perla stepped from the kitchen. "We'll go."

Mathilda shot to her feet. "No. Por favor, wait with me. We'll go together, later."

"Those who leave first are likely to get better housing and jobs. By the time the later ones come, that could all be gone."

"You too believe that this will be the start to a new life?"

Perla swallowed hard, then straightened her shoulders. "I can't let myself consider any other possibility. If it's meant to be the end, then let it come quickly. Get it over with instead of waiting and worrying and suffering."

"Her words are wise." The rabbi stood. "Speak to your husband, señora. Let me know tonight, and I will add you and your family to the list." He turned to Mathilda. "You would do well to listen to your friend and go with her."

Mathilda shook her head. "No. I have vowed to Achima to do everything I can to protect her, and that's exactly what I will do."

"How? How are you going to keep from being put on one of those transports one of these days? I can't keep you off the list forever."

She wasn't about to tell him or even Perla about Ioanna's offer. She had to bide her time until Ioanna found a place where Mathilda and Achima could hide. If she waited long enough, held on for enough time, Ioanna would have a place. That is where she hung her hope these days.

The rabbi soon departed, busy with preparing for the first transport. As soon as the door clicked shut behind him, Mathilda turned to her friend, who had three small children still clinging to her. "You have to reconsider. What you're talking about is crazy."

"David and I have been discussing this. What good is staying here going to do us? If the Nazis are telling the truth, we may have better living conditions sooner rather than later."

"And you believe that?"

"In this day and age, I don't know what to believe anymore."

"And if it's not true?"

"Then we face whatever comes our way. We're prepared. We would rather take a chance and all be together than perhaps get split up if our deportation notices come separately. Though we had no idea when the trains would start leaving, we knew we wanted to go as soon as possible."

"Por favor, I beg you not to leave me. Stay with me for as long as possible. The future is so uncertain. Something, anything, could change, and we might not have to go at all." She was grasping at bubbles on the breeze, but it was all she had.

"Then we'll return." Perla drew her into an embrace. "Te amo, sister of my heart. Your soul is golden, full of love for others. We'll pray that the times will change and that we'll be reunited very soon."

Not too long afterward, David returned home, and he and Perla retired to their bedroom while Mathilda nursed Achima and kept watch over the rest of the children.

Her eyes and throat burned as they played around her feet. They were so innocent, unaware of what awaited them. Already they had seen and experienced more than children should have to. She knew too well what trauma did to young children and how the scars of the heart ran deeper and lasted longer than the scars of the body.

If Asher had been here, would he have wanted to go right away? Maybe. He always chose to look at things in a positive light and might have been tempted to believe what the Nazis were telling them. Then again, she would have stood her ground, like she always did, and would have done her best to dissuade him, just as she had tried to get Perla to change her mind.

This was the right thing to do. The very deepest part of her bones told her that. Staying, watching, praying for change, doing whatever she had to in order to keep from getting her name called—she would do it all for Achima's sake. Praying for Ioanna to be able to hide them.

She wasn't naive. With an infant, it would be difficult to find someone willing to take the chance on having a crying baby in the house. Perhaps Mathilda would get more nourishment and so would Achima. Then she would be happy and wouldn't fuss as much.

This was her constant plea. If only Dio, high on His throne in heaven, would hear her and answer her.

"Come here, children. I have a story to tell you." They all needed a distraction.

They settled on the floor around her feet. Most of the time it was difficult to corral all of them. They must sense the tense seriousness that hovered over the flat. Each of them stared at her, their brown eyes large in their thinning faces.

This is not how childhood should have to be spent.

She shook away the thoughts. "A long time ago, in this very city, a little girl lived."

"Was that little girl you?" Bechar sat forward on his haunches.

"Si, it was me. I remember this all very well. Now, no more interruptions, or bedtime will come before I finish the story."

Each of them nodded.

"Also in that city lived a big, ugly, horrible dragon. He had a long tail with a dagger at the end of it and teeth as sharp as razors. Smoke billowed from his nose, even when he was sleeping.

"All of the citizens were very careful not to wake this dragon. If they did, he would get quite angry and might breathe fire on them."

Annette squealed and covered her ears.

"Don't worry, Annette. This isn't a scary story. Just listen, and you'll find out. Now, one day, I had enough of having to be quiet around the dragon, of having to walk on my tiptoes every time I passed him. He lived by the harbor, so he was hard to stay away from.

"I was going to show him that I wasn't afraid of him. I walked right up to him and hit him on the nose."

The group gasped.

"I truly did. He opened one eye and looked at me. Then he opened the other and lifted his giant head. He roared a mighty roar, so loud that I ran and hid behind a building. But I peeked around the corner and saw him standing on all four legs.

"He breathed flames in all directions, setting the city on fire. It was horrible. I was so sorry for what I had done. All around me the flames licked the buildings. People ran away from it. Some jumped into the water.

"I stood there. I couldn't move. Just when the orange fire was about to reach me, so hot I could already feel it on my skin, strong arms picked me up and took me away."

On that terrible day when she was small, so terrified of the inferno that was consuming her city and her home, she had hidden underneath the bed. She hadn't known what else to do. Everything around her was orange and black and hot and smoky.

Just when the flames reached her and burned her tender skin,

Papa found her. He pulled her from underneath the bed and brought her to Mama and to safety.

That was the last time she had seen him. He returned to rescue others, but he perished in that effort.

Right now, her sweater covered her scars, but nothing would ever erase them or the memory of how she got them. "You know the scars I have on my arms?"

The children nodded.

"That's how I got them. They remind me to be brave and strong, like my Papa who rescued me from that fire. When you're scared, I want you to think about me and my scars and to be brave and strong as well. In the end, the terrible dragon wasn't able to hurt me."

The children kept their attention trained on her.

"Come here, everyone, and give me a kiss. Kiss baby Achima on the forehead too."

As they did so, David and Perla exited the bedroom. Her friend nodded at her.

That was it.

They were headed to Poland and a very uncertain future.

CHAPTER THIRTY

In the dark of night, Mathilda wandered the cold, empty flat. The spare bedroom was a ghost of its former self, the sheets stripped away, leaving a bare mattress. All the clothes from the wardrobe were gone. Soon spiders would take over and weave their webs inside.

The quiet tore at her soul, ripping to shreds what little was left. The heavy mantle of silence rested on her shoulders, weighing her down. Small feet should have been pounding on the flooring. High-pitched voices ringing throughout the rooms. Squeals and laughter bouncing off the walls.

Instead, there was nothing. Even though the walls were thin, no infant cries came. It was as if the entire ghetto held its breath. The first trainload had departed. When would the next one leave? When would it be her turn? In a single instant, her life would be turned upside down.

Not that it wasn't already.

"Oh, Asher." She didn't even try to stem the tears that streaked down her face. "If only you were here. I need your arms around me, for you to comfort me, to tell me everything is going to be fine, to guide me in what I should do. It's not right that you were taken from me. Do you hear me, Dio?" Her voice rose in pitch. "It's not right."

Her scream woke up Achima, who screamed along with her. Perhaps together their voices would rise as high as Dio's throne. She went to her daughter, still bedding in the mound of blankets in the drawer, and picked her up. She kissed the soft fuzz on her head and patted her bony back. "Hush, now, hush. Mama is sorry to have woken you from your sweet dreams."

After a time, Achima quieted, only hiccups remaining. Mathilda sat on the sofa, her daughter on her lap so she could stare into her big brown eyes. Eyes so much like her father's. "My sweet, sweet angel." She could say no more as a lump swelled in her throat, almost blocking off her breathing.

No one had ever told her this was what a mother's love was like. It was beyond all thought or comprehension. It filled her and overwhelmed her and brought out every nurturing and protective instinct she had.

So together they sat in the dark, Mathilda drinking in every moment of nearness with her daughter.

A pounding at the door startled both of them. Achima cried.

"Open up. Gestapo. Open the door, Frau Nissim."

Without a conscious thought, she rose from the couch and went to the door, her entire body numb. No sooner had she cracked it open than a burly man with a bald head barged through, followed by a bevy of companions, each of them carrying a weapon.

The big one barked the commands. "Spread out. Search the entire place. We're not leaving until we find it."

Mathilda blinked as their flashlights swept the room. "What is it you want?" She already knew.

The leader turned on her as his henchmen fanned across the flat. He waved a piece of paper in his hand. "You don't recognize this?"

She shrugged and returned to jiggling Achima to stop her whimpering. "To me, it looks like a piece of paper that bread would come wrapped in."

"Take a good look at it." He shined the light on the page.

She didn't need it. He held a copy of her little paper in his hand. Perhaps the same one that had cost her husband his life. She swallowed a cry and squeezed Achima a little tighter. How could she have been so foolish? She had risked all their lives.

This was her just punishment.

She was about to open her mouth and confess her sin when Achima cried louder. Achima. Her world. If something happened to Mathilda, who knew what would happen to her daughter. For her child's sake, she had to keep her mouth shut.

Her actions had cost one person his life already. She would not allow them to cost another's. "I have never seen that before."

He shoved the paper into her face, the light he cast on it almost blinding her. "Look carefully." His bark startled Achima, and she cried harder. "And shut up that brat, before I shut her up for you."

"Then you will please lower your voice and keep from frightening her." She jiggled Achima and spoke to her in Ladino. "Por favor, por favor, my child, you have to stop crying. Mama is here and will keep you safe, but you must stop crying. Later I'll sing you a song, and we'll talk about how we will take a picnic in the country and chase butterflies when you get to be a big girl."

Her daughter calmed and nestled into the crook of Mathilda's arm. "Now I'll see that paper."

The man handed it to her and shined the light on it. There was no mistaking that she had typed the words on the page with the typewriter that was hidden in the back of the wardrobe in her bedroom. And there was no doubt that this was the last one she had written, the one Asher had taken out the day of Achima's birth.

Her breath caught in her throat, and she fought to stay conscious and lucid. "I had heard of something like this being spread around, but until just now, I had never seen it. I can assure you, I had nothing to do with this."

"So you deny writing this filth and these lies?"

"Of course. I'm nothing more than a simple woman who lacks the words to say something that well. I have a newborn to care for, and she is all I think about."

"And where is your husband?"

"I believe he is dead." The quiver in her throat was real.

"How did he die?" The bear of a man leaned in closer to her, the reek of beer strong on his breath.

"I am told he met a horrible fate. My friends refuse to tell me more."

"Why?"

"At the time, I was giving birth, and it was a difficult delivery. My daughter and I almost died, and we have barely recovered. Now my friends are gone on the transport, and I may never know what happened to my husband." *Oh, Asher, mi alma.*

"I can tell you." The German spat the words in her face.

She shook her head, more out of instinct than anything else. She didn't want those details replayed for her. Hearing them once was enough. And it wasn't a lie that Petrus hadn't told her everything. It would be too much for her to bear.

The Nazi, of course, only wanted to inflict more pain on her, and he spilled out every sordid detail. How they saw him passing the paper around. How one held him while another beat him about the head and, when he fell to the ground, how they kicked him like a ball. How they. . .

She closed her mind and focused her attention on the deep timbre of Asher's voice, the warmth and security of his embrace, and the strength of his love for her. Their wedding, when she was the happiest woman in the world. She would never have imagined their love story would come to an end in such a brutal way.

Finally, the man's ceaseless flow of words halted, and she allowed herself to breathe again.

"What? You have no reaction to what I told you?"

"I–I'm fighting to keep myself from falling apart for my daughter's sake. Thank you for the information." With every fiber of her being, she would keep the tears at bay and not give him the satisfaction of seeing her break down. That was the reaction he expected his words to have. That was the last reaction he would get from her.

The other Gestapo returned from the various rooms, each of them empty-handed. At least Asher had constructed the false back in the wardrobe well enough that they were unable to find the typewriter and her diary. The bands around her chest that prevented her from drawing a deep breath loosened even more.

"Well?" The head man's question was loud enough to startle Achima again.

Mathilda quieted her as fast as possible.

"Nothing, sir. If this woman is the one who typed that paper, who wrote those words, we can't find any evidence of it."

"If? If? You are nothing but a bunch of useless louts. They should have sent you to the front lines. At least there you could have given your lives for the Fatherland and served Germany with a modicum of integrity."

"We can continue searching." This from the youngest of the bunch, a shock of almost-white hair on his head, his mustache not fully grown in.

"Never mind. Let's take her away."

"No! You can't." Huge hands pulled on Achima. "No! You won't take her from me. I beg you to allow her to come wherever you're taking me."

For a flicker of a second, a bit of compassion shone in the man's eyes. "Trust me, it would be better if you could find someone to take care of her." As fast as it came, it was gone. "Then again, it's your choice. One more or less is of no consequence to me."

He grabbed her by the elbow, so hard it almost brought her to her knees. With the greatest of efforts, she managed to remain upright and not drop Achima.

Perhaps it would be better. . .

No. Who could take care of her? Who could nurse her? There

was no way to get Achima to Ioanna. And it would be good for them to be together. Achima was part of her. It was her responsibility to take care of her daughter.

They led her down the stairs and to the street. Once they were outside, the cold hit her. "Please, I don't have a blanket for the baby and no coat for myself. Let me go back and get them."

"Absolutely not." Her captor motioned to one of his underlings, who scurried away. A few moments later he returned with the needed items.

The young man, the one with the very blond hair, assisted her into the back of the dark-colored car, earning him a scowl from his superior.

"Thank you," she whispered. She couldn't know when she might need someone on her side, so it was nice to at least have made this connection with him.

He shut the door, and a moment later the car roared to life, racing through the inky-black streets of Salonika.

Mathilda nuzzled her daughter's cheek. "I'm so glad I have you. What would I do without you? For you, I know I have to be strong and fight. For you, I won't allow them to break me."

As she sat in the back of that cold vehicle, the numbness wore off. Her heart thumped in her chest and in her neck. Her limbs were weak, and it was a good thing she wasn't standing up. Her ears buzzed.

What were they going to do to her? To Achima?

All too soon, they arrived at Gestapo headquarters, located on the edge of the larger ghetto. The kind young soldier was gone. Or his superior officer didn't allow him near her, because he was the one who led her inside, his grip surely leaving bruises on her tender upper arm.

Achima fussed, and Mathilda calmed her the best she could. She stumbled up a set of stairs to a tiny room with only two metal chairs and a single light bulb.

The eye-watering odor of urine gagged her, and she fought back nausea at the blood-stained block walls.

She should never have brought Achima with her. She might have just doomed her daughter to death.

CHAPTER THIRTY-ONE

I hate fighting with Mom. When it was just the two of us, we had the best relationship. Jay ruined that all. Now, no matter what I do, no matter how good a daughter I try to be, Mom and I end up mad at each other. I look at Riley and her mom and envy them. They talk to each other all the time, they do things together, they just get along. I wish it could be that way for Mom and me.

—From the diary of Tessa Payton

Tessa leaned forward over the small sink in the modern black-and-white bathroom and stared at her reflection. Dark bags hung under her eyes. Since she'd last spoken to Mom, she hadn't slept well.

All this fighting was eating away at her. In the two years after Dad died and before Mom married Jay, it had been just the two of them. Together they had cried over Dad's loss and healed. Times were tough, but they managed to find joy and have some fun together.

They even took a vacation to the Jersey shore. They'd lain in the sun and played in the water and wandered the boardwalk. That had been one of the best times of Tessa's life.

And then Jay had come into the picture and ruined all that. Tessa couldn't pretend anymore that maybe Dad was still alive and would come back to them by some miracle. The pain of his loss struck her fresh. She and Mom had drifted apart. Mom had moved on with her life, while Tessa stayed stuck in the past. It took her a long time to put Dad's death behind her and focus on the future.

She applied some concealer underneath her eyes to try to hide those bags. Giannis said he had a big surprise for her today, so she went the extra mile with the makeup.

Whose eyes were those that stared at her? Dad's? She could hardly remember them. Had they been brown like hers? Mom had brown eyes, so maybe that's where Tessa's dark ones came from. Or perhaps they'd been passed down by the mysterious Jewish ancestors.

She finished making herself presentable, though her appearance told the story of her lack of sleep. Would that make her unattractive to Giannis? She shouldn't even care about such things, but she did. She'd known him a short time, but in a way, it felt like forever.

The buzzer sounded, and her heart did a little flutter, like a butterfly inside her chest. She shouldn't be developing feelings for someone who lived an ocean away from her. She shouldn't.

The wise course of action would be to keep Giannis at arm's length, to not let him worm his way into her heart. That would be smart and would avoid a lot of pain when she had to return home.

But the moment she spied him on the step outside the building, her heart did the little fluttering thing again, and all thoughts of creating distance between them flew away on the salty breeze. He grinned at her, his dimples in his cheeks, and she was done for. Riley would call her a hopeless case.

"Good morning. You look beautiful."

She glanced at her long skirt and sparkly flat sandals before gazing at him. "Thank you." He wore a red polo shirt and khaki pants. He probably had to go into work later. "I can't tell you how much I appreciate all the time and attention you give me. I take it this isn't how you treat everyone who comes to the museum?"

He reddened. "Not really. But you are a special case."

She shouldn't be allowing her heart to get carried away like it was. Then again, she'd been doing a bunch of spontaneous, almost reckless, things lately. Why should this relationship—or whatever it was—with Giannis be any different?

"You told me you had a surprise for me that you've been waiting to show me for a while. So what is it?"

"We have to take a short walk first."

"That's fine. In Pittsburgh I never walked much of anywhere except on a treadmill. It's kind of nice not to have to rely on a car. How far are we going?"

"You are full of questions this morning, aren't you? You must be patient. It is a virtue."

"Not one that I practice regularly."

He chuckled, the sound as warm as the sun on her back. "As I have learned about you. It is part of what makes you so charming. You have a zest for life, and you don't back down from a challenge."

If she blushed, her face would be red right now. Good thing she didn't. They continued their walk in silence until they came to the spice stall at the old marketplace. She inhaled a whiff of oregano and chilies and roses, all combining in one heady scent. Then she turned to Giannis. "I don't understand. What does this have to do with anything?"

"I own this building."

"You do?"

"My family has owned it for many, many years. When I inherited it from my grandfather, I decided to renovate the flat upstairs. While I didn't want to lose the character of it, I did want to modernize it. That included redoing some plaster that was chipping. Come on, let's go upstairs." He grabbed her by the hand.

"I don't understand."

"You will soon." There was that grin again. So she followed him.

He opened the door to the apartment. "We are between tenants, so that is why I can take you in here."

Because it was nestled in the marketplace, it wasn't the sunniest apartment, but the white paint and light gray floors brightened it.

"It's beautiful. You did a great job."

"Okay, I will let you out of your suspense. This flat had one very special resident eighty years ago."

Eighty years. About the time of WWII. Her breath caught in her throat for a second, then streamed out. "Mathilda and Asher lived here?"

He nodded, a dark curl bouncing with the motion. "They did."

"That explains your connection to the diary."

"When we were doing renovations, we found the diary and some of the papers Mathilda had written hidden in the floorboards, just as she describes in the journal."

"But she wrote more after they were forced into the ghetto. How did the journal get back here?"

"That I don't know, but it did. I was so excited to read it and to get to know the woman who brought life to this space. I could imagine every scene she wrote here. It was amazing to make that connection. I had to preserve it and translate it so more people could read it."

"That's amazing. This is amazing. To be where she was." Tessa moved to the window in the back where Mathilda often sat and wrote. A thin stream of sunshine lit the space. No wonder she picked this spot. Tessa peered out, and the scene below hadn't changed over the decades. There was still a clothesline full of washing out back.

Giannis came behind her and touched her back. "Does this help you picture her better?"

She spun around. "A photograph. Do you have a photograph of her?"

"No, I'm sorry, but I don't. I've searched everywhere for one, but I can't find a single picture. They must have all been lost along the way. Destroyed."

Tessa's stomach burned. "It's like they wanted to wipe the Jews from the face of the earth."

"That's exactly what they wanted to do. Some managed to preserve their memory. Others have vanished into the wind."

"That's so sad." She peered over his shoulder. "Show me where they were hidden."

He led the way to the center of the room. "We took out a wall that had been here to open up the space. This used to be the dining room." He bounced on the floorboards for a while until one squeaked. Then he bent down and lifted it up. There was a space, not very large, but big enough for a few small journals.

"Amazing."

For a while, she stood in silence, drinking in the presence of the woman who had once called this place home. Mathilda and Asher had laughed and cried here. She had found out she was pregnant here. She had been forced from this home she loved so much to another, awful place.

"She didn't come back here after the war?"

He shook his head.

"Does that mean. . . ?"

"I'm not saying anything until you finish reading the journal. It will give you the answer."

"I might have to sit down tonight and read the rest of it. I told you I'm slow, but I'm also savoring it, trying to really get to know the woman who wrote those words."

He touched her cheek. "You look tired."

So her makeup job wasn't up to snuff. "The argument I had with my mother is really bothering me. I end up thinking about what Mathilda would have done. Somehow, I think she realized how precious life and family are, and she would have found a way to make it work. She wouldn't have allowed this to linger over her head."

"It's only because of my dad bothering me and talking to me and trying to get through to me that we have the relationship we do today." Giannis finger combed his hair and sighed. "I thought

I knew better than my parents. I had gone to college, after all, and they hadn't. I had traveled the world, and they hadn't. I knew everything."

Tessa chuckled. "Mom tells me all the time that I don't know everything, and if I did, it would rock my world. Those are her words, not mine." She furrowed her forehead, never having given that phrase much consideration. "It just hit me. I don't think she was telling me that I was a know-it-all but that there was something I didn't know. Something big."

Her mouth went dry. What could it be? Maybe it concerned Dad. That would make a lot of sense. Mom might be willing to discuss the accident for the first time ever. Then again, maybe Mom was talking about all this Jewish stuff. Tessa rubbed her temples.

"Are you okay?"

"I know she's keeping a secret from me. Maybe it's time I find out what that is."

Giannis nodded. "But you're scared."

"Terrified." She couldn't even draw in a deep breath. "There's a reason it's a secret. I thought the answers lay here, but maybe they don't. Maybe they do. I don't know anything anymore. I don't even know if I'm a Christian or a Jew."

Without warning, the waterworks turned on, and tears streamed down her cheeks unchecked. She sobbed, and Giannis gathered her to himself and held her there in the place where Mathilda had lived.

What could rock her world? Did she want her world rocked? To be honest, no. No one did. That would be crazy. Even crazier, though, was living in this limbo. If she had to deal with it, so be it. Perhaps an honest conversation with Mom would go a long way in healing their relationship. Once there were no secrets between them, they could get back to the way they once had been.

She may be a college student and now a world traveler, but a girl always needed her mom. That never changed. How great would it have been if Tessa could have shared this experience with Mom? If they could have discovered their heritage together?

"I need to find out where I fit in the world."

"I understand that. It took my dad telling me that he was so excited when I was born because he would have a son to spend time with and to teach things for me to understand how much he loved me. I never saw the world from his point of view, only mine."

"I never have either." Mom was lonely after Dad died. She cried almost every night, and Tessa would crawl into bed with her, and they would snuggle. They often did that before Dad died too.

When Jay came into their lives, Mom smiled again. It meant the end of the snuggling, but it also brought Mom out of her funk. "I've been selfish. I think I need to talk to my mom."

CHAPTER THIRTY-TWO

Fear is more than an emotion. It's the captivity of your soul to the unknown. Fear is staring into a dark hole and not being able to see the bottom. Right now, it's strangling me, and I can't breathe.

—From the diary of Mathilda Nissim

For the longest time, Mathilda sat on that cold metal chair in the unheated room, cuddling Achima close so she wouldn't get chilled. Her baby's nose ran, and Mathilda did the best she could to wipe it with her coat sleeve.

No one came. There were no sounds outside the door other than occasional footsteps. Perhaps she could run out the door when all was silent. Maybe no one would see her.

If it were only her, only her life at stake, she would. She would resist like she had encouraged her people to. This was her time to stand up to their captors, to perhaps win one small victory.

Then Achima stirred in her arms. No, the risk of harm to her daughter was too great. Even if the Nazis killed only Mathilda, who would be left to raise her child?

And the chances of the Germans sparing Achima were very low.

Instead, she sat in the chair and awaited her fate.

The wound in her heart left by Asher's death ached something fierce. She imagined him sitting beside her.

"What should we do, mi alma?"

"We should pray that Dio will deliver us." He brushed a curl away from his eyes in that endearing way he had, his gaze at her lacking any

sparkle. He was serious.

"Why?" What Asher said didn't make sense. "He hasn't answered our prayers yet. It's up to us to make a plan, to figure out a way to survive."

"A plan for survival is a good thing, but isn't it even better to have a plan for eternity?"

Now he really was talking nonsense. "What do I have to plan for eternity? All my life I have been a good Jew, going to the synagogue every Sabbath and every holy day, keeping a kosher home, showing kindness to the widows and orphans."

"But is it enough? There aren't any bulls or lambs to sacrifice for our sins anymore."

"You sound like Ioanna. She speaks of Jesus dying on the cross so that we can go to heaven."

"Ioanna is a wise woman. You would do well to think on her words."

With a poof, like a magic trick, Asher was gone.

He had never really been here, but just his voice in her head, the vision of his face in front of her, were enough to calm her.

What did he mean by listening to Ioanna? When he was alive, he had always spoken about what she said and how he was thinking about her beliefs. But that was crazy. He was Jewish, a descendant of Abraham, one of Dio's chosen ones.

Now she wasn't able to speak to Ioanna anymore. May never be able to speak to her again, and she had so many questions. The biggest one was how she could believe that Jesus was the Promised One.

The door opened, and hobnailed boots clomped on the floor behind her, interrupting her musings and waking Achima. A young blond man in a brown uniform swung around in front of her. "Thank you for your patience, Frau Nissim."

She didn't have any other choice.

"Do you know why you're here?"

If she answered that question, she risked incriminating herself. She kept her lips shut and clutched Achima all the tighter.

He leaned in closer, close enough she could make out the little whiskers on his clean-shaven cheek. "It will go better for you if you answer."

That was debatable.

"Let me give you a hint." He held out a sheet of paper that had once encased a loaf of bread. One on which she herself had typed inflammatory words. "Do you recognize this?"

She stared straight ahead at the many medals on the man's chest. He was good at his job. He would get the truth from her. How long would she be able to hold out?

He stroked the top of Achima's head, and Mathilda pulled her daughter closer to her chest. To keep from blurting out words that would get her killed for sure, she bit her tongue.

"Such a beautiful child. It would be a shame for her to grow up without her mother. Or worse yet, for some tragedy to befall her. If you want to protect your daughter, you will answer me."

Mathilda couldn't swallow. She wouldn't be any kind of mother if she didn't want to protect Achima. As a parent, that was her primary job.

Yet every nerve in her body screamed at her not to say a word. Defy them. Once they had what they needed from her, she would be expendable.

She would not be a good example for her daughter if she gave in to them, would not teach her to be strong, to fight. More than anything, Achima needed to learn how to fight.

So Mathilda pursed her lips to hold back the torrent of words that dammed behind them.

The Nazi's chilly breath on her cheek sent a shiver skittering down her spine. She refused to shudder.

"Come, come, Frau Nissim. We caught your husband with this paper. He refused to tell us who wrote it. That was his downfall. He should have cooperated, and he might still be alive. My condolences on your loss."

Now Mathilda had to force back a laugh. The last thing this man was sorry for was Asher's death. He had given his life for hers. What a shame that this man didn't understand that depth of love.

Is that the kind of love Ioanna was talking about when she spoke about Jesus?

"Good thing that we were able to get your friend to talk. Levi was more than willing to provide us with the information we sought, that you were the one who wrote this trash. Trust me, I didn't want to believe that a seemingly sweet woman like yourself would put herself and her family into harm's way, that you would have it in yourself to spew such garbage."

Levi. It figured he would be the one to run his mouth to the Germans. This was his revenge. And what revenge it was. One that might well cost Mathilda her life. He truly hated her.

Her chest burned, as did the back of her eyes.

How could one of her own people do this to her? The Nazis must have offered him something—money, immunity from living in the ghetto, food. That was the only reason that made sense to her, the only one that was logical.

There were some who were desperate. Levi could well be among them. He always did like the finer offerings of life.

"So you see, we already know what you've been involved in, what you've been doing. Just admit it, and things will go well for you. And for your precious daughter."

She stiffened.

"Ah, see, I hit a sensitive spot. I knew you had a heart. Now, you can admit your guilt, or I will sit here and wait with you until you confess. I'm a very patient man."

She bit the inside of her cheek and continued staring straight ahead at the dirty wall.

This had to be a nightmare. That was all. Nothing more than a very bad dream. Soon she would wake up in her flat above the spice shop, Asher in the bed beside her.

Achima stirred, and Mathilda finally broke her stare. She glanced at her daughter and caught sight of the scars on her hand.

Papa had been willing to give his life so she might live. Live. That is what he would want for her. Though her chances for that were slim, she couldn't stop trying. Until her breath left her body, she had to continue to fight. For herself and for Achima.

Under the baby's blanket, she rubbed the rough, tough skin. Whenever she was tempted to give up, those scars pushed her forward. Papa didn't turn back when the smoke got to be too much.

She would take her lead from Papa.

She pinpointed her focus on a crack in the wall opposite her, over the officer's shoulder. Inside her head, a clock ticked. Seconds to minutes to hours. Achima fussed, and Mathilda turned and nursed her. Though she couldn't have been filled, she drifted to sleep on Mathilda's shoulder.

After what must have been several hours, her captor rose and snagged another soldier who must have been passing in the hall.

"Take this woman's child."

"No!" Mathilda shot from her chair. "You can't steal my daughter from me. She'll die without me. Please, I beg you, don't separate us."

The German raised one light-colored eyebrow. "Oh, now you're begging, are you? I like this side of you much better. Carry on."

The words had slipped from her mouth without thought. She had played into his hand. Then again, if it took begging to keep Achima with her, she would do it. "A child, especially one this small, should be with her mother. In all of this, she's innocent. She has done nothing to deserve to be ripped from her mother's arms."

Her voice had been rising, so she stopped and took a deep breath, lowered it, and switched tactics. "Are you a father?"

The man's upper lip twitched.

"You are. Think about your children. They must not be very old. Are they with you here in Salonika, or are they in Germany?"

Now was his turn for silence. The other man in the room, this one with the same-colored hair and green eyes, stood in the corner.

"I will assume they're in Germany. You must miss them a great deal, and they are sure to be missing you as well. Can you imagine having an infant of yours stripped from his mother's arms? Can you imagine your wife's heartache? Would you wish that on your worst enemy?"

A muscle in his jaw jumped. Now she had touched a nerve. Good.

"Think about that." She took her seat.

The blue-eyed officer motioned the other from the room. As soon as he had left, he pulled Mathilda to her feet, again squeezing the bruise he had left earlier on her arm.

"Listen to me." His voice was a low growl. "I believe you are guilty. I believe you wrote that paper, and I am sure that it's not the first one you wrote. You're an instigator, a rabble-rouser. But you're also a mother. Your assumption was correct. I have three children. If anything ever happened to them. . ."

He cleared his throat. "Believe me when I tell you that I could hold you here, make your life more miserable than it is now, and end it at my whim. But the time is coming when you will wish that I had put you out of your misery. There is nothing you or your people can do to save yourselves."

So it was true. They weren't resettling the people of Salonika in Poland. Were Perla and David and the children even still alive?

"Go home, Frau Nissim. Return to your hovel and prepare yourself for what is approaching. When that day comes, there will be no saving yourself or your child." He strode past her and out the door.

Just like that, they were releasing her. Perhaps Dio did hear her cries.

What was she to do? Walk out of here? Surely if she tried, someone would stop her. When he didn't come back after a good amount of time, she wrapped Achima tighter in the blanket and strolled out the door, down the hall past several soldiers who only glanced at her, and then outside.

She breathed in the clean, fresh air. Air not spoiled by rotting food and rotting bodies. A soldier now took her by her elbow and escorted her into the car and back to the ghetto.

She would prepare for what lay ahead. But she would not prepare to die. There had to be a way for her and Achima to live.

CHAPTER THIRTY-THREE

I'm much too young for regrets in my life. That's why I'm here. I don't want to retreat and miss this opportunity to visit the land of my ancestors' births and to learn more about who they are. Who I am.

I'm also too old to be coddled. I need the truth. Until I have it, I can't move forward with my life.

—*From the diary of Tessa Payton*

Tessa sat on the gray couch in her Airbnb and stared at the photograph of white domed houses overlooking a sea with several shades of startling-blue water. Then she glanced at her phone in its silver and black case.

It was crazy. She was only calling home, only calling Mom. They'd had a thousand or more conversations throughout Tessa's life, though lately—since Tessa had gone away to college—not so many. Perhaps that was Tessa's fault. Perhaps it was Mom's. Most likely, a little of both.

That was no reason for her stomach to be aching the way it was. It was Saturday morning in the States, so Mom would be sitting, drinking her coffee, maybe looking at her social media. The perfect time for a chat.

She'd thought about it all night and all day today. It was time to clear the air. Tessa couldn't put this off any longer.

She took a deep breath and, with shaking hands, pressed the number to dial it. The phone didn't ring more than twice before Mom answered. "Tessa. How nice to hear from you." Her voice held a little bit of cheer but not much.

"Hi, Mom. I'm sorry I haven't called more. I really should."

"I'm sure you're busy." Now there was more strain in Mom's words.

"So Giannis is taking me, along with his family, to their vacation place in Nea Kallikratia. It's not far from here, but there's a beach, and it will be nice to see more of the city. He'll be here in about a half an hour, so I thought this would be the perfect time to chat." She wiped her damp hands on her white shorts.

"You said his family will be there?"

"Yes. His parents and his sister. I'll be sleeping with her, if you're concerned."

"Why would I be concerned?"

But she was. Better not to get irritated about it but to move on. "I also wanted to apologize for, well, being difficult after you and Jay got together. At the time, all I saw was that he was taking my mother from me. I didn't understand that you were lonely."

"Thanks, honey, but you have nothing to apologize for, though I wish you would be more cordial with Jay. He loves you and wants to be there for you. He always has."

Tessa scuffed her toe on the gray laminate floor. "I'll try. The thing is, I already had a dad. A good one. Why would I need another?"

"Every girl should have a father figure in her life to show her what a good man is like, to help her navigate the world and understand things I could never teach you."

"I just miss the close relationship we had, and I hope we can build that again."

"I'd like that." Mom sipped, probably her coffee. "There was another hate crime against Jews the other day. Someone fired shots in a Jewish deli in Florida and killed a couple of people."

"Is that why you don't want me pursuing this? Is that why we never talked about our heritage at home?"

"It's very complicated, but to boil it down, yes. It's dangerous to be Jewish."

"And it's dangerous to be a woman, and it's dangerous to be in a certain part of the city, and it's dangerous to drive a car."

"You don't know. You don't understand."

"Then help me to understand. I'm an adult, and this is part of my story, part of who I am. What I want is to figure out how this affects me and what role it should play in my life."

"You aren't going to convert to Judaism, are you?"

"I don't know. That's part of what I need to figure out."

"That DNA doesn't define you. We've always raised you to know the truth."

A subject change was sorely needed. "When did you find out?"

Mom sighed. In the background, a chair scraped across the floor, then footsteps, then the closing of a door. Tessa waited it out until the creak of mattress springs told her that Mom had sat on the bed. "I haven't even told Jay."

"He must know if I'm over here to find out about it."

"Maybe." Another sigh. "We don't talk about it though. But maybe it is time that you and I do. Is this costing you a lot of money?"

"No. This isn't the 1980s. I can call free on Wi-Fi."

"Oh, yeah, right." She was stalling. More creaking of the springs. They needed a new mattress. "When I found out we were Jewish, it was a shock. My mother told me when I was a young adult, and then not much. Like you, I wondered what difference that made in my life. I longed to find out, but I didn't run off to Greece."

Tessa winced at the jab and clutched her phone tighter, clamping her lips together.

"For years I kind of ignored it. Then last year, I got curious, so I went to a synagogue on a Saturday morning, one in the Squirrel Hill area, Tree of Life. Services were underway both upstairs and downstairs, and I was very interested in it, though I didn't understand much. There weren't too many people there, maybe a dozen. Not too long afterward, there was a noise, like a coatrack had fallen and the metal hangers were clattering." Mom sniffled.

"I remember this." Tessa could barely choke out the words. Mom was there? How had she managed to keep this bottled up all this time?

"A short time later, an armed man came from the basement where another congregation was meeting and started shooting and yelling, 'All these Jews need to die.' The rabbi managed to help me and a few others out. Everyone else who was left was shot, and seven of the eight died."

"I'm so sorry you had to live through that."

"I still have nightmares. I probably always will, but I haven't told anyone. My mother was reluctant to disclose our background, and when this happened, I understood why. Being Jewish is dangerous, not only in Greece during the Holocaust, but right here in Pittsburgh today."

"I get that, but don't you think you should allow me to decide how to live my life?"

"It's my job to protect you. That's always been my main role in your life, and it's difficult for me to give that up. You're my only child, and I couldn't bear it if anything happened to you. Honestly, I don't know how I would survive. Look at what happened to me when I was investigating out of curiosity."

Tessa's eyes filled with tears, and her airway constricted. Here she had believed Mom's restrictions and worry were possessiveness instead of love. A love she didn't quite understand. A mother's love.

"That hate is continuing. Since then there have been many more acts of anti-Semitism in our own country. You're my world, Tessa. I know you need to live your own life and figure out things by yourself, but please understand where I'm coming from. This is really hard for me."

Tessa nodded, even though Mom couldn't see. "I do understand, kind of. I know you want to keep me safe, but you can't protect me from everything. I could have stayed in our nice suburban house and died from any number of things. I could have been in an accident like Dad."

"Just be patient and try to understand. That's all I ask. And please stay safe. I just want you home where you'll at least be within arm's reach of me."

"You should come here. We can go on this journey together."

"No." Mom's denial was sharp and fast. "I'm done investigating my background. I almost died because of it."

"That was an unusual set of circumstances. You were in the wrong place at the wrong time. And God protected you and brought you out alive."

"I'll stay in my comfortable suburban home, thank you. I have enough to deal with."

"Maybe this will bring you a measure of healing."

"Please, Tessa, don't push the subject."

Mom did have this way of shutting down when things got too personal, so it would be best for Tessa to back off. "Can you answer one more question?"

"Maybe."

"Do you know what your mother's Greek name was?"

"She didn't talk much about it. In fact, I think she hated it. Let me look. I have it written down here somewhere." The mattress creaked, a drawer squeaked open, and Mom rustled through some papers. "Here. E-P-I-D-E. I even wrote down the pronunciation because it's so unusual. *Ep-i-day.* That's how you say it."

"The church I go to here is called Epide Church. Giannis told me it means *hope*. Why did they call Yiayia *hope*?"

"That's something you would have to research. I have no idea."

"You don't know what your grandmother's or grandfather's names were?"

"No. I only got grandma's Greek name right before she died. She didn't mention her mother's or father's original names."

"This is helpful. Thanks so much for taking the time."

"Hey, I'm always here for you. I hope you know that."

"I do." They hung up, but Mom's last statement floated on the air. She hadn't been there for Tessa when an old boyfriend was making life difficult for her. She hadn't been there when Jay left Tessa at that gas station when they were on vacation.

Then again, in all those years after Dad died, she had done everything she could for Tessa. Life just changed after Jay came into the picture. He had his daughter and could well do without Tessa.

But at least she had a name. Epide Stavrou. Her grandmother, the woman who came to the States as a young child. Here was the connection between America and Greece. Perhaps this was enough to give her and Giannis a clue in their search.

Giannis. Oh no. She glanced at the time on her phone. He would be here any minute, and she still had a couple of things to pack. With how crazy and narrow the streets were here, he couldn't pull to the curb and wait for her. He'd block traffic on her street until she was ready.

She threw a few more clothes into her carry-on bag, brushed her teeth and tossed in her toothbrush, and put her hair up. She had just finished when Giannis texted that he was waiting for her downstairs.

As soon as she exited the building, he kissed her cheek and took her purple bag from her, placing it in the back seat. "Are you ready for this?"

"So ready. I love the beach and have been dying to check it out since I got here."

"Nea Kallikratia isn't like Crete or Santorini or Mykonos, but it's a beach, and I think you'll love it. Mama and Papa are there already with Eleni. They're all so excited to meet you." He started the car, and they threaded their way through the city. It was amazing how much of it Tessa recognized and for how long she knew where she was going.

Once they were out of town, she leaned against the back of the seat. "Well, I talked to my mom today."

"This is good. What did she say?"

She filled him in on what happened to Mom at the synagogue. "She's so protective of me because of Dad's accident and then because of the shooting. She doesn't want anything to happen to me. So I kind of understand where she's coming from now, but I told her I have to figure out things for myself."

"Well, I am very glad for you."

"And I have a name. She knew my grandmother's Greek name. Epide Stavrou. I hope I'm saying that right."

"This is also good, because I found immigration records for people by the last name of Stavrou from the years soon after the war. It took a great deal of searching, but I did get them. Later tonight we will have a look and see if Epide is there."

They zipped along the highway and then down country roads, past vineyards, neat rows of grapevines with dark green leaves covering the dark brown earth, and past olive groves, the leaves of the stubby trees duskier.

They came to a town, not dissimilar from Thessaloniki in its architecture. There were a few shops and a crêperie but not too much going on.

Until they reached the end of the road. There the sea opened before them, blue and green and turquoise. The sight took her breath away. "I love this place already."

Giannis laughed. "I am glad you are so easy to please."

Easy to please, maybe. But she couldn't wait to be done with introductions to the family and whatever else they had planned for the evening so she and Giannis could sit down with the new information. There had to be something they could glean from those records.

CHAPTER THIRTY-FOUR

"Oh my dear, it is so very good to have you with us." Giannis' mom wrapped Tessa in the most motherly hug she'd had in a long time. She smelled of smoked meat and oregano, a combination that Tessa was coming to appreciate, surrounded by it as she always was.

"Thank you for inviting me. I can't believe the view you have here." She stepped back and peered out the window.

The apartment was more compact and more dated than her accommodations in Thessaloniki, but the living area boasted a large window that overlooked the Thermaic Gulf. In front of them was a small harbor where fishing boats and pleasure craft were moored. Beside that was the beach, bright umbrellas dotting the sand in a neat pattern.

"Yes, we like this so much. It is a good break from our work in the city."

"What can I do to help you with dinner?"

"Nothing, nothing." She waved away Tessa's question and wiped her hands on her apron covering a flowered dress. "You go put your things in your room. You will have to share with Eleni."

"I've always wanted to share a room with a sister, so this is fabulous." She and Lily had had separate rooms at home and, for the most part, lived separate lives.

Giannis showed her to the small bedroom. The terrazzo floors were cool beneath her bare feet. The yellow walls and pink curtains were bright and cheery. A lamp with a green and orange shade sat in the corner. She squeezed by a large wardrobe and to her bed at the far side of the room.

After she had dropped her backpack and used the restroom, she joined the family in the galley kitchen.

A wonderful feast with lamb, french fries, tomato salad, beans in tomato sauce, and hummus covered most of the little counter space there was in the kitchen. Mrs. Matarasso was a small woman, barely up to Tessa's chin, streaks of silver in her brown hair, green eyes as bright as the sun and as sparkly as the sea. "We have been waiting to meet you. Come with me and tell me about yourself."

They chatted together while setting the plates and silverware outside and bringing the wonderful-smelling dishes to the glass table on the balcony overlooking the water. Eleni came in from the beach just as they were about to sit down, a blue and green sarong wrapped around her waist, matching her bikini top.

Giannis' father was paunchier and all-the-way gray. He frowned at Eleni and spoke to her in Greek. Tessa leaned over to Giannis, her wicker chair squeaking. "What did he say?"

Eleni jumped in. "He wants me to wear more clothes to the table." She laughed. "He says I will make a bad impression. But American girls dress like this at the beach, no?"

"That is not a fair question for Tessa."

She blew out a breath when Giannis stood up for her. No need to get in the middle of any discussion between father and daughter.

Prayers were said, and the family dug into the meal, Eleni at the table with her swimsuit. It didn't bother Tessa. If she lived so close to the beach, she'd probably wear her swimsuit all the time too.

The conversation around the meal was lively, some of it in Greek, some of it in English, all of it leaving Tessa's head spinning, but in a good way. In her home, there had never been such camaraderie or so much laughter.

This must be what family was about. What being home and belonging felt like.

This is what her soul had been yearning for. Perhaps this is where she was meant to be. Pittsburgh faded into the background.

Eleni and Tessa helped Mrs. Matarasso clean up the dishes. Just as Tessa handed the last dry dish to Eleni, Giannis entered the small kitchen and grabbed Tessa by the shoulders. "I'm stealing you away. How does gelato sound?"

"Perfect."

"And no, little sister, you may not come with us."

Eleni sent her brother a saucy grin. "Behave yourselves."

They strolled outside to a breath of fresh, salty air and headed down the street toward the more retail district of town. The sidewalk followed the road that edged the beach and sloped toward town. At first they passed other apartment buildings like theirs. Giannis waved to those who sat outside soaking up the last of the day's sun.

That gave way to restaurants that also straddled both sides of the road, just as in Thessaloniki. You could eat indoors on one side or under umbrellas on the beach, almost in the water, on the other side.

"This town is so charming. I love it. How do you ever tear yourself away?"

"It is hard, but I have a job I love in the city, so that helps. This is a nice place to relax."

They walked on, the sound of her flip-flops striking her heel blending in with the low conversations of the diners at the tables and the clinking of china. The farther they went, the more she fell in love with the town.

Beyond the string of restaurants and a bakery was a lovely town square with green space and sidewalks. All around, children rode motorized toys rented from a local shop. Farther from the water were more restaurants and some stores hawking souvenirs. A red-and-white-striped awning hung over the sidewalk in front of the gelato place.

Soon they were seated on a park bench, Tessa with chocolate and Giannis with pistachio. The sun was lowering in front of them, setting the water awash in reddish light.

"What do you think of my crazy family?"

"They're great. My family is so straitlaced that crazy is nice. They're all sweet, especially your mother. Your sister is a hoot."

He stared at her and furrowed his brow. His English was so good, sometimes she forgot that he might not catch all the idioms she used. "She's funny."

"I don't know what an owl has to do with funny, but okay. She is funny. She and my dad do love each other."

Tessa had to choke back a little lump in her throat. How she missed her father's love. Her life would have been so different if only Dad hadn't died. But the world didn't run on *if only*s. "That's enough about that. What did you find out about the Stavrou family? You've kept me in suspense long enough."

Giannis pulled out his laptop and set up a hot spot with his phone. "Like I said, I did find some immigration records." He typed some information into a website. "Here is what I found for anyone named Stavrou coming to America between 1945 and 1947. You said right after the war, so that's what I used."

She enjoyed another spoonful of gelato, the sweet creamy coolness sliding down her throat, before she scooted closer to Giannis and peered at his computer screen.

He scrolled almost faster than she could read, but she did catch an *E*. "Wait." He went a little too far. "Go back. I think I saw it."

He moved slower this time, and there it was. "Edie Stavrou. Aged three years. They must have changed her name. But this is strange. She came with a sister, also three years old, named Katherine. I didn't know my grandmother had a twin. I knew she had another sister close in age to her, but I didn't put it together enough to think they were twins. Another thing I guess I have to ask my mom, though you think she would have mentioned it along the way somewhere."

"Maybe something happened to the child after they arrived in America."

Tessa shrugged and licked the gelato from her pink plastic spoon. "I suppose that's possible." She scanned the records. "It says her parents were Peter and Joanne. I never knew those were my great-grandparents."

"Okay, this is good. I should be able to go back, maybe to church records, and see if I can find out more. They all changed their names when they went to America, but I can look for them with their Greek names. And I know what year Edie and Katherine were born."

"This is getting exciting. I can hardly wait to find out more. Can you do that now?"

He shook his head and closed his laptop. It was like slamming a door to Tessa's heart. "I will need to go to the municipality, to the archives in Thessaloniki. That is where all the records are kept. Like I said, I may also need to try some church records."

"I can go to the church, if you think that would help."

"That might be a good idea. The priest should speak good enough English and be able to translate for you. If I can find out where they were living, I can take a guess what church they went to."

She sat back on the bench. A young girl on a pink bicycle came whipping by, holding nothing back despite the crowds of people enjoying the summer evening. She wove among young children and strolling couples with ease.

Tessa would never have been confident enough to do that. Yet look at where she was. And who she was with. She studied Giannis' profile, almost like a Greek statue, in the dying light.

As if he read her mind, he turned to her, smiled, and pulled her close. "You have chocolate on your chin." He wiped it away with his finger, his touch creating fire on her skin.

Then he leaned over and placed a light kiss on her lips, as soft as the pale light. They sat for a moment, forehead to forehead, Tessa relishing their togetherness. This space in time could last forever, as far as she was concerned.

Of course, it had to come to an end, and Giannis pulled back. "I hope that was okay."

"More than okay." It was fabulous. Better than any kiss she'd ever had. And in this magical place, no less.

"We should head back. Eleni will want to get an early start on the beach tomorrow morning."

"I do need to work on my tan."

Giannis helped her to her feet and took her by the hand as they retraced their steps toward the apartment. "Do you think that a person can be both Jewish and Christian?"

"Of course. Just look in the Bible. Paul was both. So were the rest of the apostles. Many converts, some in Thessaloniki itself, were. Look at me."

"I forget sometimes that you come from a Jewish background. How do you meld the two, put them together?"

"It's not so much about putting them together. Christianity is an extension of Judaism. Jesus was the Messiah promised throughout the Old Testament, and He came to keep the Old Testament laws that we couldn't and fulfill the prophecies."

"I never thought about it like that, but you're right."

"We don't find our identity in the blood that flows through our veins but in Christ. That is a Bible verse, but I can't remember the reference now."

"I'll look it up tonight."

After a couple of card games with his parents and some of the best baklava Tessa had eaten while in Greece, she and Giannis parted with another gentle kiss. She almost floated to the dark room. Eleni had gone out with some friends, so Tessa had a bit of privacy.

Wow, what a day. Giannis kissed me, and I wished it would never have ended. There is magic in the air here, I'm sure of it. And I learned what family can and should be like, though I know they haven't always had it easy. But it's what I want my family to be like when I have one of my own. Maybe even with the one I have now.

Giannis told me that we find our identity not in the blood that flows through our veins but in Christ. You know, I heard that in church growing up, but it didn't make sense until now. I may be Jewish in my ethnicity, but I'm Christian in my soul.

I am who Christ has made me to be, and that's a new creature when I received His salvation. I think I found the verses Giannis was talking about. "For in Christ Jesus you are all sons of God, through faith. For as many of you as were baptized into Christ have put on Christ. There is neither Jew nor Greek, there is neither slave nor free, there is no male and female, for you are all one in Christ Jesus. And if you are Christ's, then you are Abraham's offspring, heirs according to promise."

That's from Galatians 3. God sees neither Jew nor Greek. He sees the person inside, who you are in His Son. I have to sit and let that sink in.

CHAPTER THIRTY-FIVE

This may well be the last entry I write in this diary. I will not take it with me. Yes, my name, mine and Achima's, are on the list for transport tomorrow. "It is not so bad," they say. "How can it be worse than here?"

All of me wants to believe what they say. Surely it can't be worse. The wind blows through the cracks in the windows and the flimsy walls. When it rains, which it has been doing quite a bit, the ceiling leaks endlessly. All around the flat, we have tin cans. Ping, ping, ping. The dripping doesn't stop.

Sleeping is impossible because of the cold and the noise. Just when I manage to close my eyes, Achima gives her pitiful wail. She wants to eat, and I want to feed her, but what I give her isn't enough. The two older couples who moved in after Perla and her family left aren't happy about all the crying, but what can I do?

And now my name is on the list for tomorrow. This will be my last night here, for better or worse.

Perhaps I will be reunited with Perla and David and the children. That would be nice. We might be able to share living quarters again, or perhaps I will have my own this time. We are promised zloty so that we don't go to Poland empty-handed. I will have a little money to get settled there and start a new life with my daughter.

I refuse to think about other possibilities, though I know what they are. I am not deaf, but I am choosing to be blind. It goes against everything I have written in my paper for the past years, but for the sake of my sanity, I have to think this way. If I don't, I will go crazy.

All I can do is hope that the Germans are telling us the truth, that this time their mouths are not filled with lies.

No matter what happens to me, I want to keep Achima safe and well. Wherever we go, whatever happens, that is my priority. Achima. Life has become my daughter, mine inextricably intertwined with hers.

So I will leave this diary here, and someday, when the Germans have been defeated, I will come back for it. I will write in it my joy at the downfall of our enemies. I will write in it all of Achima's milestones. I will write in it my heart.

For I leave my heart in this place, where my Asher is.

Until I return.

—From the diary of Mathilda Nissim

Mathilda had just put down her nubby pencil when a knock came at the flat's door. The old people were sleeping, as they often did in the afternoons. The transition to Poland would be very difficult for them. Thankfully, Achima also slept. Mathilda didn't have the heart to wake her. Perhaps that's why she only snoozed throughout the night.

She went to the door and opened it. There stood her friend, a scarf over her head. "Ioanna. What are you doing here? How did you get in here?"

She slipped inside and bolted the door. "I had a wagon with some bread in it. Underneath that was bricks to make the wagon look full. I told them I had come to deliver the bread to the Jews here. They let me pass without searching. When they let me go, all the air left my body."

Mathilda wrapped her in a tight hug, tears streaming down her face. "Oh, my friend, my sweet, sweet friend. It's so good to see someone I know and love, who knows and loves me. I have been so lonely." Sometimes the pain was almost too much to bear. She would pretend that Asher had gone out for a short time and would be back soon. Little tricks to keep her mind from dwelling on the truth.

All she did these days was lie to herself.

Ioanna wiped the tears from her own eyes. "I gave away some of the bread, but I kept two loaves for you." She pulled them from underneath her coat and handed them to Mathilda.

"You shouldn't have saved any for me. My name is on the list for tomorrow. I can't keep it."

"You eat one loaf today, or as much as you can. Save the other for the train. You have no idea what kind of food or how much of it you will have. It's better to be prepared."

"I'm sure they'll provide for us."

Ioanna cocked her head, a light strand of hair falling over her cheek, her eyes narrowed. "You mean like they have provided for you so far?"

All Mathilda could do was shake her head. "I have to believe."

"In what?"

That was the question. Who was there to look out for her? The Germans? Ioanna was right. They wouldn't provide food. If they did, it would be precious little. She'd learned that much these weeks in the ghetto.

Asher? He was gone. She pushed the tears down her throat. He had been her rock, the most dependable person in her life. Mama and Papa were gone too, Mama to another country, Papa to, well, wherever you went after you died.

Dio? Asher had believed so strongly in Him, but He allowed evil people to perpetrate crimes against His own people. He was vengeful and hateful. If you strayed too far from His commands and forsook Him as so many did, He punished His people in the worst ways imaginable. Wandering in the desert. Plagues, famine, war. In the end, exile. Even the remnant ended up scattered across the globe.

"I don't know what to believe in. Myself, I suppose. That's why

I wanted to fight."

"Would a handful of people with no weapons to speak of been able to stand against the Nazi war machine?"

Again, she shook her head. "If not myself, then what? What do I believe in?"

"'Believe on the Lord Jesus Christ.' That's what the Bible says. We need nothing more. He's good and faithful. He cleanses us of all our sins. The sacrifices your forebearers made weren't enough, no matter how many times they offered them."

No, they weren't. And now they couldn't even do that. There was no more temple, no more altar. It had been almost two thousand years since there had been sacrifices. So they did their best to keep the law. But it wasn't enough. She couldn't be good enough to fulfill the law's demands.

"Even your Jesus, though, is allowing this to happen. He's punishing us."

"Or maybe He's using it to draw you closer to Him. I can see that He's working in your heart and calling you to be His child."

"Am I not already a child of Dio, part of the chosen ones?"

"Blood will never make you a child of God. Only belief and trust in Jesus. He was the perfect sacrifice. He said that He is the only way to heaven. There is no other way. I have no idea what the future holds for you, but even if the worst should happen, if you trust in Jesus, if you ask God to forgive your sins and to make you His child, He will bring you to heaven to live with Him forever."

Achima cried, and Ioanna got up and put her to nurse.

"Tell me about heaven."

A radiant smile brightened Ioanna's face. "It's a place where the streets are paved with gold. There is a crystal river, and there is never any night. There's no sun because God's Son is the light. When we're there, we'll feast with our Lord. He has prepared mansions for us to live in."

"That sounds beautiful."

Ioanna leaned over and touched Mathilda's knee. "The alternative is eternity in hell, a place devoid of God's presence, a place of pain and torture forever."

A shiver ran up Mathilda's spine. "I have to think about this."

"Don't wait to put your trust in Jesus. None of us is guaranteed tomorrow." Ioanna wrapped her in a tight embrace, Achima wedged between them.

"I'm scared." Mathilda whispered into her friend's ear.

"I know. I know. But Jesus will be by your side, even when I'm not, even without Asher or Perla or your mother or father. He will be all things to you. Remember that. All you have to do to put your trust in Him is to pray to Him and tell Him all that is on your heart. That's the best gift I can give you, even better than the bread I brought."

Mathilda clung to the last connection she had in this world, the last person who knew her and loved her. The darkness outside deepened as they stood in each other's arms, silently weeping, Ioanna whispering a prayer. Though the words didn't penetrate Mathilda's heart, the soothing tone of them brought her a measure of peace. Her shaking ceased.

Achima stopped nursing and fussed at being squeezed, breaking the embrace.

Ioanna touched her cheek. "Are you sure you won't allow me to take her? She would be safe with me and well cared for. When you return, she'll be here waiting for you."

"How can I let go of my baby, my last reminder of Asher? She's all I have left in the world. They mean to rip away my home, my means of taking care of my family, and even my husband. I won't lose my daughter as well. Please, don't judge me for this."

"I understand. To have to give Katina to another woman for any length of time would be very difficult. Think of Achima though. You have no idea what's in store for you. She's tiny and frail."

"She's all I think about. Whatever we face, we will face it

together. I can't do what you ask. I can't."

Ioanna kissed Mathilda on both cheeks. "My offer will stand for as long as possible."

"I thank you, dear friend, for that. For everything you have done for us in the past few years. Without you, I'm not sure we would have survived this long. Thank you for allowing me to grieve for all that's been taken from me."

"I have to go." Ioanna wiped tears from her eyes. "It will soon be curfew, and the guards will wonder why it took me so long to deliver the bread."

Mathilda hurried to the table where her diary lay open. She picked it up and caressed the cover. "Take my journal. Hide it in my flat over the spice shop. When I return, I'll know where to find it." She told Ioanna just which floorboards to lift.

Ioanna took the book and slipped it underneath her coat. "Be careful and safe, my friend."

"May God go with you. I love you."

"I love you."

With the faintest whiff of yeasty bread, Ioanna left, the door clicking behind her, sealing yet another loss.

A snore came from one of the bedrooms and voices from the other. Mathilda needed time, so she wrapped Achima in blankets and went downstairs and outside. All around, people milled about, young and old, men and women alike. There was nothing more to do these days. No jobs or school to attend. No shopping to be done. Very few friends to see.

So they walked. She caught the eye of one younger woman with a child in her arms. The woman's eyes were blank, devoid of all emotion. Empty.

That's what they were. Empty. Like olive oil that had run out, the last drop shaken from the bottle. Nothing left to give.

She kissed her daughter's head and prayed that her eyes were not so vacant. Still, like everyone else in Baron Hirsch, she wandered with no place to go, no purpose in walking.

Just walking.

Each of the buildings, all crowded together, were old and in disrepair. Windows were cracked and paint was peeling. The drab colors matched the drabness of the skies. Here everything was muted. The colors, the noises, the feelings, almost as if cheer would be too much.

The cobblestone streets were rough, and the odors caused by lack of sanitation were almost overwhelming. Here and there were smells of death and decay. People passed her, women with their shawls over their heads, all staring at the ground. No one greeted each other. Though shouting and crying came from the buildings, outside was silent.

Oppressive.

What would tomorrow bring? What would happen? Her stomach turned to a block of ice. They were going to Poland, of that she was pretty sure. What remained unsure was if the Germans were truly resettling them or if another fate awaited them. There had been rumors of camps, but she couldn't put all her stock in rumors.

If Perla was waiting for her at the end of the line, that would be wonderful. They could face whatever was waiting for them together. She would know more and would be able to tell Mathilda what was going on. She would help. She would be a lifeline in an uncertain future.

But if the rumors were to be believed, then Perla may not be there.

Achima managed to get her hands out of the blanket and waved her little fists in the air. Her daughter. Her sweet, sweet daughter. Mathilda grasped her wrist and Achima wrapped her fingers around Mathilda's. The infant's arm was so thin, the bones right below the skin.

She had no baby fat, nothing to draw on if Mathilda's milk dried up. Nothing to keep her warm in these frigid conditions. No matter how many blankets Mathilda wrapped her in, they weren't enough to keep the chill away.

Achima could very well get sick. Then what to do? They had no doctors, and even if they did, they had no medicine. There would be no helping Achima. She would likely die.

Ioanna's offer tugged at Mathilda's heart. In many ways, it made sense. That would be the right thing to do, the logical course of action. Put her daughter first and perhaps save her life.

And rip Mathilda's heart out in the process. How did you go about releasing your child into the care of another? There were no guarantees they would survive the war. No guarantees they would ever find each other again. Achima depended on Mathilda.

Or was it the other way around? Did Mathilda depend on Achima too much? Did she place the burden of keeping Asher alive on Achima? If so, that wasn't fair for a small child. That wasn't her duty. Mathilda had her memories, her photographs, the love that still filled her heart.

She couldn't be selfish. She had sworn to Achima that she would protect her, that she would do everything in her power to keep her safe.

Oh, what a decision.

What a difficult, impossible decision.

CHAPTER THIRTY-SIX

All night long, stuck on the small, lumpy blue couch with springs poking her back, Mathilda slept very little. Even when she managed to get Achima to shut her eyes after a feeding, Mathilda couldn't.

The wind blew through the cracked windows, and Mathilda wrapped herself in the lone blanket she had. All the others, she had given to Achima. Though no rain fell, the damp still seeped in. They might never be warm and dry again.

The little round clock on the end table ticked away the seconds, the minutes, the hours until she and Achima would have to board that train bound for uncertainty. She reached to the box on the floor beside her where Achima slept and stroked her downy head. She had yet to get much hair. It was a good thing Mathilda had managed to find enough yarn to knit a small cap for her daughter.

She would need it tomorrow and in the coming days. There was no telling how cold Poland would be, but it was sure to be even chillier than here.

Mathilda whispered into the night. "Oh my precious, precious little one. You're part of me, part of the father you'll never know. A gift from Dio. After you were born, my body was empty without you inside of me, but at least I held you in my arms. What am I to do if I can't hold you close enough to feel your light breath on my cheek?

"Ioanna wants to take care of you. There are so many problems with that. You wouldn't be with me, and I need you. If I didn't come back, Ioanna couldn't teach you what it means to be Jewish. And you would never know me.

"Yet it's selfish of me to want to keep you with me when that might not be what is best for you. Being a parent is more difficult than I ever imagined. I thought all I had to do was love you, but there is so much more than that. Out of that love, I have to make the best decisions for you, regardless of what my heart is telling me to do.

"And oh, my heart is telling me to hold you close, to keep you with me no matter what, and to never let you go. My heart is telling me that I can't live without you in my arms.

"I try to think about what your father would say if he were here. He would ask me to look into your eyes." She lifted Achima out of the bed. Her lids fluttered open, and her tiny mouth puckered, as if she wasn't too happy with her mother waking her in the middle of the night. Mathilda stared into Achima's dark eyes. "He would tell me to ask myself what was best for you. To think about you not only today but also in the future.

"He would want you to have a future. He would want you to live. He would do anything he could to make that happen.

"But I'm not him. I don't have his strength. All I want is my daughter with me, the child I longed for, my invaluable gift from Dio. He gave you to me. How am I to give you to someone else?"

She pulled Achima close and held her in the crook of her arm, crooning to her, soft enough not to wake the rather deaf couples in the bedrooms. Throughout the long hours of the night, mother and daughter snuggled. Mathilda imprinted the shape of her daughter's face, the smell of her hair, the feel of her skin, on her heart.

All too soon, the sky lightened, though the dark clouds, almost like props in a primary school play, concealed the sunrise. Mathilda rose from the couch, folded the sheets and the blankets, and packed them in the bag she was allowed to bring. She washed her face and bathed Achima. She ate some of the bread Ioanna had left.

She no longer had many shoes to choose from. One pair was packed away. The other pair, low-heeled oxfords, would be the most practical. She tied the laces, put on her coat, and wrapped Achima as well as she could in the blankets she'd kept out, slipping the tiny yellow hat on her head.

One of the old ladies cried when Mathilda bid them farewell. The other remained dour and stoic and simply said goodbye. The men gave her kind smiles and wished her well.

Before she knew it, she found herself on the street, the others whose names were on the list for today also out in the early morning mist, heading toward the train station, automatons obeying orders. They shuffled their feet through puddles, not even caring that the water soaked through their thin-soled shoes.

By the time they got to Poland, Mathilda's feet would be as wrinkled as a couple of dates. She held Achima close to keep her as dry as possible.

So many of them were headed toward the rail yard. So many. How long was this train? How many cars would it have?

Up ahead, she spied Levi, towering over the others marching toward their uncertain future. He was still a bear of a man, but despite his size, the Nazis had brought him to his knees. He obeyed their orders like they all did.

One middle-aged woman who Mathilda recognized from synagogue, always regal in her bearing, came by and patted Mathilda on the shoulder. Then she shuffled on, hunched over like an old woman. The trials of the past couple of years had taken their toll on everyone.

At the end, no one would ever be the same again.

Before they left the gates of Baron Hirsch, Achima fussed, then wailed, then screamed at the top of her lungs. Mathilda jiggled her and talked to her and sang to her, but nothing soothed her. She must have sensed the nervous tension that filled the air between the raindrops.

They approached the gates, guards all around dressed in the olive-drab uniforms, guns and dogs with them. If she could, Mathilda would wail right along with her daughter. As it was, the Germans shot her cold, hard stares. It wasn't like she wasn't trying to quiet Achima.

If she couldn't get her daughter to calm down, there was no telling what the Nazis might do. She closed her eyes for a moment, picturing Samuel's broken body on the street the day of the invasion. If they did that to an old man, there was nothing stopping them from doing it to a child.

"Por favor, my little love, por favor, stop crying. I don't want them to hurt you. You must be quiet." But for all her words, all her loving kisses, Achima wouldn't be silenced.

Don't allow them to silence her forever.

With the guards at their sides, the column marched forward, down the street toward the train station. Once, when she and Asher were newly married, they had taken a train to Athens. What a wonderful treat that had been. She had luxuriated in the velvet seats and exclaimed over each new sight they encountered.

Those days were some of the best of her life. They ate, they slept, they loved.

This was the complete opposite. She was alone with little food and no rest.

The dogs pulled at their leashes, teeth bared lest anyone step out of line.

Mathilda walked at the outside edge of the river of people to give herself and Achima more air. Still, Achima cried and cried. It was amazing that she had the energy to do so. She had never wailed so much in her brief life.

A guard approached them. "Get that brat to be quiet." His Greek was broken and not much better than hers. Only the younger generation of Jewish students had been taught that language in school.

"I am trying. She won't stop."

"Stop her, or I will stop her for you."

Mathilda's hands tightened around Achima, and her heart bounced in her chest. This couldn't be happening. None of this was real. It had to be a nightmare.

Then in front of her, the middle-aged woman who had just patted her on the shoulder tripped and fell. Her high-heeled shoes had done her no good.

Just as with Samuel, no one stopped to help her. No one picked her up. They all walked around her.

When a gunshot rang out, Mathilda jerked. Achima screamed louder.

They would die, just as the woman had.

Just as Samuel. Just as Asher.

There was now no doubt in Mathilda's mind.

Here and there along the street, though it wasn't a far walk, groups of people had gathered, out of curiosity or support for the Germans, it was impossible to tell. They huddled together in their brown and black and gray coats. Most of the women wore scarves over their rolled hair, and the men sported Hamburg hats. A few umbrellas popped up like dark mushrooms dotting the edge of the road.

And then Mathilda spotted a brighter coat, a cheerful shade of green. The woman who wore it had on a blue silk scarf covered in bright yellow-and-red flowers. A sob caught in Mathilda's throat.

Ioanna.

In that instant, the path forward was clear. There was a way to help Achima, to give her the best chance at surviving this insanity.

All Mathilda needed was the courage to do this. All she needed was to pool every ounce of strength that she possessed so that she could do the impossible. The unthinkable.

The only thing a mother who truly loved her child could do.

She tried to wipe away Achima's tears, and the child gripped her finger. A bond forged in love and in trial. A bond that would never be broken. That could never be broken, no matter what the circumstances.

Mathilda brought Achima to her shoulder so she could speak to her through her own tears. It was all she could do to remain upright as the crowd around her inched forward like a slow river of lava headed toward the sea.

"My daughter, my sweet, sweet child. How I love you. I never believed a love like this was possible, but it is. Though it's very different than the love I have for your father, it's no less real and no less powerful. In many ways, it may be more powerful because it's my job to protect you.

"You were given to me for a very short time. We're only getting to know each other. But you are everything to me. Don't ever doubt that. Know that. Deep in your heart, know that you are all I could have ever asked for from Dio and even more. I thank Him for you.

"I only wish we lived in different times, in different circumstances when I wouldn't be forced into such a decision. Believe me when I tell you that I haven't reached it lightly or thoughtlessly. It is all I have pondered for the last few days. What was impossible twenty-four hours ago is now the only option.

"I want you to live. More than anything in this world, I want you to live. Be happy. Enjoy the small moments in life and cherish them. Don't take anything for granted.

"Grow strong and beautiful, both inside and out. Learn all you can. Be wise. Be kind. Be loving."

Mathilda lifted her eyes to the heavens. "Dio, grant her a long life. May she always walk in Your ways and keep Your commandments. May she know love and peace and joy. May she know how deeply I have loved her and how my love for her will never diminish."

She planted many, many kisses on Achima's cheeks and on her hands and on her head.

Then Mathilda gazed at the crowd again. She was almost to her friend. "Ioanna. Ioanna. Here I am."

Ioanna smiled, but like the sun that hid behind the clouds, then ran to Mathilda's side, heedless of the Germans who watched her like the eagles on their hats. "I was afraid I wouldn't find you."

"I'm so glad you did." They walked along together, Mathilda herded like cattle. "You need to take her. She can't come with me. If she does, she'll die, I'm certain of that. To preserve her, to do my job in protecting her, I have to do this, what is best for her."

Ioanna reached out and touched Mathilda's arm, the light brush of fingers even against her coat so comforting that it almost broke the dam that held back the emotions she had been fighting. Instead, she swallowed hard, twice, and took in several deep breaths.

"I promise to take good care of her, to tell her all about you, and to remember everything she does so that when you return for her, you won't have missed out on anything."

"Gracyas, my dear friend. That's the greatest gift you could ever give me. I can never repay you."

"You don't have to. Just return to your daughter."

"I'll do everything in my power to make my way back here. But if I don't return, please tell her about me, tell her who I was, what I believed in, and how much I loved her. That I loved her enough to give my life for her."

"I promise." Ioanna's voice cracked.

From the corner of her eye, Mathilda spied a guard approaching. "Hey, get away from there." He strode toward Ioanna. "Stay away from those pigs. Don't dirty yourself with them."

She backed up a step, out of Mathilda's reach, and she fell a pace behind. Soon Mathilda wouldn't be able to get Achima to her. She reached into her coat pocket, pulled out a note she had written last night, and tucked it inside Achima's blankets.

"Ioanna."

As soon as she had her friend's attention, she kissed Achima one last time, perhaps forever, and tossed Achima to Ioanna.

Ioanna caught the baby, turned, and ran.

Mathilda may have seen her daughter for the very last time.

CHAPTER THIRTY-SEVEN

We're so close. The truth is touching my fingertips. What will it feel like to grasp it?

—From the diary of Tessa Payton

Tessa sat at the round metal table in front of her favorite American coffee shop, sipping on a frappé. Sure, it was an indulgence, but she enjoyed it every now and again. Greek coffee was great, but this was a taste of home.

She took another drink of the cold coffee blend, a welcome relief from the unrelenting Greek sun. Giannis assured her it cooled off here in the winter, but that was difficult to believe right now.

In front of her, cars from all different countries streamed along the road by the water. At least they drove on the correct side here. Tourists filled the walk, and on the other side of the street, couples strolled hand in hand and families corralled their children or dragged them along as they headed toward the White Tower.

Nea Kallikratia had been great, but it was also good to be back in a larger city. More vibrant. More to do.

Here too were the archives she was waiting for Giannis to sift through.

She glanced at her watch. Soon she would need to leave to meet him at the museum. For right now, she stared at Mathilda's journal.

Until I return. The last words in the book. She had said she would come back and write about everything that happened to her. Did that mean she didn't come back? Or maybe the Germans found the journal and confiscated it, and it only recently made its way back to Greece where it belonged.

No matter what had happened to her, the diary had provided great insight into what the Jews in this very city suffered during the war. Perhaps some of them had sat in this very spot at one time, sipping coffee, admiring the same view.

And then their lives were turned upside down.

Imagine how afraid they must have been. Tessa would have fallen apart. They weren't sure of the fate that awaited them. They didn't know about places like Auschwitz, Mauthausen, or Dachau, but from what Mathilda wrote, they had some inkling that things weren't going to be good.

Yet here she was, a descendant of two of those Jews. They must have survived for her family to come to America. But how had they stayed alive? And how did they become involved with the Stavrou family?

There were more questions than she had answers for. She could only hope and pray that Giannis had found the answers. With a sigh, she rose and threw her empty cup into the trash can and headed in the direction of the Jewish Museum. The walk wasn't far, but the day was so warm that she was sweating by the time she got there. With the sea breeze in Nea Kallikratia, it never got this warm.

Here she was, back where she had started. She showed her identification to the guards outside the building and turned over her phone to the lady at the front desk, who called for Giannis.

When he came from the back, he smiled that dimpled grin that turned her insides to mush and kissed her on the cheek. Very chaste. Very proper.

Still, it left her wanting more.

"Come with me. I dug up some interesting information."

"That's good. It will lift my spirits a little. I read the end of Mathilda's journal, and I have so many questions. I was so sad when she said she would come back and finish it, but it looks like she never did."

"That's one of the things I discovered."

"Then let's get going." She almost skipped as she followed him to the back room.

They came to a table with several papers and books spread on it. Because it was all in Greek, she couldn't read any of it. "What does it say?"

He chuckled. "We will get to it all in good time. Have a seat."

She sat but couldn't help almost bouncing in her chair. "So?"

"You need to learn patience."

"We all know that."

"Peter and Joanne Stavrou were Petrus and Ioanna Stavrou. They came with their twin daughters, Katina, who was Katherine, and Edie. The problem with one of the twins is that I can't locate church records for her baptism or municipal records for her birth. Life was crazy at that time, and sometimes information got lost or misplaced, but it is unusual that we have that for one twin and not the other."

"That is weird." Tessa bit her lower lip. "Wait a minute. Did you say Joanne was Ioanna?"

"That's right."

"How do you spell that?"

"I-O-A-N-N-A."

"That's the name in the diary. Ioanna. No last name is ever given, but it is possible that could be the same Ioanna."

"I think it's more than possible." He reached into the brown accordion folder and drew out an old, wrinkled sheet of paper. "One of my coworkers located this. It should have been with Mathilda's journal and newspaper clippings, but somehow it got separated."

"What does it say?"

He handed her another sheet of paper, this one new and bright white:

My dear Achima,

Giving you away is the hardest thing I have ever done in my life, but I do it out of love for you. Please don't ever question that. Te amo, more than my own life.

What would I tell you if I could see you face-to-face? I would tell you to grow to be strong. I would tell you to be happy and to live a full life. I would tell you to be kind and loving to all, even if they are different than you.

Ioanna Stavrou is a wonderful woman, and I know she will take good care of you. She will make sure to give you everything I can't. Treat her like your own mother. Love her like your own mother. For that is what she is to be to you now. I could not give you to anyone who wouldn't do everything for you a good mother would do.

How your father and I wish we could be there to watch you grow up and become a beautiful young woman. Perhaps I'll return to you. I pray that will be the case and that I can be there for you, to rock you in the night when you are frightened, to take care of you when you are sick, to teach you all the things a woman needs to know.

I must go now. It's time to board the train bound for Poland. I don't know what awaits me. Te amo, my most precious daughter. Kisses, kisses, kisses, enough to last you a lifetime.

We will meet again someday. I do not know if it will be on this earth or in heaven above, but we will meet again. I'll take you in my arms and tell you how much I love you.

Praying for great health and happiness for you.

Your mother,
Mathilda Nissim

"She gave her daughter to Ioanna. This takes my breath away. She surely loved her daughter with all her heart and did the only thing she could. From reading the journal, I know that Achima and Katina were born within a few weeks of each other. Do you think that when they came to America, they just gave them both the same birthdate?"

"That makes sense. There would have been no paperwork for Achima. If they claimed the girls were twins, they might have been able to explain that something happened to Achima's paperwork."

"So you believe Achima to be Edie."

"I do."

Goosebumps broke out on Tessa's arms.

"Then Achima was my grandmother."

He nodded, and her heart raced faster than a NASCAR stock car. She covered her mouth, her hands shaking. All noise faded into the background.

All this time, she'd been reading this amazing journal written by a woman she had come to admire, who led an almost unbelievable life.

And the woman whose hands had written those words on those pages was her very own great-grandmother.

Mathilda Nissim.

Asher Nissim had been her great-grandfather.

Her breath rushed from her lungs. Asher had been murdered by the Nazis. His blood had stained the very streets she walked. She had been in their house.

Mathilda, her great-grandmother, had made the almost impossible choice to give her daughter up so that she had a chance to live.

Tessa was proof that Achima had lived. The child had survived the war and come to America with Ioanna Stavrou, the woman Tessa had always believed to be her great-grandmother.

But if Achima came to the States with Ioanna, what happened

to Mathilda? "Tell me Mathilda's fate. You must know it."

"Come with me." Giannis held out his hand to Tessa. She grabbed it and followed him out of the busy, noisy room into the solemn quiet of the museum.

Mathilda sat on her suitcase, shoulder to shoulder with her fellow Jews, packed into this rusty-red railcar like the cattle it was intended for. The clanging of the doors still rang in her ears, even as the train's wheels now clickety-clacked on their way to Poland.

The only light and air came from two wire-covered skylights, one to the right of the center of the car, the other to the left. In one corner was a bag of biscuits, wormy figs, and olives. The food wouldn't be sufficient for all these people for the journey north. Unless the Germans planned to feed them again at some point.

Which was unlikely.

Mathilda pulled her skirt to her knees and wrapped herself more tightly in her coat, vacillating between being hot and being cold.

More than anything, she was alone. Mama, Papa, her sisters, her friends, her husband, her child. Gone from her. Ripped away. The Germans could take their business, they could take their home and possessions, but the worst thing they took was those who loved her and whom she loved in return.

Now she made this journey by herself with many unknowns awaiting her. She wiped her sweaty palms on the rough wool of her coat. Her stomach churned, and she had to force the little bread she had this morning to stay down.

A strong silence fell over the group. Even though there were so many of them, not many talked. A few whispers. The whimpering of an infant that made Mathilda's milk flow. That was it.

Had she made the right choice for Achima? Only time would tell if her empty arms and her empty heart were worth it. If Achima would live. That's all that mattered.

The train puffed on, chugging closer to their destination. The odor of urine and other bodily functions filled the car, gagging Mathilda and churning her stomach even more. Beside her, a mother, father, and two children sat, the children on their parents' laps, the parents with their arms around each other.

As darkness fell outside the skylights, someone passed around the bag of biscuits. By the time it came to Mathilda in the opposite corner of the car, it was almost empty. Inside of her suitcase, she had the precious loaf of bread from Ioanna. She passed the bag to the young family beside her. The two old ladies on her other side, sisters from what she gathered, had also not partaken of the meal.

It was better if the youth were allowed the strength.

Night and day passed overhead, only marked by the amount of light streaming inside the car. They blended together. Mathilda dozed and dreamed of Asher and Achima. The biscuits and olives had run out long ago. Mathilda broke into her store of bread and shared it with the young family and the old ladies.

Long ago the infant had ceased crying. A shudder passed through Mathilda when she contemplated what must have happened to the child. Though she ached for her daughter, each passing mile showed her that she had made the correct decision.

From her reckoning, six days went by. Only once did the train stop, and the *Schupo* opened the doors for the people to get out and stretch their legs. Someone guessed they were in Yugoslavia. Did it really matter? All that was important was that she was moving ever farther from Achima.

At last the train pulled to a stop. The doors slid opened. Wild cries pierced the pitch-black darkness. Dogs barked. "*Raus!* Raus!" The *Schupo* wanted them out. Though it was night, intense spotlights were focused on them, blinding Mathilda as she hopped from the train on shaky legs to the gravel below.

German shepherds bared their teeth. They growled, low and

long. Any moment they might attack.

"*Schnell!* Schnell!" Faster, faster.

A man with his head shaved approached Mathilda. Striped clothes covered his thin body. He took her suitcase. "You'll get it back." He said the words without conviction.

Mathilda's pulse pounded in her neck. Her head swirled. "What is this place?"

"Auschwitz-Birkenau."

A red glow lit the inky sky. Snowflakes—no, ash—drifted on the air.

Suitcases piled up. One fell open, spilling photographs, memories, onto the dirt. Now buried by more valises.

Cold, cold, so cold. It bit her toes, her nose.

The Nazis barked orders in German. Nonsense. What to do?

Children, old people, women moved to one side. Si, there. She moved forward. Someone grabbed her shoulder. She shook him off.

Together they huddled. Breath rose like steam from their mouths. The cold hurt. Everything hurt.

An old man coughed. A child called for his father. A woman sobbed.

Mathilda's chest pushed in on her heart. Pain stabbed her lungs. She couldn't breathe.

Screams filled the air. Men calling names. Women sobbing. Children screeching for their parents.

Mathilda was numb.

"Schnell, schnell." The rifle-toting soldiers pushed them forward.

So many of them. Frail, hunched ladies. Small children clinging to their mothers' hands. A woman who yelled at the top of her lungs.

They marched, her boots no match for the mud. Nothing but cold.

The fight drained from her. Why did no one stop this?

Achima safe. Achima safe. Achima safe.

March. March. March.

A murmur ran through the group. "We will get showers."

Even the old lady straightened.

Hot water. How lovely. She wouldn't be cold anymore.

They entered a long, low building. Stripped off their clothes, all left in piles. Not even embarrassed about her nakedness. Thankful for the soon-to-come hot water.

The door clanged shut. A bolt slid.

Her breathing picked up pace. This was no shower.

The spigots opened.

Gas.

Dio, no! No!

Shallow breaths. Don't take in too much gas.

Light-headed.

Jesus saves. Live forever with Jesus. Just believe.

Si, Abba, I believe. Cleanse my sins. I believe in your Son. Send me to heaven to live with You.

The gas choked her. Piercing screams surrounded her.

But inside her heart was nothing but peace.

Te amo, Asher.

Te amo, Achima.

Te amo, Lord.

CHAPTER THIRTY-EIGHT

I'm so at home here. Maybe I've found the place I belong. Maybe I'll never go back to the States.

—*From the diary of Tessa Payton*

Hand in hand, Giannis and Tessa wove their way through the various exhibits in the Jewish Museum, past clothing worn by the rabbis, silver used on Shabbat, little toys the children played with.

She had been here so often now that each display was familiar to her. She had spent hours upon hours gazing at each of the placards, committing them to memory, even sketching some of the items since photographs were forbidden.

They didn't stop at any of the displays though. Her stomach tightened as they approached the one room, the one in the entire museum she had prayed that he wouldn't take her to.

The hall of names. Four walls with black stone, fifty thousand names engraved on it.

She fought back tears. "No. No."

Giannis pulled her forward, but she resisted. If she didn't see, it wouldn't be true.

"This will be good for you."

How? How could it be good for her to see her great-grandparents' names etched on this wall?

He brought her to the far side of the room, over to the right, just below the center line.

And there they were.

Asher Nissim.

Mathilda Nissim.

She collapsed to her knees, sobbing, touching their names as tears cascaded down her face, dripping onto the marble floor. This only connection she had to her ancestors.

Ancestors who the Germans had murdered.

She knelt and cried until her knees ached. Then Giannis helped her to her feet and held her close.

As Asher had once held Mathilda close.

"I am so sorry. I understand this is hard. For many of us, we grew up knowing what crimes the Nazis committed against those who came before us. You have just found this out, and it must be difficult to comprehend."

"Why? Why would they do this? How could they be so cold, so unfeeling, so ruthless as to kill people only because of the blood in their veins?"

He rubbed her back. "That is a question I cannot answer. Only God knows. One day He will make it known to us, but today is not that day. All we can do is learn and tell others what they would tell us if they could."

"I know how Asher died. What about Mathilda?"

"She left on transport number nine on April 10, 1943, with approximately twenty-eight hundred other Jews, packed eighty into a car with very limited food supplies. For six days, they traveled in such a fashion. The conditions were deplorable. They arrived on the evening of April 16, 1943. Mathilda was sent straight to the gas chamber."

Again, sobs shook Tessa, and once more she found herself in Giannis' arms. "My poor great-grandmother. Poor Mathilda. Poor, poor Mathilda. How awful. So terrible. She shouldn't have died. She should have come back for Achima."

"Thank goodness that she had the sense to give Achima to Ioanna, otherwise you wouldn't be here. Her greatest wish came true. Achima lived and had a daughter of her own, who had a daughter of her own."

"My mother. I wonder if she knows this. Knows what happened to the strong, beautiful woman who gave birth to her own mother. Wow. Achima was my mother's mother. This is…"

"It is so much to take in. I understand."

They remained in the hall of names for a while longer. Each one inscribed on the wall was a person with a story. Someone who laughed, who loved, who lived.

He led her to the wall to their right, near the left-hand side on the top. David Yacoel. Perla Yacoel. Bechar, Annette, Isaac Yacoel. They all perished.

So many like Mathilda who didn't want to die. Who had so much more life in front of them, only to have it snuffed out by hatred and evil.

The same hatred and evil that still permeated the world. That had touched her mother in a similar fashion to the way it touched her grandmother and great-grandmother.

They were Jewish. There was no denying it. And they had an amazing story to share with the world.

Once Tessa had regained her composure, she thanked Giannis, who promised to stop by with some food that evening, and made her way back to her Airbnb. She took the route that brought her through the old Jewish market and past the house where her great-grandmother had once lived.

She paused in front of it, staring at it, memorizing each line, each window. Part of her past.

A past that brought her to today and who she was. Neither Jew nor Greek but one with Christ. For that, she had Ioanna Stavrou to thank. She raised Achima—Edie—to know and love the Lord. She passed that to Mom who passed that to her.

What a legacy. One that she would pass to her children someday.

After snapping a few pictures of the building with curious

onlookers staring at her, she finished her walk to the apartment and, instead of taking the elevator, climbed the four flights of stairs and let herself inside.

The air-conditioning was glorious, and she flopped on the couch until she could cool off. She should try to take a shower before Giannis arrived.

She hadn't been settled for long before her phone rang. Mom. Could she handle talking to her and telling her their family story when she was just processing it herself? Still, Tessa answered.

"Oh, thank goodness I got you. Jay—" Her voice cracked.

Tessa went cold all over. "What is it, Mom?"

She sobbed for a moment before collecting herself. "Jay's in the hospital. He's had a heart attack. A bad one. The doctors are waiting to stabilize him a little before they do surgery. They don't know how much damage there is to his heart. Please, I need you."

Tessa's heart tore at the panic and concern that laced Mom's words. Not even when Dad died had Mom been quite so frantic.

Even while Tessa was chasing the past, the present continued. And sometimes the present needed you more than the past. "I don't know how fast I can get there. I'm not next door to an international airport."

"Just do what you can. Please."

"Is he conscious?"

"No." More sobbing from the other end of the line.

"Okay, Mom, hang in there. I'll be home as soon as I can. I'll let you know my flight details as soon as I have them. And I'll pray for you and for Jay."

A moment of silence stretched before them. "Thank you, Tessa. I love you."

"I love you too. Keep me posted if anything changes." Code for *if he takes a turn for the worst.*

As soon as she hung up, she flipped open her laptop and searched for flights. No matter how hard she tried, she wouldn't be able to get home until late the following evening Pittsburgh time.

By the time she had a flight booked, called Mom, and worked on straightening up and packing a bit, Giannis was at the door.

He'd hardly set foot inside when he put the bag of food on the coffee table and reached for her. "What is wrong? You are crying. Do not be upset about what I showed you."

"I am upset about that, but there's more. My stepfather has had a serious heart attack, and my mom is frantic. She needs me there. I have to go home, and I have a flight booked for the morning. Can you take me to the airport? I'm afraid it's going to be pretty early. Like eight o'clock."

Giannis pulled her close, though he did chuckle. "You think no one here gets up that early. I will take you to the airport. I'm so sorry about this. Will it be difficult for you to go home?"

She snuggled closer to him so she wouldn't forget how he felt in her arms, how he smelled of the spices that perfumed this city, how soft his lips were on hers. "Right now, it's all about keeping my mom calm. I hope nothing happens to Jay while I'm traveling. It's not easy to get from Thessaloniki to Pittsburgh."

"I will pray that he will be fine. And I will pray for when you talk to your mom."

"Yes. Thank you. It's time that we work out some of the problems between us. I need to tell her how I've felt all these years but also what I've learned about myself and about her while I've been here. This has been the best experience of my life."

He released her and opened the bag, pulled out two Styrofoam containers, and handed her one. "I remember that souvlaki is your favorite Greek meal. I am glad that you can have it on your last night here."

"My last night." She sat on the couch with her legs tucked underneath her. "I'll miss this place, but someday I'll return. I promise you that."

"And I will miss you."

"I'm going to hate not being able to see you every day."

"We need to talk about our relationship."

Oh goodness, they were in a relationship. She couldn't help the smile that crossed her face. The feelings she had for Giannis were real.

And now she had to leave and cross an ocean. With so much distance between them, would this mark the end of it all? They didn't know each other very well yet. It might not be strong enough to sustain the strains of a long-distance relationship.

Yet it was worth a try.

Giannis, however, might not feel the same way.

"I hope I am not too forward, but I would like to keep in touch with you. To see where this might lead." He toed the laminate floor with his tennis shoe.

Tessa gave a half chuckle. He'd never been this nervous before. "That would be nice. We could FaceTime and even have movie-night dates. Though it will be the afternoon for me. And like I said, I will be back. I don't know when, but I'll make it happen."

They ate their souvlaki with plastic forks. "What will you do? Will you go back to school?"

"That's not really an option." She loaded her fork with chicken, rice, tomato, and yogurt. "I cleaned out my bank account. I have some left, but not enough for a semester at a private college. Right now, I have to focus on the present and let God take care of the future. What about you?"

"They are building a large new Jewish Museum in a more modern part of the city, so I am busy working on what exhibits we'll have. I'd like to work on one about Salonika Jews who went to America. Your story deserves to be told."

"Not my story but Mathilda's." She stared out the balcony doors as the shadows deepened. "Her voice has been silenced for almost eighty years. It needs to be heard again. She has so much to tell the world today."

They finished their dinner, and Giannis helped her clean. In the morning, all she would have to do would be to take out the trash.

"How about one last walk to the White Tower?" Giannis put away the broom he'd been using to sweep the kitchen floors.

"That sounds perfect. Is the place with the triangulars still open? I need one last one."

"You and your sweets." He came and kissed her on her forehead. "I think they are. We will go find out."

They strolled along the waterfront, the tavernas and bars still crowded, the nightlife just ramping up. When they came to Dimitriou Gounari Street, just before the White Tower, they turned and soon came to the building with the bright blue facade and black-and-white tile floors, where they bought her favorite treat.

They strolled the couple of blocks to Navarinou Square and sat on a bench facing a small fountain, the water almost as blue as the gulf by Nea Kallikratia. Behind them were the excavated ruins of the Palace of Galerius. Pittsburgh couldn't hold a candle to Thessaloniki.

This place, these people, this man beside her, had become part of who she was.

Thessaloniki had changed her forever.

CHAPTER THIRTY-NINE

It had been a long, teary—at least on Tessa's part—goodbye at the Thessaloniki airport early that morning. Then an even longer flight with two layovers. What a relief to walk out the doors of baggage claim in Pittsburgh and find Riley standing by her little red Toyota.

Riley caught her in an embrace. "I missed you so much. I'll bet you have a million things to tell me, but frankly, all I'm interested in is Giannis. Wow. I never thought you would go and find someone on the other side of the world."

Tessa climbed in the passenger side and settled herself for the trip home. "Giannis is great. We're going to continue to see each other as much as we can and try to find out where this is all leading."

"I'm happy for you."

They drove through the darkened streets for a while. As it was almost midnight, most shops and restaurants were closed. "This is weird to be driving in a car. Except for when we went to the beach and a couple of taxi rides, we walked most places in Thessaloniki."

"You might be having reverse culture shock."

"Maybe." Tessa bit her lower lip. "Did you know that two of my great-grandparents were killed in the Holocaust?"

"Is that what you found out? How horrible. I'm so sorry."

"The journal I was reading, the one about Mathilda Nissim. It turns out she was my great-grandmother."

"No way."

"Yep. How weird is that?"

"Amazing. It's like God led you right to her."

He had. He'd brought her to the place she needed to be at the time she needed to be there. And He gave her a sense of belonging and identity. The place she was going might not be much like home anymore, if it ever had been, but she did have a place that was hers in Christ.

For the first time in a long time, peace flooded her.

She allowed her eyes to shut, and when she opened them, Riley had pulled into the driveway. She helped Tessa bring in her suitcase, gave her another big hug, and drove away into the night.

Mom met her at the door. "I could have picked you up." The dark circles underneath her eyes weren't from the poor lighting.

"You have enough on your plate." Tessa hugged Mom. "Jay is your priority right now."

"Thank you. You must be exhausted."

"Frankly, I'm more hungry than tired. I slept a little on the plane."

"It's going to take you a while to get your days and nights straightened out. How about some eggs? They won't take me long to make."

"Sounds fabulous, thanks. But I can make them. I've been sitting for a long time."

"I need to keep busy. I can't sleep much."

"How is he?"

"Holding his own. They think they'll be able to do the surgery tomorrow."

"That's good news."

"Yeah." Mom rubbed her eyes. "I hope he makes it."

For all his faults, her mother really loved Jay. For Mom to lose a second husband would be devastating. "I'll pray for him. I'll be with you at the hospital tomorrow."

"Are you going to be up to it?"

"There isn't another place in the world I'd rather be." And that was the truth. No matter what she had discovered in Greece, who she might be falling in love with there, right now her place was beside Mom. "Forget the eggs. Let's both try to get some sleep. We can pick up a breakfast sandwich on the way to the hospital."

"That sounds good." Mom kissed her on the cheek and hugged her tight. "I'm so glad you're home."

"I'm glad too. I have so much to tell you, but that can wait." She made her way to her bedroom, still all pink and frilly like it had been when she was ten, and plopped on the bed, clothes and shoes and all.

Before she knew it, Mom was shaking her awake. "Do you still want to come to the hospital with me?"

Tessa sat up and rubbed her eyes. "Of course. Just give me a few minutes to try to find some clean clothes." She hurried through getting dressed and presentable, and soon she and Mom were on their way.

Lily met them when they entered the ICU waiting room, her eyes red. "Hi, Janet. Hi, Tessa. Glad you made it."

"Me too." She hugged her stepsister. "How are you? Were you here all night?"

She nodded, her somehow perfectly curled blond hair bouncing, and pointed to a couch where a blanket and a pillow sat. "I just wanted to be near him."

"Of course you did, dear. But you need to make sure you rest as well." Mom hugged Lily and fussed over her, bringing her a cup of coffee from the pot at the far end of the room and sending Tessa to the cafeteria to round up some pastries.

If she had expected things to change, she had been so very wrong. Everything was the same. It was Lily who got all the attention while Tessa was left running errands. Tessa who got forgotten and left behind.

She found some packaged Danish and bought a couple of varieties so Lily would have a choice. When she stepped into the elevator to return to the waiting room, she noticed a sign by the buttons that said CHAPEL. She pushed that button, and when the car arrived on that floor, she made her way to the small, quiet room with a cross at the front.

She slid into one of the pews near the middle of the chapel and placed the bag on the seat beside her. For a moment, she sat and stared at the cross. Had one of her Jewish ancestors encountered Christ? Or maybe Paul? Had they been jeering for the Savior to be slain, or did they silently weep for what their people were doing to the Messiah?

Those were questions she would never have answers for. And not the reason she had come here. She bowed her head.

Oh Lord, please help me to be kinder to Lily. Over the years, she's made it difficult for me to love her, but that's not an excuse. I think of all the people who were nice to me in Greece who had no reason to be except because of You. That's what I want to be like.

Maybe I'll never truly belong in this family, but it is still my family, the one You placed me in for a reason. Help me to find out what that reason is and to accept my place here.

I do thank You for Jay. He did his best to be a father to me, and I didn't always make it easy on him. I allowed my hurt and my jealousy to get the better of me, and I ask Your forgiveness for that.

Please guide the doctors that will be doing the surgery, that they will be able to fix his heart and that he and Mom will enjoy many more years together. Make him healthy and strong soon.

Help Mom to endure all this. It has to be so difficult for her. Don't put her through becoming a widow once more. Give her strength and peace.

And help me to be a comfort to all of them. Help my words to be kind and loving and for my feelings to match.

In Your Son's name, amen.

She rose, went back to the elevator, and made her way to the waiting room. Putting into practice what she had prayed, she smiled when she handed the bag of pastries to Lily. "I got you a couple of choices. Or maybe you'll want them all."

"Thanks," Lily mumbled.

Tessa joined Mom on the couch across from Lily. "They took Jay back a little while ago. The doctor said this could take some time. Are you sure you don't want to go home and get some rest?"

"I'm not that tired. To me, it's the middle of the afternoon."

"Right. That's confusing."

They said little to each other after that, Mom lost in her book, Lily lost on her phone, and Tessa lost in the HGTV show on the monitor mounted on the wall.

By the time noon rolled around, Tessa could have eaten a horse. The screen in the waiting room showed that Jay was still in surgery, and the nurse took their information, so she and Mom went for lunch. Lily decided to go home and take a shower.

Mom got a salad from the cafeteria, and Tessa got a hamburger. Her last real meal had been the souvlaki Giannis brought the other night. "I'm glad it can be just the two of us for a while."

"Lily is really hurting. She's scared because her dad is all she has left. It wouldn't hurt you to be nice to her."

Tessa bit her tongue. It would be wrong to pray to God, asking Him to help her be nice, and then turn around and say some unkind things. "I'm trying. Really. But I like it when it can just be the two of us."

"Me too. I'm glad you're home. I missed you so much."

"Why did you hide the fact that we're Jewish from me?"

Mom stabbed a couple of pieces of lettuce with her fork and dipped them in the dressing on the side. "I told you. The incident at the synagogue freaked me out. The less you knew about it, the further I kept you from it, the safer you would be."

"Did you know that your grandparents were killed by the Nazis?"

Mom sucked in a breath and flicked her gaze to Tessa's face. "What?"

She shared what she had learned. "You should go sometime and see the city where we come from. You should stand in front of that wall and pay your respects to your grandparents."

"It's too dangerous. You told me about the guards outside. Why do you think they're there? Because anti-Semitism wasn't wiped out at the end of World War Two. It's still here. I was probably never told for the very same reasons. And when I did find out, I almost died, just like my grandmother."

"We can't be frightened to live our lives. If we are, that's not really living."

"A pretty meme to make but not very practical in today's world."

"But true. Mathilda, your grandmother, lived life to its fullest. She was strong and capable and fought for what she believed to be right. In the end, she did what she had to do so that you and I could be here right now. We are the result of the very painful decision she made to give up Achima. By giving her daughter life, she also gave life to many generations to come."

Mom put her fork down and stared at Tessa. "You're right. I suppose she found herself in a very difficult place, and in the end, she did what was best. I don't envy her having to throw her daughter into her friend's arms. I could never have let you go. Especially after—"

"After Dad died. I know. I have to believe, though, that a mother's love is strong enough to do what you have to do for your child, even at great cost to yourself."

"Tessa." Mom opened her water bottle and took several long drinks from it. "There's something I need to tell you. I should have told you long ago, but at first you were too young, and then I had kept it from you for so long that it became impossible to say the words."

Mom's tone was so serious, goose bumps popped up on Tessa's arms. "You can tell me anything. I'm tougher than I look." Though her hamburger wasn't sitting in her stomach very well at the moment.

"Well—"

Mom's phone dinged with a message from the hospital. "Jay's

out of surgery. We need to go upstairs and speak with the doctor." She pushed away from the table.

"What were you going to tell me?"

"Later. This wasn't the time or the place anyway."

CHAPTER FORTY

The screen on Tessa's phone proclaimed it to be four o'clock in the morning. Four in the blessed morning. She hadn't been able to sleep past this time in the three days she'd been home, other than the first morning. For how tired she was, you would think she would be able to stay in bed most of the day.

Not the case.

Maybe if she got up and got something to eat, she'd be able to go back to bed in an hour or so. Her stomach was telling her it was lunchtime.

Careful not to step on the spots on the floor that creaked, she stole down the hall lined with family photos. She didn't need a light because she had memorized each one. There was one of her and Mom. One of Jay and Lily and his late first wife. And one of the four of them as a blended family.

She stopped short.

There wasn't a picture of her, Mom, and Dad. Why hadn't she ever noticed that before? How strange. Maybe she could find one and hang it on the wall. If Jay had a problem with it, too bad.

She inched down the stairs to the kitchen with its gray cabinets and white countertops and stainless-steel appliances. No wonder she gravitated toward HGTV. She lived in a house inspired by the network. She went to flip on the under-cabinet lights.

"Leave them off."

She about jumped high enough to hit her head on the ceiling. "Mom, you scared me to death."

"Sit with me." Like a four-year-old afraid of the dark.

"Okay." Tessa, her hands still shaking, sat on the barstool beside Mom. The dim light coming from the displays on the stove and microwave illuminated several candy bar wrappers on the counter. Had Mom dug into her chocolate stash at this hour of the night? Or morning, or whatever it was?

"I can't begin to imagine what my yiayia must have suffered. How horrible the conditions were for her. When you left for Greece, I was afraid you might stumble on information like this. After all, less than two thousand out of fifty thousand people survived. The odds weren't in favor for our family."

"No, they weren't. That wall where all their names are etched is chilling and moving at the same time."

"I ordered a book, and I've been reading it, about a young woman who was taken to Auschwitz from Thessaloniki. She managed to survive, but she described the conditions in the ghetto and what it was like on the train. Horrific. That humans should treat each other like that."

"I saw where the ghetto had been and the train yard as well. I even stepped foot into the apartment where Mathilda and Asher lived."

Mom perked up. "Really?"

"You should have been there."

"Maybe I can go one of these days."

"That would be nice. Giannis would be happy to show you around. I'm glad you're interested in our family history."

"I always have been. It's just... I guess it's just that I'm a coward. I don't want people to start hating me because I'm Jewish. And I know they would. I know people who would right off the bat."

"That's terrible. I can't believe anyone we know would be that way, would think anything less of us because of our ethnicity."

"I said in the hospital the other day that I had something to tell you."

"Yes." Tessa drew out the word.

"It's about time you heard what I have to say. Why I'm so fearful of our family background. And why I think you should give Jay a second chance."

Tessa clung to the edge of the padded barstool. "What?"

"Your father. . . I know you admire him greatly and think he was the best man that ever walked the earth."

"He was a great dad. Like the time I fell off that overturned bucket and broke my arm. He was at the doctor's office with me."

"That was me." Mom fiddled with one of the chocolate wrappers.

"Oh." The picture of Dad being there had been so clear, but she had been only five, so she might not have remembered it correctly. "There was the time he took me fishing. That was so much fun." That had to have been Dad. Mom would never get near mud or a worm.

"I pushed him to do that with you, and you were gone for a total of thirty minutes. It's a ten-minute drive to the lake."

"I guess. What are you trying to say?"

"I allowed you to believe that Dad was a wonderful man because I didn't want you to end up scarred because of what truly happened. I lied to you and allowed you to live in a fairy tale because I thought it would make you happy."

"Mom, you're scaring me." She couldn't draw a deep breath.

Mom covered her face and sobbed. All Tessa could do was to rub her back and wait until she could talk. That didn't stop Tessa's arms and legs from shaking. Whatever Mom had to say about Dad wasn't good. Quite possibly, her world could be rocked.

Again.

At last Mom sat up, got a handful of tissues, and wiped her face. She stood on the opposite side of the island from Tessa. "I guess I just have to rip the Band-Aid off. Your dad didn't die in a car accident."

Tessa furrowed her brow. "What was it?"

"He didn't die at all."

Tessa gasped, not comprehending. "What do you mean?"

"He was abusive and a drug addict. When I met him, he was wonderful, but after we were married, he injured his back and became addicted to pain killers. They changed him. He became vengeful and spiteful. He spewed hate every time he opened his mouth at every minority you could imagine. Including Jews."

"Not Dad."

"Yes, Dad. This was right around the time I found out I was Jewish. That's all I knew. Yiayia wouldn't tell me more. Here I was, living in fear of a man who would do who knows what to me because of who I was. I was terrified he would find out the truth. The abuse continued until I couldn't take it anymore. He left and never looked back."

"Dad is alive?"

Mom shook her head, still grasping several tissues in her hand. "He died of an overdose shortly after the divorce was final. I'm sorry. I was so scared of being Jewish that it took me years to go to that synagogue. Then the shooting happened. And then you took that DNA test and went all the way to Greece. I was only trying to protect you."

Only trying to protect her. Isn't that what Mathilda had said over and over in her journal when talking about Achima? That her greatest job as a mother was to protect her daughter. She was willing to give Achima to another woman, even knowing she may never see that daughter again, so that the child had a chance to grow up healthy and happy.

But the truth about her father landed like a kick to the stomach. She bent over the cold countertop for so long that she got chilled. Had her memories been so vague that she'd twisted them to fit the picture Mom painted of him? And she did paint a rosy picture.

That would explain why there were no photos of the three of them in the hall upstairs. "He hated Jews?"

"Everyone who was different from him. Everyone. He boasted of it, puffing himself up. It was the drugs talking, but it was awful. He talked about killing them, doing away with 'their kind.' He had firearms in the house, so I had to take him seriously. If he ever found out my heritage, that my mother was fully Jewish, he would have killed me."

"And that's why you never told me."

"You were little when he left, and I had no words to explain to you what had happened to him. Then, as time passed, I couldn't see any sense in popping that bubble. I wanted you to live a beautiful life."

"It's going to take me some time to come to terms with this."

"You don't hate me, do you?"

For a long time, Tessa stared at her hands touching the smooth stone counter. All she could think about was Mathilda and Achima. Mathilda had no idea if her choice would be the right one or the wrong one. Achima could have grown up hating her mother. "Did Yiayia hate Great-grandma?"

"You mean because she took her from her mother? That's something I didn't know until you brought me that information, but we went to my yiayia's house all the time. She and my mother talked on the phone every Sunday afternoon, even if they had just seen each other the day before. I would say they had a very close relationship. Great-grandma didn't tell Yiayia about all of this until she was an adult, but Yiayia always spoke fondly of her mother. I never remember her uttering a single angry word."

"That's because she was a mother. Mathilda, your yiayia, did what she had to do to protect her daughter. And that's what all the women in this family have always done."

"So you understand?" Again, Mom was pleading.

Tessa chewed the inside of her cheek. "Not all the way because I'm not a mother yet. From what I gather, there is no other love or connection like that between mother and daughter. But reading

Mathilda's journal gave me some insight into that relationship and what lengths a mother would go to in order to do what she feels is best for her child."

"Thank you for that." Mom blew her nose. "You can see why I would want to keep you away from everything related to Judaism and that it didn't start with the temple shooting. And why I lied to you about your father. I should have told you when you were older, I really should have, but by then so much time had gone by that it was difficult to find the words. How would I even start the subject?"

"I wish you had. Maybe it would have helped me to look at Jay in a different light. Maybe we could have had a closer relationship these past few years."

"I'm sorry, sorry to have kept it from you all this time." A few tears trickled down her cheeks.

"Oh, Mom." Emotions, jet lag, whatever, got to Tessa, and her own tears fell. She went to her mom and hugged her, holding on tight, allowing the tears to wash away all the years of hurt between the two of them.

Dad had been. . .not a good person. Not the man she believed him to be. The thought left a bitter taste on her tongue. Pain pounded behind her eyes. Then again, Jay wasn't always the best person. She stepped away from Mom. "Why did you marry Jay?"

"He loves me and is good to me. He loves you too and wants what's best for you. True, he doesn't always come across that way or communicate very well, but he does."

"He left me at that gas station."

Mom shook her head. "Not on purpose."

"But it took so long for you to come back for me. I was so scared, so afraid that I had done something to upset him and make him want me out of his life."

"Honey, no. It wasn't him; it was Lily. She told us you were with Jay's parents in their car when she knew that wasn't the case.

Did you ever stop to think why she didn't get a phone until she was sixteen or her driver's license until she was seventeen? Jay was devastated that she would do that to you. Don't you remember how he was the first one out of the car when we found you and how he scooped you into his arms?"

Apparently there was quite a bit that she didn't remember or didn't remember the right way. "I guess I have a ton to think about. Things aren't the way I always believed them to be."

"Part of that is my fault, and I'm sorry. You're right. We should have had a better relationship so that we could have discussed all of this. You put on such a happy front that I didn't know you were still struggling all these years later."

The *sorry*s flew like dandelion fuzz on the wind. "You know what? Let's not be sorry anymore. I have to process what Dad was like and reconcile what Jay is like, but what happened is in the past. We can't change it. All we can do is move forward."

"I'd like that. You, Tessa, are a very special young lady. I'm proud to be your mom." They both bawled a little more, healing, cleansing, restoring.

Once they had dried their eyes, Tessa yawned. "Is it okay if I go back to bed for a little while before we head to the hospital?"

"Of course." Mom smoothed back Tessa's hair like she had when Tessa was little. The simple gesture touched a place deep inside, a place long cold and walled off, and opened and warmed it again.

Tessa kissed Mom's cheek. "I love you."

"I love you too, my butterfly. I love you too."

CHAPTER FORTY-ONE

Jay gained strength every day and was finally moved from ICU to a regular room. During that time, Tessa hadn't been allowed to visit him, but now Mom had gone home to rest, and Lily had to work. That left Tessa alone in the waiting room that had become a second home.

She'd learned not to drink the coffee from the pot in the little kitchenette in the corner. She must have gotten spoiled by what she'd had in Greece. This just wasn't the same. The skyline out of the two large corner windows was familiar, and she knew where every lump was in the couch that she and her family occupied underneath those windows.

By now Jay would be awake because they would be bringing his lunch soon. The time had come. She adjusted her ponytail, picked up her phone, and trekked down the hall to Jay's room. She waited until he answered her knock to enter.

He was sitting in bed, his bald head shining under the fluorescent lights, his lunch tray in front of him. Plants lined the windowsill, get-well cards stuck between them. He turned toward her and smiled. "Great to see you."

"Good to see you too. Your color is much better."

"I haven't felt this healthy in years. I guess that this block in my artery had been causing problems for a long time, symptoms that I ignored until it was almost too late."

"I'm glad you're still with us." Tessa pulled up a chair beside his bed. "What are they serving you?"

"I ordered broiled chicken and green beans. My new diet to keep this from happening again."

For a while, he ate his lunch, the TV in the background on some sports talk channel, the discussion about the upcoming football season. Tessa couldn't sit back in the chair and relax. Putting off the talk they needed to have served no purpose. "There are some things I need to say to you. First of all, I'm sorry for the way I behaved growing up."

He put his fork down and waved her away. "I don't need your apologies. You were a tween and then a teen. That's normal. Your mom said that she told you about your dad. You know, I didn't handle the situation the right way either. All the feelings you were having were normal, but I didn't know how to deal with them."

"And I've been angry at you for things I shouldn't have been. Things that I remembered the wrong way. I thought you were trying to take the place of the most wonderful man in the world, and I was angry at you for that. The grief counselor I was going to at the time told me that, but it never sunk in. I just continued being angry."

"I did what I could, but I could have loved you better."

She finally unclasped her hands and slid against the back of the seat. "Strange as this may seem with my going to Greece to discover my past, with you, I don't want to get stuck in what came before. Let's move forward from here. This will be a new starting point for us. I need to thank you for stepping in like you did and trying to be a father to me. I'm still not too old to need one if you'll have me."

Jay reached for her hand. "I would like that. This is a time of new beginnings, a time to learn from the past and move forward."

"I know you won't love me quite the same as Lily, but I do hope you will love me."

"Where did that come from?"

She told him about the incident at the gas station, the one

that continued to haunt her. "As you may have been able to guess, Mom and I had a good talk the other morning."

"I love you girls just the same, and I wish you would have known that before now. Yes, it was hard at first. You believed your dad to be this wonderful man who had died in a terrible accident. I didn't quite know what to do with that, and you were trying to deal with everything that had happened. But never doubt that I love you as much as Lily. Maybe I didn't show it as well as I should have, but I do. I truly do."

All Tessa could do was nod.

"So tell me about your trip to Greece."

"You're not mad that I took the rest of my college money?"

"At first I was. You had worked hard to get to where you were and then, to me, it looked like you were throwing it all away. Then again, what should I know? I dropped out of college my sophomore year to backpack across Europe. I saw myself in you, and I couldn't deny you the right to do what you needed to do for yourself."

"I will finish."

"I trust that you will. And your mom and I will be there for you every step of the way. We'll help you financially if you need it."

"I appreciate that." She opened the photos on her phone and shared them and her story with Jay. With the man who could have been, who should have been, the father she really needed.

They laughed for a while and chatted about all she had found out. He held her hand when she cried, telling him what happened to Mathilda.

Little by little, his laughs were softer and his smiles less bright. He was getting tired, and so was Tessa. "Why don't you rest for a while? I'll go to the waiting room and see what I can do about online classes for the fall."

"Sounds good." He was asleep before she even left the room.

She returned to the waiting room and plopped down on the

sofa, then opened her laptop. Only a couple of classes stood between her and graduation. Maybe the school she'd been attending would allow her to finish those as independent study. Her time abroad might even count for something.

Someone entered the room, tennis shoes squeaking on the tile floors, but she didn't glance up. Hmm. The first thing to do would be to email her adviser and see what he suggested. She hadn't pulled up her email program before a shadow fell over her.

This time she did turn her attention from her computer. When she did, her mouth fell open. Before her stood a tall man with dark, curly hair, both dimples deep in his cheeks as he smiled.

"Hello, Tessa."

"Giannis." She set her laptop to the side, jumped up from the couch, and threw herself into his embrace. "I can't believe you're here. What are you doing here? I'm so glad you came."

He laughed, and in that chuckle was all the music of Greece. "I missed you." He nuzzled her neck for a moment before kissing her on the cheek and then backing away. "And I brought another puzzle piece for you to meet."

At that moment, Tessa caught sight of the woman standing beside Giannis. She'd gone unnoticed in Tessa's joy at seeing Giannis. "I'm sorry to have snubbed you. I'm Tessa."

"Hi." The girl with dark hair and green eyes, just about as tall as Tessa, held a hint of familiarity. Like Tessa should know her but didn't. "I'm Madison Cohen."

Tessa shot a glance in Giannis' direction.

Madison tugged her T-shirt over her blue jean shorts. "I guess you're wondering why Giannis brought me here."

"Kind of."

Giannis cleared his throat. "I went by your house, but your mom said you were here. And she wanted me to tell you that she'll come as soon as she freshens up."

"Okay. But I doubt you came all the way from Thessaloniki to tell me that."

There was that beautiful laugh again. Tessa couldn't get enough of it. "No. You have to hear Madison's story."

"This is strange." Madison inhaled and exhaled, her shoulders rising and falling with the motion. "I was in Greece this summer on an international business internship. I knew all about my Greek Jewish heritage, so I went to Thessaloniki where my family is from when I got a few days off."

Giannis stood up on his tiptoes, then down. "She walked into the museum and asked what information we had about her great-grandmother."

All at once, the last piece dropped right into place for Tessa. "Your great-grandmother is one of Mathilda Nissim's sisters."

Madison smiled. "Yes. Linda Recanati. She came with her mother and other sister before the war to live in Chicago. My great-great-aunt never married or had children, but of course, my great-grandmother did."

"We're cousins." Tessa couldn't contain the grin that stretched from cheek to cheek.

"We are. I don't have much family, so I was thrilled when Giannis told me about you and what you had discovered. Now that it's August and everything is shut down in Greece for the summer holiday, I decided to come home and look you up on the way. Giannis offered to come with me."

He shrugged, an impish light in his eyes. All that pitter-pattering of hearts she'd only read about in romance novels, she finally experienced. To keep from bursting, she turned to Madison. "So you live in Chicago?"

"I do, and I hope that means we'll be able to see each other from time to time and we'll be able to get to know each other. We always wondered what had happened to Great-grandma's sister. It's terrible, it really is, to think about what she must have gone through. We never knew she had any children, so it's wonderful to find a living relative."

Just then Mom came into the room, bright and fresh from a night in her own bed. She set even more plants on the windowsill. "I keep telling the people from church that we have enough, but they keep coming. And there isn't an inch of space for more plants in Jay's room." She turned back to the three others. "So what is this? Are we having a party in here?"

Tessa let out a little chuckle. "Not a party but a family reunion."

Mom glanced from Tessa to Madison to Giannis. "Well, I've met Giannis, just briefly."

"It has been nice to meet you, Mrs. DeSantis."

"Call me Janet. I recognize you from the pictures Tessa shared with me. I'm glad you're here. I've heard so much about you."

"You have?"

Heat rose in Tessa's face.

"And who is this?"

Tessa shook off the new, strange feelings overcoming her. "Mom, I would like you to meet your cousin, Mathilda's great-great-niece Madison Cohen."

"What?"

Giannis and Tessa told the story again. After a few minutes, Mom and Madison were chatting away, so Giannis and Tessa stole out of the hospital for a walk on the grounds. "I can't believe you're here."

He held her hand, his warm and strong in hers. "I really missed you."

"I missed you too. But to come all this way."

"Everything in Greece is shut down in August. It's holiday time. The museum is open, but I have two weeks off. Many of the shops are closed around this time too. The ones for tourists are not, but some of the others are. There's a big festival right now."

"I wish I could have been there."

"Maybe you can be." He led her to a bench in a garden that was filled with black-eyed Susans, bee balm, and coneflowers, a riot of yellow, red, and purple. "I have been thinking about the exhibit I am working on for the new museum, the one about Greek Jews in America. You are the perfect person to help me with it."

"Me? I only found out I was Jewish a few months ago. I don't know enough. Madison would be a much better choice. Besides, I promised Jay I would finish college."

"Could you do your classes online?"

"Actually, I was thinking about doing that anyway."

"Look at all you discovered in a short amount of time. Now it will be easier with resources for you."

"How can I leave Mom here in America alone? I don't know."

"Think about it and let me know. That is all I ask. You could have all of August off. And she could come to visit you there."

"She has said she would like to do that. I can't begin to tell you how much better our relationship is. It still needs work, but there's the chance it could be even better than it was before. And Jay..." She relayed the conversation she'd had with her stepfather that morning.

"I am so happy for you." He pulled her in for a kiss.

She kissed him back, a thrill running from the tips of her toes through her body. How could she say no to this wonderful, wonderful man?

CHAPTER FORTY-TWO

February 2022

A light evening breeze blew, and the sun set below the hills surrounding Jerusalem. A few chairs had been set up in the garden of the hall of names in Yad Vashem. Madison and her fiancé were there, as were Mom and Jay. Giannis was beside Tessa. On her other side were Riley and Aunt Fran and Uncle Max, the guests of honor tonight in this very sacred place.

Here, thousands of names were etched into stone, and photographs encircled a round room and stretched as high as the ceiling. These names weren't like those on the wall at the museum in Thessaloniki. These names were of those who made sure that a remnant survived, that the Jewish people weren't wiped from the face of the earth like dust before the wind.

People like Tessa's great-grandmother Ioanna Stavrou. Some of her great-great-nieces and nephews, including Manos and his siblings, were also in the audience, witness to what courage in the face of great danger looked like.

It looked like a mother and daughter who had lost their way but had found it again. It looked like cousins by blood and by love who together made up family. It looked like a group of Greek Christians who didn't realize until a few years ago what their great-great-aunt had done for a frightened, desperate, determined Jewish woman.

Tessa glanced at all those seated here. If not for Mathilda's incredible courage, if not for Ioanna's fearlessness, none of them would be here. Mom and Tessa would never have been born.

One of the museum's VIPs rose and retold Mathilda and Ioanna's story from the beginning of their friendship before the war until Mathilda tossed her infant daughter into Ioanna's hands. How Ioanna had run, how she and her family had left Thessaloniki soon after the war and had fled to Turkey and then on to the United States.

Tessa clung to Giannis' hand and choked back her own tears. She owed Ioanna her very life. Through Ioanna's actions, Mathilda and Asher lived on. Tessa touched her heart.

The Yad Vashem representative called Aunt Fran, Uncle Max, and Riley to the front and handed them a plaque to commemorate what Ioanna had done.

Tessa could no longer hold back her tears. Mom pulled a bunch of tissues from her purse, kept one for herself, and handed one to Tessa.

The short ceremony ended, but the people brought together by Mathilda and Ioanna lingered. Together Mom and Tessa laid a wreath of flowers in front of the slab on which Ioanna and Petrus Stavrou's names were carved.

Forever, the world would remember their sacrifice.

When Mom came to Greece in the fall for Tessa and Giannis' wedding, she would be able to see her grandmother and grandfather's names etched into the wall in the Jewish Museum. The COVID pandemic had halted work on the new one, so it remained where it had been when Tessa had first stepped through that door.

She and Giannis had been apart for almost eighteen months because Americans couldn't travel, but now she had finished her degree as she had promised Jay and was working beside Giannis in Thessaloniki.

Because of a courageous decision almost eighty years ago, her life was now full of promise.

Thank you, Mathilda.

February 23, 1963

To my dearest Mama,

In your letter to me, you told me what you would say to me if you could see me face-to-face. You said you would tell me to grow and to be strong, and so I have. Today is my twentieth birthday, and I think you would be proud of me.

You told me to be happy and to live a full life. That's what I intend to do. I may be young, but I have met a wonderful man who loves me with his whole heart. On my birthday next year, we're getting married. We have so many hopes and plans for the future, one guided by God. We love to travel. I don't know if I will ever get to Greece, but even if I don't, I'll cherish each moment that God gives me, whether it be large or small, and hold it close to my heart. Life can change in an instant, as it did for you, and I will live without regrets.

You told me to be kind and loving to others, even to those who are different than me. And so I will try. Whenever I see someone with different color skin or different eyes or hair, I don't turn away or tell them they can't sit beside me on the bus. For you, I smile and invite them next to me and talk to them. When I have a home of my own, I'll invite them there.

Maybe I should be afraid. It was wise of Mama to wait until I was an adult to tell me about my heritage as it saved me so much heartache as a child, and so I will wait until my children are old enough to handle the truth before I divulge it to them.

You told me that Ioanna was an amazing woman, and so she is. Mama has been wonderful to me. I may have just learned my true birthdate, but I never felt excluded or unloved or treated any differently than my sister. Mama took me in and kept her promise to raise me as her own.

I wish I could have known you longer than just the few weeks we had together after my birth. I hope that I was some comfort to you after my father's passing. How wonderful it would have been to know both of you.

In a way, I feel that I do. I know you in the tilt of my chin, or so Mama says, and in the way I stamp my foot when I'm angry and in my determination to accomplish whatever I set my mind to.

War robbed us of the chance to be together in this life. Mama has told me how she shared the Gospel with you. I pray that you understood and accepted the Savior, that even now, you're rejoicing with the Lord in heaven. When I walk through glory's gates myself someday, I pray that I will see you there, waiting for me, and that, at the feet of the Lord, we will be reunited.

Thank you, Mama, for all you told me. I cherish your words.

Your beloved daughter,
Achima

AUTHOR'S HISTORICAL NOTES

One of the reasons I love reading and writing historical fiction is because I enjoy seeing how an author takes real people, places, and events and turns them into a novel. So here are the answers to some of your burning questions about the facts behind *What I Would Tell You.*

Who was real in the book? Dr. Merten, the German representative in Salonika, was. It was with him that the Jewish Council negotiated for the terms of the release of the men held in labor camps. Even though the money was supposed to go to Germany, it is rumored that he kept some of it for himself and buried it in northern Greece. He was responsible for the deportation of the Jews. He returned to Thessaloniki in the 1950s and was tried and convicted of war crimes. Though he was sentenced to serve twenty-five years, he was extradited to West Germany and set free.

Rabbi Zvi Koretz was also a historical figure. Born in Galicia and educated in Vienna, he became Salonika's chief rabbi in 1933. As he was Ashkenazi, he was generally not liked by the city's Sephardic Jews. He was arrested in Athens right after the occupation, then released, then arrested and imprisoned in Salonika before being released again. He was arrested a final time in the spring of 1943 while trying to delay the deportation of the Jews by offering the Germans more Jewish property. He was sent to Bergen-Belsen and then to Theresienstadt. Though he survived the camps, he died three months after being liberated.

What places in the book are real? Salonika, also known as

Thessaloniki and Thessalonica, is a beautiful Greek city on the Thermaic Gulf, boasting a rich history stretching back thousands of years. My daughter and I had the honor of visiting there in August of 2021. Roman ruins fill the city. Just about every place I mention in Thessaloniki is real. The Kapani market still exists and is a lively place to buy spices, fruits and vegetables, meat and fish, olives, and tourist items. My favorite was the spice shop, so that's where I chose to have Asher and Mathilda live.

In the contemporary story line, the man at the restaurant in the Kapani market is real and looked like I described him. He was always there, handing out menus, trying to get people to eat at his restaurant. My daughter and I went by him so often, he got to know us. We did eat there, and the food was fabulous. If you're ever in Thessaloniki, be sure to find him and eat at his establishment.

The triangular dessert that Tessa loved so much is a treat my daughter and I enjoyed three times in our weeklong visit. The key to them, according to our tour guide, is not to have them filled with cream until after you order. The best place to get them is Trigona Elenidi. As you might be able to tell, if you want to eat your way through Thessaloniki, I can tell you how to do it.

The Jewish Museum of Thessaloniki is as I describe it. As of the writing of this, it has not yet moved to its new location. We did have to turn over our phones, much to my disappointment, so I wasn't able to get any photographs. Instead, I took pages and pages of notes. All of it was fascinating, but the room filled with names on walls of stone took my breath away. It drove home the magnitude of the human toll the Holocaust exacted.

Baron Hirsch was a real section of town, though not much remains today. The same is true of the rail yard. The wall with the figures painted on it is real. Unfortunately, so are the swastikas sprayed over the very moving mural.

Nea Kallikratia is a very charming seaside town and is much as I described it. Several nights my daughter and I sat on the beach no more than three feet from the waves and had dinner. We also enjoyed gelato on the bench in the town square while kids rode rented motorized cars. The scene with the girl on the bike was ripped from real life. She amazed me.

What events were real? On July 2, 1942, the men were rounded up in Liberty Square on one of the hottest days of the year. The Greek sun is intense. They stood for hours, forced to perform humiliating exercises. Then the registrations began. No men were actually taken away the same day. I had Asher leave then for dramatic effect. It was over the next several days that all able-bodied men were taken from Thessaloniki and sent to labor camps.

When I was there in 2021, Liberty Square was being revitalized into a park with a memorial to the Jewish men who died there. Fencing surrounded the entire square, and I couldn't look inside. On the harbor side of it was a small plaque and an iron menorah with the forms of men and women making up each of the seven candleholders.

While the details of the ransom for the men in the work camp are pretty much as they happened, it would have been almost unthinkable for the council to have a woman among them. It was actually a group of men who got together and came up with this plan. The Germans extracted a heavy price from them, including sacred land. They did believe they had time to move the bodies, but they didn't. Aristotle University still owns the land. There is a small green space at the university with a small, ill-kept memorial. I did hear talk that the memorial would be enlarged and better cared for. When I was in Thessaloniki, I thought it was swanky to be walking on marble sidewalks until I learned where the marble came from.

The Jewish cemetery was a very important place to the people. They didn't give it up lightly or easily. As I researched why this might be, I came across Jeremiah 16:3–4: "For thus says the Lord concerning the sons and daughters who are born in this place, and concerning the mothers who bore them and the fathers who fathered them in this land: They shall die of deadly diseases. They shall not be lamented, nor shall they be buried. They shall be as dung on the surface of the ground. They shall perish by the sword and by famine, and their dead bodies shall be food for the birds of the air and for the beasts of the earth." This was such a terrible pronouncement that professional mourners wailed every day at the cemetery and the dead were buried the day after their death.

While the release of the men was secured, their return home was short lived. The first transport left the train station across from the Baron Hirsch ghetto on March 15, 1943. Most who survived were aboard that train. It took until August, five months, to complete the deportation of Jews from Salonika.

The mass shooting at the Pittsburgh synagogue happened on October 27, 2018, and because I wanted to include it, it's the main reason the contemporary part of the story takes place in the Pittsburgh area. The shooting at the Jewish deli is fictitious, though there was a shooting at a Jewish grocery story in New Jersey in December 2019.

The scene at the Thessaloniki airport when Tessa arrives really happened to my daughter and me almost exactly as I describe it. It was the only hiccup in our entire trip. You'll never know how relieved I was to see the driver holding the sign with my name.

I tried very hard not to turn the contemporary story into a travelogue, though as you may have been able to tell, I fell in love with the city. From the warm sun (there's just something different about it) to the kind people to the amazing culture and history, it's a fabulous place to visit. I'm so thankful I got to experience it, and I hope you enjoyed experiencing it along with me.

ACKNOWLEDGMENTS

First of all, thank you to Becky Germany, Abbey Bible, Laura Young, and all the marvelous people at Barbour Publishing for allowing me to spread my wings and fly on my own with this book. It's been one I've wanted to write for so long. I'm so glad I got to do it with all of you.

Thank you, Becky Fish, for being such a terrific editor. I really learned from you and enjoyed working with you. I appreciate the hard work to help make this book be all it could be.

Thank you to my amazing agent and friend, Tamela Hancock Murray. Your excitement over this story helped to sell it. Thank you for believing in me and encouraging me along the way. I couldn't ask for anyone better to represent me.

Thank you to Dawn, my sweet friend and fellow bibliophile, and now my amazing first reader. Your insight was spot on and just what I needed to hear. I appreciate your time, your effort, and your graciousness. Little did we know when we met in the parking lot at school how God would bring us back together.

A huge shout-out to Diana, my longtime critique partner. You're the best, and it's always a blast to chat books and writing with you. Thanks for taking the time to read this, for pointing out all kinds of flaws and errors, and for encouraging me.

Thank you to everyone on my Liz Tolsma's Reader's Facebook group for cheering me on and for helping to spread the word about *What I Would Tell You.* Your support of me is deeply appreciated.

Thank you to all of you who took the money to buy this book, the time to read it, and the effort to review it. Without you, I wouldn't be writing. Okay, I'd still be writing, but it sure is nice to know there are people who will be reading my work.

I don't know where I would be without my daughter and travel buddy, Alyssa. Probably still standing in front of the building our Airbnb was in, trying to figure out how the lock worked. I'm glad you had been in Athens for the summer already and knew that you have to turn the key three times. Who would have guessed? The memories we made those two weeks are some of the sweetest of my life. I can't think of anyone who I would rather have had this adventure with. You were so patient with me as we walked many miles in some terrible heat to see all I needed to see. Your knowledge of Greece was a lifesaver. I love you!

A huge thank you to Eleni Sismanidou, our tour guide in Thessaloniki. This story wouldn't be what it is without the places you showed us and the insights you gave us. And the tips on the best places to eat! You went above and beyond the call of duty. It was, by far, our most memorable day in Greece.

Thank you to my husband, Doug, for holding down the fort while I was away and taking care of Jonalyn that entire time on your own. I know you don't believe in heroes, but you're mine.

And finally, all praise to God for this gift and this responsibility, for the doors He has opened, and for the opportunities He has presented me, all beyond my wildest expectations. *Soli Deo gloria.*

Liz Tolsma is the author of several WWII novels, romantic suspense novels, prairie romance novellas, and an Amish romance. She is a popular speaker and an editor and resides next to a Wisconsin farm field with her husband and their youngest daughter. Her son is a US Marine, and her oldest daughter is a college student. Liz enjoys reading, walking, working in her large perennial garden, kayaking, and camping. Please visit her website at www.liztolsma.com and follow her on Facebook, Twitter (@LizTolsma), Instagram, YouTube, and Pinterest. She is also the host of the *Christian Historical Fiction Talk* podcast.

Other Barbour Books by Liz Tolsma:
The Pink Bonnet (True Colors series)
The Green Dress (True Colors series)
The Gold Digger (True Colors series)
The Silver Shadow (True Colors series)
A Picture of Hope (Heroines of WWII series)
A Promise Engraved (Doors to the Past series)